WEATHERMAN

ML NYSTROM

HOT TREE PUBLISHING

WEATHERMAN

DRAGON RUNNERS MC
BOOK 7

ML NYSTROM

HOT TREE PUBLISHING

DRAGON RUNNERS MC

Mute

Stud

Blue

Table

Brick

Dodge

Weatherman

MACATEER BROTHERS

Run With It

Ready For It

Hold It Close

Risk It All

Give It To Me

THE DUTCHMEN MC

The Price of Redemption

The Price of Forgiveness

The Price of Peace

The Price of Atonement

For information, contact the publisher, Hot Tree Publishing.

WWW.HOTTREEPUBLISHING.COM

EDITING: HOT TREE EDITING

COVER DESIGNER: BOOKSMITH DESIGN

E-BOOK ISBN: 978-1-923252-17-2

PAPERBACK ISBN: 978-1-923252-18-9

To Mr. Roger Spencer, Mr. Frederick Fuller, Ms. Bonita Lackey, Ms. Travis, and all the other teachers who inspired me to put words on paper.

CHAPTER 1

"I asked for onion rings, and they gave me fries. I had to call over the manager. If I wanted fries, I would have ordered fries. I wanted onion rings."

The rotund woman gestured wildly as she sat in my salon chair with her head half wrapped in square foils. I had to step back to prevent another color brush from getting knocked to the floor.

Burna Jones kept talking while the other patrons listened, or at least pretended to. "I told him he needed to give me what I asked for, and you know what he said to me? He had the nerve to say that I ate the fries. Of course I ate the fries! I was hungry, but that's not the point. I wanted onion rings, and he shoulda give 'em to me for free."

I tried not to stare at the bulging collar of flesh around the woman's neck as it flopped in tandem with her words. It was hard to ignore it. *Just keep quiet, Opal, I* told myself as I combed up another section of hair to spread jet-black color on her steel-gray strands. Tambre Bearclaw, the salon owner and my boss, had warned me that the best way to deal with Burna was to put her in the chair, use the darkest color on the palette, and keep quiet.

"Don't try to suggest anything else or she'll throw the biggest hissy fit you've ever seen," Tambre had advised in a whisper when I first met the difficult woman. "No one wants to work with her and her nasty attitude, so we take turns. Think of it as a rite of passage or initiation."

"I told that man I'd be giving his restaurant a one-star review and speaking my mind on the internet," Burna continued. "And I did just that. Let's see how his business handles it. I bet he'll be callin' me with an apology real soon." She finished her narrative with an emphatic "*mm-hmm*" and crossed her arms below the drape ballooning around her hanging chin.

"That new woman workin' at Randy's is hard to understand sometimes," another woman remarked from the depth of the shampoo sink.

"No excuse for givin' someone fries when they ordered onion rings. These young people are just too damn lazy to work."

I gritted my teeth. I had nightmares of when I worked fast food years ago as a young teenager. It got so busy and backed up sometimes that occasionally we messed up orders. Getting cursed at by customers over how many chicken nuggets came in a paper cup was one reason I left. Getting groped by the manager was another.

I exchanged glances with my friend and roommate, Kimmie. Both of us had moved to Bryson City, North Carolina, earlier this summer, just after graduating from cosmetology school in Red Wing, Minnesota. It was a big culture shock to go from a relatively flat area of the country to this mountainous region. The roads twisted like crazy, and there were times that I couldn't understand the thick Southern accent some people had, but both of us needed a fresh start somewhere that no one knew us and our pasts. The instructor back in Red Wing had an older relative in this area who told her about the job openings in a local salon.

We were a long way from home, but this place was just as good as any other.

We had agreed to let the past be the past and not to talk about it. "New town, new people, new lives" had become our motto. I did my best to follow that line of thought, I really did, but sometimes at night, when I lay in my bed and listened to the sounds my baby girl made while sleeping, memories would roll through my brain like a movie scene, and I had to jam a pillow over my face to keep my tears from coming out.

I finished Burna's color job and twisted the dial on the timer. "I'll be back to check on you in a bit. Do you need anything? Water?"

"Get me a Diet Coke. I don't want all those carbs in the regular ones. Makes you fat."

Kimmie made a choking noise and covered it by examining her client's nails closely.

Tambre was in the back room taking inventory and spotted me as I came in. Without breaking her stride, the older woman opened the fridge and pulled out a can of the preferred soda. She handed the cold drink to me with a conspiratorial wink. "You handle that battle-ax really well. Burna has been known to chew up and spit out store clerks for anything she doesn't like. She makes the Karens-in-the-wild look tame."

I took the can and plucked a paper-wrapped straw from a counter drawer we used for extra condiment packets, plasticware, and other bits. "I've dealt with worse."

Tambre gave a quiet hum. "I think she likes you for now because you don't try to correct her or change her mind. That's how I deal with her, too, but she will eventually bite at you. Try not to take it personally. She's been this way for years."

I smiled at my boss. Burna Jones was easy compared to some of the other people I used to be around.

Molly appeared in the doorway. "Hand me one of them sodas, would'ja? It's hotter than the devil's front porch out there. Cutter's already bitchin' 'bout keepin' his tomato plants watered. Lord, wish it would rain soon and shut him up. A good soakin' shower and not these little teaser sprinkles."

The perky woman turned to me with barely a break in her speech. "Tam is right about Burna. That bitch tried to get my friend Melissa Wall fired from her job over at the movie theater. Complained she didn't get the extra butter on her popcorn that she paid for and made a big stink about it in the lobby. I can still remember the look on Hilda's face. She was sooo embarrassed."

"Hilda?" I asked. Only a month had passed since I moved here, and even though I'd met a lot of people, Hilda wasn't a name I remembered.

"Burna's granddaughter. Lost her parents on the Tail when she was little. Drunk driver, if I'm rememberin' right." Molly shook her head. "The Tail of the Dragon is hard enough to run when you're sober. Why some dumbass decided he could take it after downing a six-pack or three is beyond me. Left that poor little girl to be raised by the bitterest woman ever known to God or man."

I could relate somewhat to both women. My childhood hadn't been rainbows and unicorns either. I had no clue who my dad was, and my mom only earned the title because she gave birth to me. If I thought about it, I could feel sorry for myself and become permanently angry about life, but I chose not to. I'd made other choices I regretted, but I'd also come to accept my mistakes and learn from them. I had my own little girl now, and I was determined to give her a better life than the one I started with.

The cold of the soda can bit into my fingers a little, and I smiled at my boss. "I'd better get this out to Burna, then, before she decides to get me fired too."

Tambre gave me a pointed look and a wink. "No

chance of that. You've got a great eye for color and a deft hand. Plus, you're here on time and get the work done. Burna's a regular customer, but I need good, reliable help just as much or more than I need her."

I nodded but didn't say anything back. Yes, I needed this job as much as Tambre needed me here, but I'd been burned too many times to completely trust anyone. In my experience, words meant nothing without actions behind them, and I'd had earfuls of promises that seldom panned out. There were only two people in the world who I knew had my back 100 percent. One lived in Minnesota with her new man. The other one?

I couldn't think about him right now. If I did, I'd never make it through my workday.

I handed the drink to the dye-covered woman, who didn't bother to say thank you. The timer ticked away on the rolling work tray. I glanced at the waiting area and saw no more walk-ins had come in. Kimmie was chatting with her client as she stroked a clear coat over the new set of acrylic nails she'd just finished. Bex and Deandra were busy on two other women, chatting and smiling as they discussed the last of summer break and the upcoming school year.

I picked up a broom and swept my area clean, then sent a quick text to Lori to check on Pearl. I didn't like the idea of leaving my baby girl with a stranger, but I had to work. Luckily, she loved being at Lori's place and giggled a lot when I dropped her off. I was the one who cried when I left her.

Gossip flowed freely around me, and it was hard not to eavesdrop.

"Did'ja hear about Morris Cumber's son's wife's cousin?"

"My husband complains about the kids not eating, but he's the one who's the pickiest at the dinner table."

"Ground beef is on sale over at Ingles this week."

"I'm headin' over to Walmart for school supplies later."

"The Dragon Runners are having a party on Saturday night."

I stiffened a little as I bent over to scoop the clippings into the dustpan and dump them in the small trash can at my station. Everyone knew about the Dragon Runners Motorcycle Club in this town. They owned quite a number of businesses and had connections that ran deep.

The first time I met Betsey, the reigning MC queen, she scared me a little. She came in the salon with her jeans and cut the day I interviewed and got hired. Her heeled boots clacked confidently across the wood floor, and I noted the regal way she carried herself. I'd had Pearl with me, and the redheaded woman squealed. Yes, *squealed*.

"Lord have mercy, what a cute little girl. Here, let me hold her for a minute."

Pearl had no problem grinning and reaching for her. Betsey had hitched out a hip like an expert and propped Pearl on it. "Who's a pretty girl? Oh my, look at all them teeth. Aren't you smart? Yes, you are! Yes, you are!"

Pearl had gurgled and grinned at the bubbling lady. I'd fought tears as I was reminded of my favorite person I'd left in Minnesota. Mama J was the mother of six children and had been my best friend and support when I needed it most.

It was Betsey who solved many of my moving problems. She'd turned to me and rapid-fired a handful of questions.

"You're the new girl? Where are you staying? There's an apartment across from Soap-n-stuff that's open for rent. You need a good daycare? Lori, down at the tattoo parlor, is doing a daycare now at her house and might have a spot. Lord knows, she an' Table don't need no money, but she likes takin' care of kids."

In no time, Kimmie and I had moved into a two-bedroom apartment over a storefront in the downtown area of Bryson City. It had been renovated and was cute, though a bit small. I shared a room with Pearl, of course. The window had a full view of a huge, stately house that was a local craft store on the bottom floor and a family home on the others. Betsey's son, Blue, his wife, Psalm, and their kids lived there. Psalm made the most amazing soap.

Lori was married to Table, another biker in the club. They owned and operated Dragon's Ink, a tattoo place not too far from the salon. Their house sat farther out of town, with a big fenced-in backyard that butted up to the river.

Town news and happenings surrounded me on a daily basis in the beauty shop. I heard all about the women of the Dragon Runners MC. It seemed they had their own club, and a strong one at that. So far, I'd not involved myself more than I had to. My emotions were too raw, and the move across the country to such a different place was still too new. Some days were better than others, and I could smile and be happy. Some were so hard, I barely kept myself upright.

The timer dinged, and Burna shifted in the chair, making the fake leather squeak. "Young lady! I'm done!" Her shout across the salon had several sets of eyes rolling.

"Coming, Ms. Jones."

"It's about time." The woman sucked up the last of her soda and handed me the empty can. "I have a lot to do today."

"I'm sure you do. Let's go get you shampooed and cut."

A COUPLE MORE SCHEDULED JOBS OF COLORING, CUTS, AND one perm later, I was finished. My day was long, but I had a nice pocketful of tips and a slow cooker of *kalops* waiting for me at home. I picked up Pearl, who was all smiles and giggles, from the sitter's and then drove to the apartment. Kimmie was already there and dolling up to go out again.

"Bex got invited to go to the Lair tonight and said I could come with her. I bet they'd let you in too. Betsey loves kids and would probably take Pearl for a while so you could enjoy yourself."

I rested my girl on my hip. "Thanks, but I'm good staying here."

A few years ago, I lived to stay up all night and party with no limits. It was the lifestyle I chose and one I remembered well. My past still haunted me and probably would for the rest of my life, but I could either choose to wallow in self-pity or move on.

I'd done all the wallowing I ever cared to do.

Kimmie left a few minutes later, and the apartment quieted. I cooled the mashed potatoes and meat to feed Pearl, and she messily crammed the food into her mouth. She was getting so big and growing more every day from an infant into a toddler. She crawled like a cheetah and pulled up on anything that would hold her weight, taking tentative steps before plopping down on her padded rear. Potty training was around the corner. Her blonde hair was long enough to clip up in a small bow-shaped barrette at the top of her head. Her blue eyes and mischievous grin reminded me of her biological father, but she mostly looked like me.

"How's my little Pearl? Did you have fun at Lori's?"

Her answer was a short "En-gah," and she showed me her baby teeth before she stuffed a carrot piece in her face.

I giggled with her.

One of my biggest joys in life was this time at night with my little girl. We splashed and played while I gave her a bath, and she fell asleep as I rocked her and hummed whatever song was in my head. Mama J—Janice—taught me so much about how to be a good mom. Reading, singing, playing games, being involved. So much of this time was precious, and I hoarded every minute.

I held my sleeping daughter and listened to the rhythmic squeak of the plain wood rocking chair as I moved it forward and backward. I had some money in the bank, but I needed to stretch it out as long as possible, keeping some back for emergencies. Kimmie's family had shipped us some living room pieces and kitchen stuff that was used but in good shape. Goodwill supplied the rest. I'd spotted the wooden rocker when Pearl and I spent a day puttering around the local flea market. The first piece of furniture I ever bought just for me. It was old and a little rickety, but a little wood glue and a cheap cushion fixed it up nicely. Some people might find it a little weird, but I loved that rocker. I wondered how many children had been soothed to sleep by its back-and-forth motion. How many bedtime books had been read in it? How many quiet nights had the rhythmic creaking calmed a troubled mind?

I transferred Pearl to her crib, which took up most of my bedroom. My next splurge had to be a new mattress and box spring, as the one I used now was worn and dipping in the middle. A twin-sized this time—no need for anything bigger, and the current double took up too much space. I had plans to save up and eventually get us our own place. One with a yard and a fence and a dog. My dream house. Something I once touched with the tips of my fingers long enough to imagine the possibility before it was torn away.

Pain ripped through me, and I stifled a sob. Pearl fussed and squirmed to find a new position, and I held my breath. She farted and quieted down. I smiled.

"She's getting big," an invisible voice whispered in my ear. Its warm tone spoke with caring admiration and a bit of pride.

"Yes, she is," I whispered out loud.

Silence answered back.

I changed into a sleep shirt and carefully climbed into my bed. Pearl was such a good baby and seldom woke at night, but I still didn't want to make any noise to disturb her. I settled on my side, mentally sorting tomorrow's schedule and tasks on repeat until I fell asleep.

I did not acknowledge the two tears that tracked down my face.

CHAPTER 2

Weatherman backed his bike into a spot in front of the garage and cut the engine. He lifted the heavy helmet from his head and shook out his sandy blond hair. His job at the news station had him keeping it stylishly short at all times, even though he preferred to have it longer.

I guess I won't have to keep to a dress code soon. He only had a few weeks left at that job. It wasn't a bitter ending to this part of his career, but a necessary one.

The custom paint and spray booth was at the far end of the garage complex. They did everything at this facility from simple oil changes to complex restorations. It started as a ramshackle dump and grew into a thriving business under the leadership of Brick, the current president of the Dragon Runners MC. Over his lifetime, the club had acquired a number of diverse businesses besides the garage and bar, including a campground, a tattoo parlor, and a hair salon.

He opened the door to the building where the spray booth was located. Dodge was bent over a car, taping off another part of an elaborate spider on the hood.

"That's gonna look damn good at night. I bet it scares the shit out of someone."

He stepped into the spray booth and closed the door behind him, keeping a good distance away. Dust and other particles could ruin a good paint job, and from the intricate detail of the spider, Dodge would probably throat punch anyone who messed it up. The booth's exhaust was off for now, so the two friends could carry on a conversation.

"I hope so. I'm charging him enough." Dodge peered at one of the arachnid's black legs and swore, peeling off a section of blocking tape and repositioning it. "You just get into town?"

Weatherman chuckled at the man's fastidious attention to detail. He slipped his hands into his jeans pockets and leaned back against the coated cement wall. "About a half hour ago. No one's up at the Lair, so I thought I'd stop here before heading to the house."

"How's your mom?"

Weatherman sighed. This was his reason for leaving a promising career as a meteorologist at the station. He hadn't set out to become a TV personality, but the station plucked him up as an intern before graduating. Later, they hired him straight out of school, claiming his good looks and articulate voice were what they needed to draw their audience. It helped that the camera loved him. He had a slim, athletic swimmer's build, along with piercing eyes and wavy blond hair. He'd had to live in Knoxville in order to take the job, but he was okay with that, as it wasn't too far away from home. All was well until his mother got sick. "She's taking her first chemo in the morning."

"Good luck to her and to you, brother."

Weatherman dipped his head in acknowledgment. "She's got a long way to go, but the doctors say it can still be beat even at stage four. As soon as I finish my contract, I'll move back permanently. Until then, I'll keep commuting."

Dodge tapped the tape in place and checked again, satisfied with its placement. "Sorry you have to give up your dream job."

He shrugged. "It's my mom." Yes, it sucked, but for his entire life, it had always been just the two of them. His dad left long ago, before he was born, and he could count on one hand the few times he'd seen or spoken to the man. Child support had been paid regularly, at least, and his mother had squirreled it away into some high-yield money market investments. They ended up being a nice-sized nest egg for school and whatever future he wanted to claim. Not rich by any means, but comfortable enough not to worry.

It didn't matter to him, because he'd never lacked for anything growing up. Natalie Turner had worked as a bank teller all her life to make sure he never had to suffer. When he was a young child, she would come home every night to cook dinner with his "help." He remembered the fun he had shaking chicken legs in a bag of seasoned flour as she cheered him on. Later, they would play a game together, and she'd read to him before bed. She never closed his door or hers, so he could hear her breathing from her room. As he grew up, she chose to never date anyone, even though men asked her out a lot. Almost every activity she did was kid oriented. School book fairs, swim meets when he made the team at the Y club, science projects—everything in his life, she was involved. Some kids might consider that to be smothering, but Weatherman regarded those memories as precious.

"I can always get another position. The station said I could come back when I want. *If* I want."

"I hope it works out," Dodge said as he straightened. "I'm almost ready to spray. You wanna stick around for a bit, or you got other stuff to do?"

"I gotta go get a haircut, and then I'll head over to the house. Moving sucks."

Dodge chuckled. "I hear you. Take care, and I'll see you at the Lair later."

Weatherman blew out a breath. His afternoon plans didn't include going to the Dragon Runners' headquarters tonight for any length of time, but he might stop in to see his mentor. Of all the Dragon Runners, Table was his biggest influence. He'd met the man by chance one night back in high school when he and his mom lived in Asheville. He'd been out with his girlfriend at the time and two other friends when they spotted a car barreling down one of the many twisting mountain roads. The shiny line of fluid trailing behind the vehicle told him why.

"Holy shit, look at that!"

"She's going way too fast."

"Watch out!"

His friends had screamed and panicked while Weatherman—Bryce back then—concentrated on staying with the careening vehicle, hoping the driver stopped before the brakes completely drained. Ultimately, the car crashed into the guardrail on a sharp curve. Only by the grace of God did it not flip over the rail and tumble down the mountainside. He'd stayed with the woman he now knew as Lori and waited with her until her boyfriend showed up with help.

That was the night he met Table and found his future with the Dragon Runners MC.

"It's not easy getting into the club, and not everyone is cut out for club life," Table had told him. "You're serious, I can talk to my people. If it's mostly about your mom, you just let me know if she needs somethin' and I'll take care of it."

He prospected right out of high school during his freshman year at the University of North Carolina at Asheville. He learned that Lori had been abused by her ex-husband and went into hiding from him. Thankfully, she found Table and the club, who protected her and gave her a new life. But somehow, her ex found her, and then all hell broke loose. Table even took a bullet for her and nearly died. Brick, the club president, somehow fixed the situation, and nothing else came of it. Eventually, Table and Lori moved to Bryson City and began their life together.

Through summer classes and several semesters of credit overloads, Bryce graduated early, and his good looks, along with his natural charisma, landed him the perfect job as the weather forecaster at a TV station in Knoxville. His mom had always wanted to live in Bryson City, which was fortunate, as the Dragon Runners MC was headquartered there. Some kids wouldn't want their parents around, but Bryce was okay with it and, in fact, encouraged Natalie to move close to him.

Only a year into his promising career, life threw a major curveball at them. Natalie's lung cancer diagnosis had them both reeling, and he'd made the decision to end his budding career for now to take care of her.

Weatherman fired up his bike and caressed the handlebars. His Softail Harley only seated one, but his cruiser had an extra spot. He used to take his mother on the occasional trip, but she was too frail now. So far, the cancer hadn't metastasized to other parts of her body, and the doctors said it was treatable, but still very serious. Natalie had a long, difficult road ahead of her.

"One step at a time," he said to himself as he strapped on his helmet.

The summer heat brought a sticky humidity to the air as he rode away from the garage. Most of his furniture and personal belongings were in storage for now. The little two-bedroom house his mom bought was small, but he planned on living there until she got back on her feet.

Or not.

No, he wasn't ready to face that part yet. As long as Natalie Turner had the capacity to breathe, she could heal, and he wouldn't give up on any shred of hope.

With that thought, he pointed his bike in the direction of Tambre's place and headed there.

CHAPTER 3

"DID YOU GO TO THAT NEW RESTAURANT THAT JUST opened? What's the name?"

"Smoky Mountain Bistro, if I'm not mistaken. Real fancy food, but damn, it is good!"

"Burna Jones said she didn't like the way the place looked."

"Hmph. Burna Jones doesn't like anything."

I listened to the shop gossip as I painted another section of hair on my client's head and then carefully wrapped the foil. There was something therapeutic about doing this routine basic highlight job. I found it soothing to watch the repetitive motion of spreading the thick lightening paste over the strands and listen to the crinkle of the foil as I folded it into an even, compact rectangle.

The bell tinkled, and of course, the newcomer was greeted by a wave of curious eyes. Normally, what I saw and heard were waves and shouts of "Hey, girl," but the woman in the door was dismissed coldly.

So, not a new person, but someone everyone knew and shunned.

Except Tambre.

"Good afternoon, Donna. How are you?"

Donna tilted her head back and ignored the snubs. "Hey, Tambre. I got a little problem." She reached up and tugged at her dry strands. "I did my roots at home to save some money, an' it didn't go so good."

"Hmph. Ain't enough bleach in the county to clean some stains," the woman in my chair muttered under her breath. Her remark was brief, but the ugly tone made me take a longer look at the woman standing at the front of the salon.

She could have been anywhere between thirty-five and forty-five. Her clothes consisted of short-shorts and a ripped T-shirt over a spaghetti-strap cami, but her breasts hung low and loose. She was pretty, but underneath the heavy makeup, there were deep lines and shadows of hard living. The straw-like consistency of her greenish-blonde hair made me wince.

"This is bad, Donna. We can try a deep keratin treatment and see what happens." Tambre's voice held a note of compassion for the woman. It made me love my boss even more.

"How much?" Donna asked warily.

"I'll work something out with you. Go sit in my chair, and I'll get you set up."

I finished with my client and set the timer. Kimmie

worked on a set of nails for a new client and gabbed about some new bar she'd found and how much fun she had going there.

I took a few minutes to text Lori about my daughter. Most of the time, Pearl was a happy, content baby, but this morning, she was a bit fussy. I put it down to cutting molars and made a mental note to pick up some baby Tylenol on the way to get her later.

I stretched my back and several bones popped. Standing on my feet for hours on end really did a number on my legs and back. I'd given up on anything stylish and cute and instead wore Skechers with arch supports nowadays.

The bell over the door rang out, and the eye-wave greeting started again. This time there were squeals of pleasure.

"Hey, Weatherman!"

"When did you get in?"

"How's your mama?"

I bit my lip. The salon patrons treated the woman sitting in Tambre's chair, currently getting her hair slathered in a thick creamy mask, like a pariah, while they fawned over the man. It bothered me.

"Mom's doing okay now. She's got her first chemo treatment tomorrow morning, though. I expect she'll be feeling rough for a few days."

His voice was deep and resonant, with a pleasant sound. I imagined he could charm the pants off any of the women who were currently drooling on their capes. Not me. I was immune to men at this point in my life. I had my daughter and my growing reputation as a colorist and stylist. That was enough. Frankly, I didn't want anything to come along and mess it up.

"Hey, Tambre, any way you can work me in for a quick trim?"

Did you not see the full waiting area? I turned away and picked up the broom, intent on ignoring him and keeping my hands busy.

"I'm working on Donna right now, and Marilee is waiting for me," she replied.

No, I said in my head. *Please not me.*

"Looks like all the chairs are full, but if Courtney doesn't mind moving to the shampoo station while her color times out, I bet Opal can get you sorted."

I closed my eyes in resignation. I didn't want to cut his hair, whoever he was, but when my boss asked me to do something, it was a good idea to comply. I put a smile on my face and leaned the broom back against the wall. "You bet."

I had to lock my knees when I finally took in his appearance. Taller than me by at least a head, nice masculine build but not bulky, clean hair and face with high, sculpted cheekbones and full lips. He could be a model in a magazine ad.

Though it was his eyes that nearly sent me to the floor.

Greenish-gold hazel gazed back at me. Eyes nearly the same shade as someone else I knew. *Used* to know. Someone I kept in my private memories, just for me.

"Good afternoon, Opal. I'm Weatherman." He reached out a square-shaped hand for me to shake.

I just stared at it. White noise filled my head, and my belly twisted as if a snake were coiling up to strike. I'd cut and styled plenty of women. The last man whose hair I cut…

"Opal?"

"It's okay, baby. You got this."

The guiding voice helped get my focus back. Yes, I could do this.

I forced something resembling a smile and made myself take his hand for a brief shake. "Yeah, hi. Have a seat, and I'll go get a fresh cape."

When I came back out from the storeroom, I spotted two of the ladies in the waiting area giggling, blushing, and sneaking pics with their phones of the man in my chair. Was he some sort of celebrity? *Not my problem or my business. I'll just give him a cut and let everything else go.*

"Your hair isn't too bad. Why don't you go to Morris's Barbershop like all the other men in town do?" I asked.

He grinned, showing off perfect white teeth. Either he had fantastic genes or a great orthodontist. "Last time I went there, he did a number on me. Looked terrible on the air, and I had to wait until it grew out enough to fix it. Nope, I'd rather get it done right."

"On the air?"

"I'm the evening meteorologist for the WXVI news

station in Knoxville. Well, for the next four weeks, at least."

So he *was* a sort of local celebrity. "Oh," I replied. Kinda lame, but popular or not, he was still a stranger to me. That laser smile of his pierced me, and not in a good way. "You sure you trust me? We just met."

"I trust Tambre. She wouldn't hire someone she didn't believe could do the job."

He was sitting in my chair already, the cape in my hands.

Just cut his hair, I repeated to myself. *Simple sweep and taper. Easy peasy.*

I sprayed him down and combed through his locks. Most of the time, I tried to chat with my clients, but I just wanted to get him done and out of my life. The sandy-colored strands threaded through my fingers as I point-snipped away, lifting the layers and checking the fall. The other man I'd trimmed liked his hair military short.

"Can't take the Army out of me, baby."

I still heard his voice from time to time. Still pictured his smile with that overlapping front tooth. Still remembered when he took me in his arms the first time. Grief hit me out of nowhere, and my scissors dropped to the floor.

Tambre called out, "Opal, are you okay?"

I shook myself off and fought back the wave of tears that threatened to flow. "Yeah, you bet."

I picked up the shears and cleaned them before resuming my work. Thankfully, Weatherman stayed silent. If he talked to me or asked me questions, there was no way I could get through this job or even answer him.

A few minutes later, I was done. I'd made it through without losing control completely, although I would probably shed some tears later.

I brushed off the cape and took it from around his neck. He stood up and straightened his clothes, and I finally noticed the cut on his back. A biker. Another member of the Dragon Runners MC.

Uff-da, will I ever get away from motorcycle men?

He followed me to the register.

"That will be twenty-five dollars." I recognized that my tone was much sharper than it needed to be, but at the moment, I couldn't help it.

He handed me two twenties. "Keep the change. I apologize if I made you nervous."

"You don't make me anything," I said rather acidly. The generous tip threw me off. Experience had taught me that men who were generous usually had expectations.

His chuckle had the sound of irritation rather than mirth. "Seriously, what is your problem?"

"I don't have a problem. I just don't like doing men's hair."

"So, it's not me."

His statement brought me up short, and I didn't know what to say. My actions were already rude, and anything else I had to say would make me the bitch of the year. He hadn't done or said anything bad, so technically I had no reason to be this angry with him. The behavior of the salon patrons wasn't really his fault, yet I wanted to hate this man. Hate him with a passion because he reminded me of someone else.

Before I could come up with a reasonable response, the timer on Courtney's hair dinged. "Thank you for the tip. I gotta get back to work. Have a nice day."

I turned and left him at the counter. A few seconds later, the bell sounded over the door, and I assumed he was gone.

Kimmie hissed at me from her station. "What the fuck is wrong with you? He was hot as hell!"

Yes, he was hot. My hormones agreed, but that attraction made me hate him more. It didn't make sense, but that's where I was. The snake in my belly coiled up, and I had to keep moving before it talked to me.

"Whatever," I flipped back. I had a client in my chair who was paying me a lot of money for her hair, and that's where I focused my attention. Courtney had resumed her spot, and I reached for the foils, ignoring everyone else.

New town, new people, new life.

I repeated the words over and over again.

New town, new people, new life.

New town, new people, new life.

So what if I had the perfect hue of his hazel eyes on my mind?

CHAPTER 4

WEATHERMAN CRINGED AT THE RETCHING SOUNDS COMING from the bathroom. It was impossible not to, as the small cottage didn't allow much privacy. His mom's house sported two bedrooms with a single bathroom between them, a living space, and an eat-in kitchen. The yard wasn't particularly spacious either, but that cut down on maintenance. Most of it was covered with raised garden boxes filled with flowers or vegetables, and the yard itself wasn't much more than pathways through them. This was what his mom had always wanted—a neat, nice house with lots of things growing around it.

"Mom, you need help?" he called out.

"I'm fine, sweetie. I'll be out in a minute."

He pressed his lips together as the toilet flushed. Chemo fucking sucked. Three infusions in the last three weeks, and this was her reaction every time. What would the next three do? The daily radiation had four more weeks to go, then more scans, more hospital time, more infection risks, more of everything.

He wanted to scream at the unfairness of it all. His mom had worked hard all her life to provide for the both of them. Many times she'd had to take on a second job to make ends meet, yet his memories were happy full ones. All the chapter books they read before bedtime on school nights, board games every Thursday evening with the neighbors, Saturday afternoons at the children's museum, swim meets and soccer games at the Y, hanging at the pool in the summer with the other kids who lived in the apartment complex. Everything his mom did involved him, and he would forever be grateful to her for her sacrifices in raising him.

Natalie came out of the bathroom. She'd taken the time to comb what was left of her bobbed brown hair and wash her face, but she was still in the long zipped-up bathrobe she'd put on that morning. It was almost noon. It was rare that she would still be in pajamas at this hour, as the woman was a powerhouse when it came to working. "I don't know what's got into me. I'm just so tired."

He looked at his mom's pink scalp showing through the brittle strands. "Chemo, Mom. It's the chemo working."

"Well, I wish it would go faster and get rid of this mess. I got things to do. Cain't be lyin' around in bed all day."

His heart pinged. "It's okay to take some time off, Mom. You've earned it."

She shuffled over to the sofa and sat down with a groan. "Never thought I'd be sittin' on my butt so much in my life. I feel useless."

Weatherman couldn't help the chuckle. "You've never been useless, Mom. Why don't you watch one of those romance movies you like so much. Hell, you can binge all day. No one to stop you."

Natalie sighed and propped her feet on the coffee table. "If I'm gonna sit here and indulge myself, I might as well get something done. Hand me that basket over yonder. The one with my stitchin' in it."

Weatherman lifted a large round basket filled with cloth, colored threads, and other sewing and knitting implements. Some things never changed. His mother worked a lot with fiber arts, and seldom had he ever seen her without a project in her hands. "Cross-stitching? What are you making?"

"Just finishin' up stuff I hadn't gotten 'round to doin'. Might as well make my time productive."

She picked up a white square mounted in a hoop and poked through a box of needles. "You go take care of your business. Emma said she'd come by tonight and bring me some food from that new place downtown. The one where some old diner used to be."

Weatherman smiled. He'd heard all about the Smoky Mountain Bistro from Dodge. Apparently, he had a thing going with the owner. Good for him. It was about time his friend found a worthy woman to be with.

Thoughts of the new hairdresser he met a few weeks

ago at Tambre's place came unbidden to his mind. Prickly attitude and sporting a chip on her shoulder the size of Texas, he wondered how such an unpleasant person could work in as social an environment as a salon.

Opal. Opal was her name.

Weatherman donned his cut, settling the material at his back as if putting on armor. He didn't wear it at the TV station, but otherwise, he always had it on, declaring his membership. "I'm gonna check on a couple local jobs. Might talk to Chief Wilson and see if the rangers have any openings. I'll go by Table and Lori's for a bit before I head off to Knoxville."

Natalie picked up a card of green thread and unwound a length. "I don't like the idea of you out fightin' fires or lookin' for poachers."

"It's what I trained for, Mom. Both areas. I got all the certificates, and it pays well. Most of the time, I'll be sprucing up campsites and walking trails. Not all that glamorous, but I have to do something."

Her fingers trembled as she poked the end of the thread at the eye. Weatherman held his breath and willed it to go in. He was wary of helping her too much. His mother was a proud woman and needed to keep as much of her dignity as she could. There would be a time soon when she would have to give in and let people help her. Until then, he'd let her thread her own needles.

Thankfully, the thin green line was on target. Natalie relaxed when she saw her success. "There now. All done. Well, git on with yourself. You're burnin' daylight."

Weatherman smiled as he leaned down and kissed his mother's forehead. "Love you, Mom."

"Love you, too, son."

CHAPTER 5

Weatherman pulled up to Dragon's Ink and entered Table's establishment. He'd spent some time at the forestry department headquarters and had a long talk with the chief. The training he'd done during his high school years and college summers paid off, and as long as he passed the physical stamina test, he was assured of a job. It also helped that they were short-staffed.

The buzz of the tattoo gun mixed with classic AC/DC. Table bent over a client's shoulder, coloring in an elaborate python coiling around the guy's arm. The 3D effect was stunning and made Weatherman want something like it. The other piece Table had done for him was very simple, just the words of his college's motto scripted on his forearm. *Levo Oculos Meos In Montes* — "I lift my eyes to the mountains."

"Hey, Weatherman. Bring any rain with you?" Table called out as he dipped more ink. The sweating man in the chair took a breath and grimaced as the buzzing started up again. "It's drier than a mummy's ass out there."

"Not this time. How's life with Lori?"

Table grinned from ear to ear. "Gets better every day. God knew what he was doin' when he sent her to me."

Weatherman's lips broke into a wide smile. "I'm happy for you."

"Thanks. How's your mama?"

"The doctor said the side effects could be mild or severe, few or many. From what she's going through right now, they're at the severe end."

"I'm sorry to hear that, brother."

Weatherman sighed. "Yeah, me too. It can't be helped, though, and there aren't a lot of alternatives. At least we have a chance of beating it."

"Your mom's always been a fighter. Wish there was better news, but I get it. The club will stand by you and her, whatever happens."

A burn started in the back of Weatherman's eyes. He'd lived most of his life with only one person he could count on for anything. Now, he had a whole family ready to have his back whenever he called and then some. "I understand Lori's running a daycare kind of thing."

Table huffed and wiped the man's arm. "Ain't no 'kinda' about it. My house is filled with so much kid shit that I have to camp out in the garage to keep my man card. She's got two other mothers who trade off days. I've been out lookin' for a place to make into a center for them." He wiped again and shook his head.

"God knows I love my woman and my kids, but I'm tired of steppin' on plastic blocks and stacking cups."

Weatherman laughed aloud. In the five years Lori and Table had been together, they had produced two boys in addition to Angel, Table's daughter by his first wife. This was a surprise, as they didn't believe Lori could get pregnant. Angel was now in first grade. Cameron was four, and Mitchell was two. Currently, Lori was pregnant again, and more than one remark had been made about Table and Stud being in competition to see who could produce the most children.

The client let out a bark of comradery. "My kid has a bazillion Legos. I swear the damn things breed overnight. Them little pieces are the perfect size and shape to dig into the soles of your feet when you're not lookin'." He groaned. "How much longer you thinkin'?"

"I can go all night, brother, but if you're ready for a break, I am too."

The client nodded. "Yeah, I think I'm done this round. Great job so far. Even my wife likes it."

Table chuckled as he wiped the man's arm with antiseptic. "That's good. I'd hate it for you if she didn't. I won't go over aftercare this time. Been down this road a time or two, eh?"

The man laughed. "Yeah, I know the drill. Courtney's thing is her hair. Gets it done up every few weeks over at the salon. My thing is my ink. Don't know what I want after the snake is done, but I'll figure something out."

Table swiped the credit card, and the client left with his arm swathed in white gauze and plastic wrap. The tattoo artist turned to Weatherman. "Wanna go to the house and grab a bite?"

"Sure. I got time before I gotta hit the road."

Table squirted sanitizer on his hands and rubbed them together. "Sucks that you got a two-hour commute ahead of you."

"I'll take the southern route back to Knoxville and ride the Tail. Only a few more broadcasts and I'll be here permanently. Interviewed today with the forestry service. All I gotta do is pass the test and I'm in."

"Can you handle it with all that's going on?"

Weatherman took a deep breath. "Helps clear my head to have something else to focus on."

Table nodded. "I get that, brother. Let's get over to the house. Lori's itchin' to see you."

They rode in tandem down the road, Table leading and Weatherman just behind him. Greenery flashed by as the bikes roared over the asphalt. Signs of the season changes were there despite the late-summer heat. The vibrant greens of the mountains had started to change to fall colors.

Table pulled off at a hidden spot next to a nondescript mailbox. The house was nestled deep in a forested area and wasn't visible from the main road. Weatherman glanced up at the state-of-the-art security cameras that dotted the driveway. It opened to a mountain dream spot. A perfectly manicured lawn surrounded a gorgeous modern two-story home in the middle of a clearing. A separate four-car garage and storage shed sat next to it. Few people knew Lori's past and that she'd inherited a very substantial amount of money. She and Table had this place built special for their growing family. It was a little slice of heaven, tucked away with one of the area's many creeks running through the backyard.

Lori came out of the house with a baby nestled under her arm and partially on her pregnant belly. Weatherman smiled as a tiny blonde dynamo burst through the door past her and sprinted over the grass to him.

"Uncle Wedder!"

Weatherman winced at the moniker his mentor's daughter gave him. She had trouble saying "Weatherman" and had dubbed him "Wedder" when she started learning how to speak. The name stuck. "Hey, poohbear. How's my favorite girl?" He scooped her up, and she hugged his neck hard enough to choke him.

"I'm good. I started big school, and it's a lot of fun."

"School *is* a lot of fun. It can be hard sometimes, but learning new things is always a good time."

He took note of the child on Lori's hip. "Is there a new kid I don't know about?"

Table walked up and leaned in to kiss his wife. "This little cuteness is a client's kid. Pearl. Belongs to the new hairdresser over at Tambre's place." He slipped past Lori and entered the house.

So, Opal had a daughter. Weatherman looked at the baby. Her big blue eyes watched him with open curiosity. Her pale hair stood up in two wispy pigtails wrapped in pink ties. She had a sippy cup in one hand and a stuffed alligator with bulging eyes in the other. Weatherman could see the resemblance to her mother and knew when she grew up, she would be a knockout.

He wondered briefly about the father. Was he the reason the hairdresser was so prickly toward him? He didn't recall a wedding band, but perhaps she didn't wear one. Or Daddy wasn't in the picture at all. He could relate, and it made sense. "Opal and Pearl. That's cute."

Lori blinked. "Oh, so you met Opal? I can't imagine what that poor woman is dealing with. Single mother, moving so far away from everything she knew in her life. It's a big step."

So, she was a transplant, from the northern Midwest by her accent. Weatherman filed that bit of news away, his curiosity piqued.

Table came back out with two beers and handed one to Weatherman. "You did the same thing, baby girl. Left a whole other life behind and ended up here."

"I was running from something." She hitched the little girl higher and frowned. "Come to think of it, I bet Opal is too. I get the impression that she's had a rough time."

The adults moved through the house to the deck that overlooked the backyard. It was a preschooler's fantasy land: a swing set, plastic dinosaur jungle gym, sandbox, and big kiddie pool filled the fenced area. Angel ran to the giant storage bin they used as an outdoor toy box and started rummaging through it. The two boys tumbled out of the house and joined her.

Weatherman burned to ask questions about Opal. Rough time from what? Abusive husband? Deadbeat father? What about her family?

The scant information he had told him she was essentially by herself. Just her and her daughter. He understood firsthand how hard that life could be. He also understood that she'd landed in the perfect place to start fresh, with a ready-made family. If she would allow it, of course. Dodge's woman, Fauna, had been brought into the fold recently, and that had taken some effort. Some ongoing drama still lingered there, but everyone in the club supported them as a couple.

Table held out his beer. "To finding new places and new people."

Weatherman clinked the neck of his bottle against Table's before taking a long sip.

Lori asked Table about his day and then shared hers. "I ran into Burna Jones at Target this afternoon. She was tearing into a clerk over the price of composition note-books and having a major fit about three-ring binder colors." She shook her head and settled herself on a metal patio chair. "Hilda is a freshman this year, and the teachers have long lists of specific supplies they expect the students to have. Poor girl had to listen to her grandma rant about how much everything is costing her."

Pearl dropped the sippy cup and examined the toy alligator's eyes.

Table burped lightly. "Burna Jones is never happy. Told off Dillon Johnson after he mowed her lawn. Said he didn't do it right 'cause the lines didn't go in the direction she wanted 'em to. Now she's having trouble finding someone to do her yardwork."

"I almost feel sorry for her." Lori settled Pearl in a webbed playpen and handed her the dropped cup.

"I feel sorrier for Hilda."

Weatherman took a swallow and watched as Pearl pulled herself up to a wobbly stand. She gazed at him and pointed. "Bah-bah-bah-bah." He smiled at the little girl and winked at her. She grinned back, then sat back down on her diapered rear end and started playing with her alligator.

He chuckled. At least this one liked him, unlike her mother.

They talked about random stuff. The club and its upcoming events, the extreme dry weather, the local high school football team and their Friday night games —anything and everything except his mother's battle. It was nice to have a respite for a moment. Weatherman appreciated their efforts.

The kids came up for juice boxes, and Lori waddled into the house to get them snacks. Table put his beer aside as one of the boys crawled onto his lap and poked at the Dragon patch on his cut. Weatherman also put his half-finished beer down and noticed Pearl had grabbed onto the playpen edge again, standing steady while looking at him. She really was a cute kid.

She gave him a coquettish smile and dropped her

head to hide her eyes, only to pop back up and giggle. Weatherman covered his own eyes and flipped his hand open, and she let out huge belly laughs. He played peekaboo with her until Lori came out with several plastic bowls of Goldfish crackers and Teddy Grahams. Pearl plopped back onto her rear and munched the treats.

"Your mama is on her way to get you, pretty girl. Can you say 'mama'?"

"A-mah," Pearl agreed.

Weatherman decided that was his cue to leave, although he was tempted to stick around to see how Opal would react to him being there. What would she think about the innocent game he'd just played with her daughter? He bet she would get huffy and might even blow a gasket. That held some entertaining curiosity, but he did need to get on the road.

"I gotta get going."

Table stood up and flipped his oldest boy upside down to dangle him by his feet. Cameron squealed with delight, and Mitchell jumped up and down, shouting, "Me too! Me too!"

"You okay to ride?" the big man inquired as he descended the back steps with his boys into the thick grass of the yard.

Weatherman nodded. "Half a beer won't be a problem."

"I meant the other sh… stuff in your head. You clear enough?"

Weatherman understood the implied invitation to

crash overnight if needed. More beers, more small talk, more distraction. It meant a hell of a lot to have that kind of support from the person who acted more like a big brother than a friend. "I'm good. I'd feel better getting back tonight rather than dashing tomorrow morning. Thanks for everything. I'll see you soon."

He gave Lori and Angel a quick hug. The boys continued wrestling with their dad and opted for waves from the yard.

As he walked to the driveway, he couldn't help but play one more round of peekaboo with Pearl.

CHAPTER 6

"I saw this ad on Facebook 'bout a new cream that treats cellulite. I'm thinkin' 'bout orderin' some."

"Hmph. You know all that mess is nothin' but a scam."

"My son is a starter on the football team. I swear he's doubling my laundry."

"The marching band rehearses three times a week after school. I gotta take snacks over for them next Wednesday."

I lifted another section of hair from the client at my station and swiped the mahogany color on it. The salon buzzed with gossip this late afternoon. September was in full swing, and the women had shifted to fall mode. Classes, teachers, football games, and an upcoming community-wide Halloween party that the Dragon Runners sponsored. That event was a long time away as far as I was concerned, but I got the impression that it was a big deal.

Tambre came over to my station. "How are you, Agatha? Is your husband coming in for your birthday?"

The woman in my chair nodded her foiled head. "Yeah, he got his leave approved. It's hard sometimes, and the boys and I miss him, but if all goes well with this promotion, he'll get an assignment stateside, and we'll move to where he's stationed. Fingers crossed that it'll be soon."

"I hope he stays safe out there." Tambre touched a wrapped foil to check it. "Loving a military man ain't easy, but you got yourself a good one. Opal here is one of the best colorists I've ever seen. She'll get you ready for the reunion."

I preened a little at the compliment. It meant a lot that Tambre trusted me with the people here in the shop. This was the second time Agatha had been in my chair and the first time I'd colored for her. "Always glad to help. Where are your boys?" I asked.

She smiled as she held still for the next section to be painted. "Chad is in the first grade, and Tori is in preschool at my church until one. This is my only free time for shopping, haircuts, personal doctor appointments, and all that happy stuff." She laughed out loud, making the foils rattle. "I swear, I live my life by Google Calendar."

I laughed with her. I figured us to be around the same age, roughly twenty-six, but she seemed far older. Probably because she had two kids, a husband, and a house. We chatted about kids, daycare, nighttime routines, and other parenting tips as I worked.

I thought about it as I set the timer. Many of the women here had children and spouses, and I heard hours of their complaints.

"He never listens to me."

"Spends all his free time in the garage or in front of the TV."

"We never go anywhere or do anything."

Perhaps being single wasn't a terrible thing. Did it bother me? I paused at the thought as I entered the break room to get my water bottle from the fridge. I had the beginnings of a great career in a skill that would never grow old. I had my daughter to raise. I had friendships developing in this small town. Yes, I admitted, I did get lonely from time to time, but for the most part, I was good with my own company. Did I need a man in my life? Not really.

Did I *want* a man in my life?

That question I couldn't answer.

The timer buzzed a short time later, and I smiled at Agatha's grinning face. The foils came off easily, and I piled them into a shiny mountain on the working tray. A quick shampoo and conditioning later, she perched in my chair and grinned widely as I picked up my comb and tools.

"Oh my, that color came out really nice. I love it!" She beamed as she tilted her head from side to side. "Do you have any recommendations for a new look that fits me?"

I regarded her reflection in the giant mirror at my station and pondered for a moment. "Since you like shorter styles, I'd do a reverse bob with a long side sweep. It draws the eye upward and slims the face."

Agatha laughed and tapped her rounded chin. "I need all the help I can get. Let's do it."

I smiled back. "You bet."

The comb gently glided through Agatha's freshly colored strands before she spoke again. "I'm so glad you moved here. Such a blessing. My older brother is single. His name is Robert, but we call him Bobby. Brother Bobby, to be exact. He's the new preacher over to the big church on First Street. I'll introduce you to him sometime soon. What church did you grow up in?"

I hesitated. Yeah, I was aware of religion, Jesus, and all that stuff, but I'd never really gotten into that scene. "I didn't grow up in a church."

I should have lied. Agatha grabbed onto that statement like a starving man to a sandwich.

"Well, that settles it. I'm bringing Bobby to see you next week. He'll probably invite you to his church, and you can watch him preach. When he's up in the pulpit, he needs a proper haircut 'stead of them whack jobs he gets from the barbershop."

My stomach danced with trepidation. The last thing I wanted right now was to meet men. Any man. I just got my life on track and wasn't planning to get off it. Didn't I just decide I was okay with being single?

"I'm not sure I'm ready to start dating."

"Are you divorced?"

An unexpected rush of emotion joined the chorus line kicking in my gut. This wasn't the first time someone made assumptions about my past. I had no intention of explaining anything, and I kept most of my thoughts to myself. It was easier to let people guess the worst—and in truth, they weren't that far off. "He died."

I could barely get the words out.

Agatha thankfully let it go. "I'm so sorry for your loss. How long ago?"

"This past winter."

"Oh, I'm so, so sorry. My deepest condolences." She said it with such sincerity, I believed her.

Whether that meant she gave up on her brother and me or not was a crapshoot, but I needed to get my head under control. I smiled and faked my way into a good attitude. "Thank you. Now, let's get this party started."

I picked up my scissors and started shaping.

The salon kept buzzing all day. Appointments, walk-ins, the latest gossip—it all flowed around me as I worked. These women were involved in so much, and every one of them had stories to tell about life, love, and family. Many times, I considered myself an outsider looking in, but it was nice to be somewhat included in this extended group.

Molly came by with bags of zucchini. "Here, y'all. Grab as much as you want, 'cause I'll have more tomorrow. Cutter done lost his mind plantin' that much. We got all sorts of squash coming out our ears. Anyone want tomatoes or cucumbers for picklin'? Them vines is still producing like crazy."

A few women poked through the bags. Another one

said something about pumpkins and cushaw abundance to come. I had no idea what a cushaw was, but apparently it was a popular item here.

Molly looked around and frowned. "Where's Kimmie?"

Tambre came from the back with a concerned expression on her face. "I'm not sure. She was supposed to be here a half hour ago and hasn't called."

I swept up my station and kept my head down, hoping they wouldn't ask me directly about my roommate. She was going out more and more during the week, staying out late and coming home in the wee hours of the morning. It bothered me, as I had firsthand knowledge of the path she was on and what the end of it held, but I didn't have the power to stop her.

Kimmie's timing radar must have been on. She ran into the salon, out of breath and disheveled. "Sorry, sorry, sorry, I got caught in a tangle on the highway. Damn construction zone!"

Molly laughed. "No worries, girl. Let's get started, 'cause I got a time limit."

Tambre's smile of relief didn't quite reach her eyes.

CHAPTER 7

THE MUSIC IN HIS EARBUDS DIDN'T COVER THE SOUNDS coming from the bathroom. Weatherman dressed for work and gritted his teeth as his mom was violently sick. She vomited from anything she tried to put in her stomach. Even drinking a glass of water brought it on.

Every.

Fucking.

Treatment.

He hated it. Hated that he could do nothing about it but listen to his mother deal with this painful routine. Her reactions were so bad, the doctors gave her extended breaks between infusions, but that only seemed to increase the suffering.

"Mom, you need me?" he called out as he lifted the pot from the stove and poured the heated water into a glass pitcher filled with ginger tea bags.

"I'll be fine in a minute."

A moment later, Natalie appeared in her zipped-up

robe and slippers. Her hair was gone now, and she wore a scarf wrapped around her head. Weatherman pressed his lips together, knowing this bothered his mom a lot, but again, there was nothing he could do about it. This feeling of helplessness bugged the shit out of him and made this whole situation worse.

She slowly made her way into the living room and sat in her big recliner. "I hate this crap."

Weatherman agreed. "I'm sorry you have to go through it, Mom." He poured some tea into a glass filled with ice. "I hope this will help settle your stomach."

"Doctor told me to keep my fluids up no matter what or else I gotta get an IV," she groused. "I don't want any more needles to deal with than I have to. Bad enough with this damn portacath in my neck." She took a cautious sip of the brew. "Yeah, that's good. Thank you, dear."

"No problem."

She contemplated the glass in her hand. Mickey Mouse danced under the hundredth-anniversary logo. "You remember when we went there, when you were around six or seven."

Weatherman smiled. "Yes, I do. We walked right into the Main Street Parade as soon as we got there. I was fascinated and a little scared. First time I'd ever been on a plane."

"I wasn't exactly a world traveler either. I figured driving would take too long outta our vacation time, so flying was a better way. I let Disney Travel make all the arrangements. Kinda nice just to pay one price and let someone else take care of it."

Weatherman sat on the sofa next to the chair. His mother continued to sip at the tea, which she seemed to be keeping down so far. "I remember the rides, the shows, the food. Space Mountain was my favorite, I think, but then we went to Animal Kingdom the next day." He smiled at the memory. "That was a great time."

"We had some good ones, didn't we? How 'bout the camping trip in Chattanooga?"

Weatherman laughed. "Oh shit, yes. We got the tent set up, and it rained like hell for three days. Flooded the whole damn campground. We still did the caverns and the aquarium but slept in the car. I still remember it was a fun trip."

"Sometimes you have to adapt."

Weatherman's chuckles continued as he picked up his own glass of tea. He remembered how that phrase came from his mother's mouth many times during his childhood. When she had to figure out a janky DIY repair at their apartment because the landlord couldn't be bothered. When she had to leave work and take him to the emergency room because he'd fallen off his skateboard and broken his arm. When she got laid off from the bank and needed to come up with another income source for several months.

Sometimes you have to adapt.

Weatherman regarded the glass in his hand. This one had Dixie Stampede printed on it. "We did so many camping trips all over the place. Georgia, West Virginia, Ohio, Kentucky—some really cool places. If you had a trip you could go on right now, what would you choose to do? Camping again or something nicer?"

"I liked the camping thing, but if I had the strength and the time, I'd go on one of them big tropical cruises. One that has the little paper umbrellas in the drinks. Never had one like that." She paused. "I always thought I'd do that someday, but I'm not so sure I'll get that chance now."

Pain cut into Weatherman's heart, clean and sharp. No, he wouldn't acknowledge that thought by saying it aloud. Uttering those words would put some weight behind that possibility, and he wasn't ready for that. Not yet. Not when there was any ray of hope.

His mom had been a powerhouse of a woman his entire life. The person to give him roots so he could grow wings. He would forever be grateful for all the sacrifices she made to give him the best life she could. And now, when faced with the ultimate challenge, he wanted to give back all he was able. "I'll make sure you get your cruise, Mom. You just gotta work a little harder to beat this thing."

Her laugh was loud and weak at the same time. "I'll do my best, dear, but it's not up to me. Emma should be here soon. Why don't you go get your ass outta here before you're late? You want to give me something? Go find me a daughter-in-law who's gonna take care of you when I'm not around."

There it was again. "Mom, I wish you wouldn't say shit like that."

Natalie sighed. "Sweetheart, if I had the choice, I'd be here forever just to see all the great things I know you're gonna do. Reality is, I might not. I promised you I'd fight the good fight as long as I could, and we'll see if that's enough. Lord knows I'd love to see you with someone special and with kids of your own."

Weatherman sniffed. "I'm working on it."

"Hey, y'all," a voice called out. A minute later, an African American woman in scrubs came in the door carrying a plastic grocery bag of yarn. "Hey, Miz Natalie. I brought some yarn I found on sale over to Walmart. Lord ha' mercy, them people there is crazy. I saw a woman shoutin' down one of the clerks over a buy-one-get-one candy bar. She wanted the free one without paying for the first one." Emma shook her head. "Don't make a lick a' sense."

Natalie laughed. "I'd spend good money for that kind of show."

Emma did the routine of checking vitals, then asking about symptoms, aftereffects, and general health. Weatherman stood from his spot to allow her to work.

Natalie joked about her sickness. "I always wanted to lose that extra twenty pounds, but I didn't think it would come off this way."

He had to laugh to keep from crying.

Emma chuckled. "Now that we got the business end of things done, let's get down to what's really important. I hope you'll put down the cross-stitchin' and show me how to cable knit today."

Seconds later, the TV was on some afternoon talk show, and the two women were bent over needles and yarn.

Weatherman watched as Natalie inserted what looked like a big toothpick through the pile in her hand. "I'm gonna go for a ride and head over to the station. I'll see you later tonight, yeah?"

Natalie didn't look up as she twisted the multicolored strands around her fingers. "Okay, dearest. Be safe."

He left the small house and mounted his bike, pointing it in the direction of the highway. In a few minutes, he opened up the throttle and relished the wind against his face shield. Only now could he allow the tears to fall from his eyes.

He cursed long and loud at the unfairness of life. His mom had worked so damn hard for decades and now was battling to keep her life when she should be enjoying retirement. *It's not right,* he screamed in his head as he barreled down the road.

He took one curve a little too fast and skidded slightly. He corrected quickly before it became a problem, but he did slow down. The last thing his mom needed was a call that he'd been hospitalized for being a dumbass.

Off in the distance, he spotted a car on the roadside shoulder. The trunk was open, and a woman rummaged in the back. As he passed it, he saw the flat tire. He wasn't in the mood to deal with people, but a lone woman trying to change a tire on her own prompted him to turn around and go back to help her.

He pulled up behind the car and recognized Opal, the unpleasant woman from the salon who'd cut his hair a while back. Pearl's mother.

As disagreeable as she'd been, he'd thought she was pretty when he first saw her. Hell, she was what he would call hot, but her standoffish and downright hostile attitude turned him off. Big-time. On the other hand, she was a single mom with all the frustrations that came with the title. Perhaps she'd been having a really bad day when he entered the salon. He was willing to give her the benefit of the doubt but planned on steering clear of her. Even so, as much as he preferred to keep riding, his sense of right wasn't so skewed as to drive off and leave her there.

She turned, and for a brief moment, he saw a flash of fear in her eyes.

Fear? Of him?

It didn't last long. Those baby blues shut down in an instant, and she stood straight.

"What do you want?" Her tone was Nordic cold, and Weatherman had the urge to turn around and leave. It pissed him off, and in his present state, he would probably lose his temper at her and say things he would regret later.

"I thought you might need some help. My mistake."

She huffed a bit but relaxed her face. "Actually, I do. I don't know how to change a tire, and my cell phone is dead."

Weatherman let part of his ire go. It wasn't her fault that life was rough now. He shouldn't take it out on her. He inhaled through his nose and blew out a calming breath. "I'll take care of it. Got a jack back there?"

She lifted a tool bag from the spare tire well. "Is this it?"

He stifled a smile. If he laughed at her ignorance, she might throw it at him. "Yeah, it is. Step back, and I'll get this done."

"Okay. Hold on a minute." The bag clinked as she handed it to him and then walked to the back of the car.

Weatherman opened the drawstring and examined the contents. Just as he'd thought. The crappy, flimsy stock tools that came standard with the vehicle. He hoped they would hold up long enough to get the job done.

As he placed the jack under the frame, Opal came back around to the side of the car with something in her arms. Weatherman had to stop and look. Pearl peeked out at him from a pink blanket and grinned her baby teeth at him. Automatically, his eyes darted to Opal's left hand to confirm the absence of a ring.

She didn't miss the curious look. "I'm a single mom. Is that a problem?"

Weatherman focused back on his task. "Not at all. I was raised by a single mom, so I know firsthand how tough it can get."

She bobbled the baby but didn't say anything. No snappy rejoinder. There was a lot going on behind her eyes. He was somewhat curious but didn't ask. She might answer, and if she did, then he'd get to know her. If he got to know her, he might develop an interest in her. If he developed an interest in her, that would detract from his obligations to his own mother. Still, he had a soft spot for single moms.

The flipping jack handle on the loose crank wrench slipped like crazy as he lifted the car but miraculously didn't break. Somehow it held, and he prayed it stayed that way until he got the tire done. He nearly threw his back out forcing off the nuts, but he got them loose after several minutes of yanking and swearing at them with the floppy nut wrench. The spare tire was one of those cheap fifty-fifty styles, but at least it would get her to the garage.

"You should get a T-handle nut wrench. Better torque in case you have to do this by yourself someday." He put the poor tools back in the bag and pulled the string shut. There weren't any towels that he could see, so he wiped his hands on his jeans.

"I'll check into it." Her tone came out contrite. She took a breath. "I'm sorry for being so mean to you. It's...." She sighed. "I'm not in a really great place right now, but I'm trying."

He relaxed his stance and his attitude, as he definitely related to that statement. "I get you. My life isn't where I want it to be either, but time only has one direction—forward. It will get better." He closed the trunk and turned to face her. He didn't know how she would react if she knew he had met her daughter at Table and Lori's place, and even played peekaboo with her. "What's your daughter's name?"

She smiled at the dozing child. "This is my precious Pearl."

Opal and Pearl. It really is very cute, Weatherman thought as he watched Opal's face soften. Her clean wavy hair was pulled back from her face in a high ponytail, making her appear more like a teenager than a mother somewhere in her twenties. One fat lock hung over her forehead and framed her thickly lashed eyes.

Beautiful.

Weatherman cleared his thickening throat. "You're ready to go as far as I can tell. Know where the DRMC garage is located? Drive there and I'll follow you to make sure you get there without any more problems."

Her eyes darted to him, and her full mouth thinned as she pressed her lips together. "Thank you, but I can take it from here."

Weatherman pointed to his cut. "How much do you know about motorcycle clubs?"

He watched her shut down. Physically. Immediately. Completely. The light drained from her eyes, and her body locked tight.

"More than I ever wanted," she stated, her words devoid of any emotion. "I need to go. Thanks again." She turned to leave.

"Hold up." He reached out a hand to touch her

shoulder and get her attention. Her reflexes were lightning fast.

"Keep your hands off me!" she hissed and stepped away.

He held both hands up, palms toward her. "Whoa, whoa, whoa, lady. Calm down. I was just going to say the Dragon Runners have a code when it comes to taking care of the women in this town. You see a man wearing this emblem, you can trust that he won't leave you on the side of the road until you're safe."

The baby started fussing, making Opal more upset. Her face screwed up in frustration as she jiggled the toddler. "I don't need anyone taking care of me. I appreciate your help, but that's all you're gonna get from me. Just my thanks."

What the hell? His tone became acidic. "I didn't ask you for anything, did I?"

That stopped her. "No," she begrudgingly admitted. Pearl let out a squall. "Now see what you've done?"

Weatherman threw his hands in the air. "I give up. Get yourself to the garage and take care of that tire as soon as possible. I'm outta here."

He turned to his bike and strapped on his helmet. Out of the corner of his eye, he watched her put the baby in the car seat and then get in the driver's side. The car cranked up, and she drove away without looking back.

"Crazy woman," Weatherman declared as he revved up his bike. Her defensive reaction to him made him wonder what had happened to her to make her that way, but it wasn't his problem. "Not my circus, not my monkeys. I got enough on my plate to deal with right now. I don't need something else to worry about."

He still followed her until he saw her pull into the garage before breaking away to go to the station.

CHAPTER 8

This was so not my scene. Kimmie had been at me for days, pushing and pushing and pushing until I finally gave in. I hadn't mentioned anything to her about Tambre's concerns, but she'd been coming into work on time recently and seemed to have cleaned up her act. She continued to go out almost every night, though. It bothered me, but there wasn't much I could do about it. Being the supportive friend was a role I thought I needed to play for her and for myself. That was one reason I was outside the River's Edge Bar on a Friday night with Kimmie while Deandra babysat for me. My goal was to be done and home by midnight at the latest, and Kimmie had already made fun of me for making this plan.

"Jeez, you used to be fun. Now you're like some old person."

I never thought twenty-six was old, but in her eyes, I guess I was. As a working mom, I had to prioritize my time to take care of my daughter and my job. Anything else stayed on the back burners, and some of them were turned off permanently.

I shut off my car and took a deep breath. Kimmie rummaged in her purse and pulled out a plastic bag with three tightly rolled joints in it.

"You'd better not think you're gonna smoke those in here," I snapped.

Kimmie huffed as she pulled one out and placed it between her lips. "Fuck, Opal. What's wrong with you?"

"Nothing's wrong with me. I just don't want the smell of pot in my car."

She found a cheap lighter and flicked the wheel with her thumb. It sparked a few times but didn't ignite. "Damnit, I'll save these for later. Got 'em from a guy over at that other place in Maggie Valley. Real shithole, but damn, they know how to have a good time! Let's get inside and get a drink. Hopefully some lucky guy in there can get the stick out of your ass for a change."

I bit back a nasty retort and asked myself for the hundredth time, *Why did I come here?*

The gravel crunched as we walked across the parking lot to the log cabin–styled building. It was bigger than I'd expected, with a long line of bikes in a regimented row along the front. Music spilled out from the door, and I recognized the tune, but I couldn't name the song. I saw through the opening that Stud stood up front with a bass in his hands and was singing into a mic. I'd met him and his wife, Eva, when they brought their girls in for cuts. He was one of the hottest men I'd ever seen. His full mouth made this half smile that had this sexy come-hither vibe to it. The ladies in the crowd squealed like obsessed teenagers. Then Eva arrived, and I saw that smile was totally for her.

My heart jumped a little. Someone smiled at me like that. Once.

"For fuck's sake, Opal, come on!"

Kimmie's impatience started to irritate me. I had to be at the salon by nine in the morning for a cut and special color palette that would take me about four hours to do. Bad idea to start that kind of work if I was too tired, or even worse, hungover. "I'll be the designated driver. I don't want to do any drinking."

She threw her hands in the air and huffed out an impatient breath. "Fine. You do you. I'm gonna have some fun. Feel free to leave me anytime. I can get a ride from someone."

She disappeared into the crowd toward the bar. I found a clear spot at a back wall and parked myself there to watch and listen to the music. It had been ages since I'd been to a bar. It didn't really scare me, but I was still a little nervous.

The people were piled in thick, and many were dancing. I spotted some of the other Dragon Runners members by their cuts. One of them sat at the bar sipping a white ceramic mug of what I assumed was coffee. Huge, dark, and menacing, his eyes scanned the crowd constantly. Another one was behind the bar along with Betsey. I remembered someone calling him

Bruiser, but I hadn't really met him yet. She spotted me and waved me over. I played dumb and waved back. Then she got too busy filling orders to bother with me.

I glanced at my phone sometime later to find out only a half hour had passed by. I was sure it was more. The lights, the noise, the gyrating bodies—it was getting to me. I found myself thinking about the burn of a fireball shot as it made its way down my throat. Then the second and the third and the fourth and finally the numbness that followed. It had been so long since I'd done anything like that, and the sudden craving caught me off guard.

"Just one drink won't hurt," the voice in my belly urged. One that had been dormant but never completely gone.

No, I said internally, with a firmness that didn't quite hit the mark.

"You can take tonight to relax. Go back to boring tomorrow."

Stop talking to me.

"Maybe Kimmie will let you buy a joint off her. She obviously needs the money."

Stop.

"You've been working so hard. Pearl is safe at home. You'd be okay letting your hair down."

Stop!

I almost said it out loud. Shouted it for that matter. Yeah, one drink might be okay, but it could lead to another. Then another. Then another. And when that wasn't enough, other stuff would follow. I would not be going down that road, but it was hard. Especially when a rum and Coke appeared in front of my eyes in a big square hand.

"Here you go, baby doll. You look like you could use one of these."

My eyes focused on a large wide man with a slight gut hanging down over his belt. His flannel shirt screamed country farmer, not biker, and the cowboy hat on his head seemed like overkill. He stood very close to me. Closer than I wanted.

"No, thank you," I shouted, hoping to be heard.

I wasn't.

"Ah, doan' be like that. It's Friday, and we're here for a good time!"

His boyish grin might be cute another time, but at that moment, I found it disturbing. "I'm sorry, but I'm not drinking tonight."

"Come on now, baby doll. I'll make sure you get home safe."

The leer, the sparkle, the words—I recognized this tactic. It was far too familiar. "It's not a good night for me."

The grin fell a little. "You should lighten up some, else you ain't gonna get anywhere."

Anger rose up in me. In the past, I'd handled these situations much differently. Now, I didn't want to handle them at all. "I'm not looking for anything, anyone, or anywhere tonight."

"Then why'd you come here?"

Good question. "I don't know. My friend needed a

wingwoman, but she's abandoned me, so I guess I'll leave."

"Who's your friend?"

"Her name is Kimmie."

His belligerent frown turned up into a knowing smirk. "Kimmie? Pink hair? I met her last weekend over at Reaver's bar in Maggie Valley." His bushy brows waggled a few times. "Now *that's* a woman who knows how to throw down and go down."

A vision of my friend on her knees ran through my mind. I didn't need to hear more about Kimmie and her private life. I wanted to keep my own focus, and at the moment, that was to get away from this bully. "That's great for her, but I'm not into that anymore. Have a nice night."

I turned to leave and was promptly jerked back. My upper arm burned from the meaty hand that was wrapped around it.

"Don't you walk away from me, bitch. I'll say when you can leave."

I wasn't proud of it, but the anger in me drowned in a sea of fear. Memories assailed me and emotions flooded my brain, paralyzing me with the pain of being overpowered and helpless. This was not new, and I felt myself being pulled back into something I didn't want any more. The snake in my belly uncoiled and hissed as it awakened.

"If you need help, you know where to find it."

The sibilant voice laughed at me. It knew I was losing. Should I just give in and get it over with?

"Don't do it, sweetness," another voice spoke up in my head. One that was both welcome and dreaded.

So much whirled through my brain, I couldn't figure out how to react. Run? Give in? Fight? Take the drink and throw it in his face? Or toss it back and down the lot?

In the end, it was decided for me.

A flash caught my eye just as a fist connected with the man's face. He yelled, "Motherfucker!" as he let go of my arm and stumbled back. Weatherman stepped in front of me, shielding me from the asshole.

The snake grumbled but returned under its rock. The other voice went silent, but I got the impression of amusement.

"The lady said no once. She shouldn't have to repeat herself."

Only one other person had ever thrown down for me like this. Stood between me and danger.

And because of me, he would never do it again.

The asshole wasn't backing down, and neither was Weatherman. The man outweighed the biker by at least fifty pounds, yet this David and Goliath scenario kept going.

Then another Goliath came to stand next to Weatherman. The biker who'd been sipping coffee at the bar stood larger and taller, and his face seemed to swell with anger like the Hulk's.

The pretend cowboy backed off with a sneer, attempting to save some sort of face. "Ain't no cunt worth this trouble. Plenty more to choose from."

I wanted to slap him.

I didn't have to, as the big bar bouncer did it for me. The asshole crumpled and didn't get up.

"Thanks, Mute," Weatherman said to the behemoth, getting a thumbs-up in response before turning back to me, his eyes filled with fury. "Come with me."

I followed him outside, not sure why I was also mad as hell. What was it I had that drew jerks to me all the time?

Weatherman whirled around, catching me short. "What the hell are you doing here?" he demanded. His harsh tone rubbed me the wrong way.

"I came with my friend Kimmie." I didn't tell him I only did it because she'd badgered me. He didn't need to know any more of my business than that.

"Kimmie? The one with the pink hair? Ah, hell." He crossed his arms and stood over me. "Do you know where your friend is right now?"

No, I didn't, but I wasn't going to admit that to him. "I think she went to the bathroom."

"If you turn around and look at the Jeep Cherokee in the back under the pin oak tree, you'll see her giving a blow job to one of the oil refinery crewmen who comes here on weekends. She best hope Betsey doesn't find out she's turning tricks out here."

Cold dread hit my stomach like a lead anchor. Sure enough, when I glanced at the Jeep, I saw a head of pink hair bobbing up and down in a man's lap. He had his eyes closed and his head back as she worked him.

I spun away from the sight with a slight cry and

squeezed my eyes tight. If it hadn't been for Weatherman's arms catching me at my elbows, I might have fallen. The image still showed behind my lids, embedded in my brain. Panic clawed its way up my throat.

"Take a breath, baby."

I took in a deep one, filling my lungs as I'd been taught to do. Count to four, exhale over eight.

"Shit. I'm sorry I threw that at you. Wasn't a good idea." His trite tone sounded regretful. "You just don't strike me as a woman who hangs out in bars."

Gut punch. Whatever air I had taken in left me. "You don't know me well enough to know what kind of woman I am."

His eyes glittered down at me. "You're right. I don't know you, and it's not right for me to judge you for taking some time for yourself. Single parenting isn't easy, and you never get time off. But I can tell this is not where you want to be."

I shook my head and let my anger go. "No, it's not. I would rather be home with Pearl. Kimmie's been pushing for me to go somewhere with her, and Deandra volunteered to watch Pearl so I could."

I looked up, meeting his eyes. He stood close, and we both noticed at the same time that he still held my arms. He didn't let go, and I didn't pull away.

In that moment, I felt safer than I had in a long time. I also felt more vulnerable, and the odd combination brought its own level of anxiety.

He took a breath and let it out slowly, his fingers

lightly massaging my forearms in apology. "I'm sorry for jumping your shit earlier. It's not my place to say who or where you can hang out. It can get rowdy at the River's Edge sometimes. You saw that tonight."

He moved closer to me. "I'm not sorry for stepping in."

"I could have handled it." The words came out like the lie they were. No way could I have dealt with that asshole on my own.

"Yeah, maybe, but you shouldn't have to, and you won't when any Dragon Runners man is around. Even if I wasn't here tonight, you think Mute was just gonna let a man put his hands on you uninvited?"

"I guess not."

"No guessing, babe. We take care of our own."

Time stopped. The world around me silenced and ceased to move. It seemed to be waiting. Waiting for me to decide something. Something bigger than me. Something that had the potential of greatness or disaster. A risk I'd taken in the past, and it nearly killed me.

"It's okay to let your heart beat again."

"Have you had anything to drink?"

The dual voices, one in my head and one from the man in front of me, started time flowing again. I dropped my eyes and shook my head. "No." It was the same answer to both of them.

"Do you want to drink? I'll stay with you if you do."

"No. I don't drink. I can't, and I won't." My voice came out defensive and harsh, but I couldn't help it. I hoped he planned on letting that go, as I had no desire to explain why.

Weatherman made a noncommittal sound in his throat. "If you're ready to leave, I'll follow you home."

"I can't leave Kimmie."

"I'll text Bruiser. He'll keep an eye on her and keep her safe. Give me your number, and I'll text if I hear something."

"I'm not—"

"Babe, let me do this for you."

"Babe, let him do this for you."

The two voices were too much to resist. "Okay, but you can only follow me as far as the street. I'll go up to my apartment myself."

I recited my number. His thumbs flew over the phone's screen, my own phone pinging with an incoming message a moment later before he tucked the rectangle into his back pocket. "I just texted you so you'll have my number too. Let's go."

The single headlight stayed with me the ten minutes or so to my place. He didn't follow so close that I thought we'd collide, but his presence was constant in my rearview mirror.

I parked on the street and glanced over to where his bike idled as he straddled the seat. I couldn't see his face behind the face shield, but I sensed his eyes on me. This was confirmed when he flicked two fingers at me. I waved back automatically before tapping my code into the electronic lock to the outside door and heading up to my apartment.

A few minutes later, I watched Deandra head to her car from the upper window. Weatherman was still there, waiting until she got into her car and drove away. His helmeted head tilted back as if checking on me one last time, and then his red taillight disappeared down the road with a throaty growl.

Pearl was dead asleep, but I was wide awake and buzzing with energy. I puttered around the apartment, putting a few dishes away from the drying rack and wiping the counters. Kimmie was so seldom home anymore that most of the mess in the apartment was mine and Pearl's, so it didn't bother me to do nearly all the cleaning. I swept some crumbs into my palm and brushed them into a rather full trash can, debating on whether to take the bag down to the dumpster in the side alley or wait until the morning.

My phone beeped with a message, causing me to jump.

Weatherman: Bruiser texted back to say he put two prospects on Kimmie. She's totally wasted, so they took her to the Lair to sleep it off. They won't hurt her. She's safe.

I let out a heavy breath. The hairs on the back of my neck told me there was more to come, but at least my friend was okay for now.

Me: Thanks for letting me know.

Weatherman: No problem.

I caught my lower lip between my teeth as I took it one step further. Too far, maybe, but something compelled me to send one more text. Just one.

Me: Thanks again for helping me, and sorry for being so bitchy tonight. I'm still dealing with some baggage, and I don't usually talk about it to strangers.

The three dots stayed still for a moment or two, and I thought he was either asleep or going to ignore me.

Weatherman: You've cut my hair. I changed a tire and punched out a guy for you. We exchanged phone numbers. I think it's safe to say we're not strangers anymore. Sleep well, and I'll see you soon. I'm due for another cut.

Weatherman: For what it's worth, I'd keep your baggage to myself. If you need to talk about it, I'll be around.

CHAPTER 9

Chief Wilson shook his head while Ranger Fine lost his breakfast in the bushes. Weatherman pulled at his uniform collar and swallowed several times, determined not to copy the other officer. No wind blew, so the smell of rotting meat from the pile of bear corpses hovered in the air, coating everything in its sickening stench.

Heads. Hides. Paws. All taken, the rest left to putrefy out in the open. Poaching had been a problem for a long time, but this absolute butchery brought the issue to a whole new level.

Weatherman swallowed the saliva in his mouth and forced control on his emotions. Between his mother's illness and the encounter with Opal at the bar, he was ready to punch another asshole. A bear poacher would be perfect.

"Who called it in?" Chief Wilson asked. His disgust was plain on his face.

Many people in the area hunted. Deer and wild turkey mostly, but some tried for bigger game. Hunting permits and limits were strictly enforced, and most hunters followed the rules, but there were those out there who didn't care and collected trophies like tourist mugs. There were some years when certain animal populations were severely restricted. This season for bears was one of them. Weatherman didn't have a problem with hunting, as most of the people he knew did it to fill their freezers. But the scene in front of him had nothing to do with feeding families.

Officer Fine spoke from his bent-over position. "Couple tourists found 'em. They got lost hiking off the trail and stumbled on this shit. Got one o' them fancy location tags and left it here so we could find the place."

Wilson barked a single laugh. "Be nice if more hikers had them things. It'd make findin' 'em a lot easier." He sighed as Weatherman started taking pictures with his phone. "What a damn waste. Second site with shit like this. Same MO. That makes thirteen bears total that's been killed."

Weatherman winced. "There are babies in this pile."

"Son of a bitch." The chief jammed a hand over his face and pinched the bridge of his nose. "I'm gettin' too old for this shit. We got any leads at all?"

"Only ones are Walt and Clem Gustler. Someone phoned in a tip about them showing off some bear paws at some backwoods hooch bar in Maggie Valley. Can't confirm it, though. The moment any of us roll up to talk to anyone, they all go blind and develop amnesia."

The senior officer glared at Weatherman and frowned. "In other words, ain't no one remember nothin' or seen nothin'."

Weatherman nodded and put his phone in his back pocket. "All we got is a pile of dead bears."

"Ask around your people in the club and see if any of them heard somethin'. Ya'll have deep roots in these mountains. Maybe someone knows something."

Weatherman nodded again. "I'll talk to Brick, and he'll put the word out. This shit won't make him happy."

Wilson grunted. "I've known Brick since before you was born. Something or someone disturbs the peace in this town, they better hope the law finds them first." He hitched up his pants under his slight overhanging belly and turned to the green-faced officer. "You done puking yet? Go grab the camera and get'chur ass over here. We got work to do."

LATER THAT NIGHT, WEATHERMAN LAY BACK ON HIS queen-sized bed. It barely fit the small room, but he was content for now. The house had air conditioning in the form of two window units, but the nights were cool enough that they weren't needed. Good thing, as the noise from the fans would mask his mother's breathing. Just as in his childhood, the bedroom doors were left open, and he could hear her in the other bedroom. Only now, her lungs were constantly laboring and rattling. It bothered him a lot that even the simplest of bodily functions had become a struggle to perform, and there wasn't anything he could do about it other than listen.

He flipped over for the four hundredth time and punched his pillow. Restlessness invaded his mind and shut down any chance of sleeping. Visions of the dead bears danced in his head accompanied by the harsh sounds of his mother's breathing. He wished he could go outside, jump on his bike, and ride, but the weight of his responsibilities sat heavy on his chest, preventing him from getting up.

Opal came to his mind. He didn't know why he thought of her in that moment, but she slipped into his thoughts easily, like a hand in a glove. She also had a lot on her shoulders. Single mom, new place, new people, trying to make a life for herself and her daughter with zero family support. That took enormous strength and bravery, which few people had, especially if she had other baggage to deal with on top of it. He admired Opal for taking charge and doing whatever she needed to for her child, just like his own mom did.

The sounds of his mother's shallow breathing drifted into the room. He shifted once again to his back and checked his phone to see it was just after midnight. He wondered what Opal was doing.

It's late, dumbass. She's sleeping at this hour.

No, even if it was a possibility, the prickly woman wasn't interested in anything else but her own goals, and he didn't have time to get to know anyone, let alone dating.

Sometimes you have to adapt.

Yes, but not today.

On impulse, he opened his contacts and scrolled to her name.

Weatherman: Hey, are you up?

The three dots stayed still.

What the hell am I doing? He moved his thumb to close the app when the dots started bouncing.

Opal: Yes, Kimmie just came home and woke up Pearl. I'm trying to get her back to sleep. Anything wrong?

"Anything wrong?" How 'bout everything?

Weatherman: There's a lot on my mind.

Opal: Want to tell me?

Weatherman: I don't want to get into it too much. I had a really rough day at work.

Opal: I understand. It gets tough sometimes at the salon, too, especially when Burna Jones comes. She's never happy unless she's complaining about something.

Weatherman: Yeah, I've seen her in action.

Opal: I used to be pretty negative about a lot of things myself. I believed life had nothing to offer me, but someone helped me see there was good in the world. All I had to do was reach for it and I'd eventually find it."

Weatherman: Have you? Found it, that is?

Opal: I don't know, but I hope so. If not, then I can start again tomorrow, right?

Weatherman inhaled deeply through his nose, then blew out slowly with pursed lips. His wild emotions were calmer now. Opal wasn't exactly a close friend, but she was no longer a stranger. As the saying goes, any port in a storm is a good one, but he sensed that she understood what he was dealing with better than most.

His mom coughed and turned over, breaking his thoughts about the pretty hairdresser.

Weatherman: Yeah, you're right. Tomorrow is a new day. Is Pearl asleep yet?

Opal: Yes. I should be able to put her down now.

Weatherman: I should let you go, then. Thanks for texting with me. It helped a lot.

Opal: You're welcome. Good night.

CHAPTER 10

Summer in the North Carolina mountains was muggy and hot. Fall wasn't turning out to be much better. From the gossip in the salon, I figured out that this season had way less rainfall than normal. Everyone talked about how low the rivers were and how some tributaries had all but dried up. Nights were only a little cooler, and the tourists flocked to raft what was left of the river, swim in the lowered lakes, and ride the trains.

The salon stayed busy with people coming and going all day. My chair was constantly full, and I was happy to have a roster of clients who came to me regularly. Cuts, color, perms, styling, wedding parties—all sorts of jobs filled my days, and the tips didn't suck.

Pearl was walking all the time now and getting into everything. I had to watch her like a hawk in the small apartment, as sitting still was no longer an option. She pulled up on anything that held her weight and grabbed at whatever caught her curious eye. Anything within her grasping range had to go on higher shelves. She was eating like a little pig, and it seemed like I had to buy her new clothes every week as fast as she was growing.

I was happy, or at least content for now.

The only blemish was my roommate. Kimmie was going out and drinking. A lot. Many nights she came home late or not at all. Sometimes Pearl woke up with her noise, and more than once, I had to rock my girl back to sleep, barely keeping my own eyes open while I did it. I tried to talk to Kimmie about her choices, and for a while, she would straighten up, but then the call of the bars and the men got too much for her and she went right back to them.

I was pretty sure it was because she was lonely. I had my daughter to take care of, which left me little time outside work to consider having any kind of companionship. There was only so much I could do for my friend. I hoped she recognized the path she was on soon before she did more damage to herself.

The bell at the salon's door rang as Betsey came in. "Hey, y'all. How's everyone doing?"

A chorus of "Just fines" and "Real goods" echoed back.

I was finishing up the last of the Coates triplets. The two ten-year-old girls and one boy were into competitive swimming and spent a lot of time in chlorinated water. I treated them with an apple cider vinegar rinse followed by a deep argan oil conditioner before I did the trimming.

I wondered when I should look into getting swim lessons for Pearl as I whipped the cape from Morgan's shoulders. "All done, kiddo. I hope your meet this weekend goes well."

The kid hopped down and darted to join his sisters.

"I got a big favor to ask you," Betsey said as I picked up the broom.

"You bet. What can I do for you?"

"Weatherman's mom ain't doin' too good. Them cancer treatments are takin' a lot outta her. He said her hair has all fallen out. I want to get her a nice wig, but I don't know nothin' about them. Tambre said you helped a client get one a while back. Can you help me?"

Weatherman's mom has cancer? This was news to me, but then again, I hadn't seen much of the man since his bar rescue. Shop gossip said he'd taken a job with the forestry service and was working as a ranger and volunteer firefighter. The physical stamina test was tough, but Weatherman had passed it. I wasn't surprised. He didn't appear to be out of shape.

I dumped the hodgepodge of hair trimmings in the trash can next to my station. "I'll be glad to help as I can. I have a friend from school who works with a wigmaker. She told me hand-tied human hair ones are the most comfortable and versatile, plus with good care, they can last up to a year. They're also the most expensive, though."

Betsey let out an odd "Psshht" sound, and her nails clicked as she wiggled her fingers in a dismissive gesture. "The cost don't concern me. Takin' care of my people does. Can you get me a pretty one similar to what her real hair used to look like? I have some pictures."

She pulled up Facebook on her phone and scrolled through several images until she found the one she wanted. I saw an older woman with light brown and gray hair cut in a classic pageboy style with blunt bangs in front. Perfect to hide the netting seam. It was a simple look that wouldn't take a lot of extra time to maintain. A younger teenage Weatherman with a high school letter jacket stood hugging her from behind. There was no denying that he got his good looks from his mom.

"What's her name?" I asked.

"Natalie. Natalie Turner. It's just been her and her son for a long time. When Weatherman joined us, she came along too."

Something clicked into place. He'd been short-tempered the morning he found me with the flat tire. Of course, my gut reaction then didn't help, but it made sense now. His mom was sick. I had no relationship with my own mother, but I saw what it was supposed to be like when I lived with my friend Mama J in Minnesota. That woman would give her life to save her kids—and nearly did one night last winter. Weatherman must have been feeling this deep with his mother. This probably affected everything in him.

The women of the Dragon Runners MC were also prime examples of motherhood. Betsey took everyone under her wing no matter what. Tambre, Molly, Kat,

Eva, Psalm, Lori—all of them showed such family devotion and care as I'd never seen in any other bunch of people. It was humbling. I understood a new restaurant owner in town, Fauna, was on her way to becoming part of this group as well.

At one time in my life, I thought I had a big family with the Dutchmen MC. I'd wanted it to be true and craved it like I was starving. I was so close to having it, but then it was ripped away one snowy night. I'd resolved myself to never realizing that dream, but it was nice to see other people living it, I guess.

I had too many sins in my past to ever have a golden future.

"I'll make some inquiries and email you some pics," I told Betsey. "I'll make sure Natalie gets the best."

She smiled. "I knew I could count on you. We're so damn lucky you decided to make our mountain town your new home."

I got a little flustered at the praise from the MC queen. Part of me liked that I was appreciated. It was rare that anyone did. The other part of me had red flags flaring like crazy. Usually when someone gave me compliments, there was a hidden motive.

Fortunately, the bell rang again, and I turned to the new customer as Betsey waved goodbye. It was a man I'd not see before in the salon. He was attractive, but in a wholesome boy-next-door kind of way, not the drop-dead-gorgeous-rebel vibe I got from Weatherman. He was slightly taller than me with a slim build, pleasant face, dark hair, and brown eyes that peered at me from behind wire-framed glasses. "You must be Opal. My sister, Agatha, has bugged me for weeks to come get a haircut from you. I'm Pastor Robert Tisdale."

Oh shit! Uh… shoot. "Nice to meet you… um… Pastor."

He smiled with a slow blink. Not one of those sexy, cunning blinks. One that radiated kindness and understanding, like a big brother or therapist. It was nice.

"Nice to meet you too. Most people call me Bob or Bobby. Do you have time now, or should I make an appointment?"

My next color was in an hour. "I have time now. Please." I gestured to my chair. "Do you need a shampoo or just a cut?"

"I washed it this morning. It should be fine, but thanks for asking."

That serene smile stayed on his face as he sat, and I draped the cape over him. I noticed there were several sets of eyes stealing glances at him over magazine covers and cell phones. I saw one woman take a few pictures. Didn't any of these women have lives outside the salon?

I combed through his thick dark hair. His cut was basic layers and not complicated at all. He sat still as I threaded the strands through my fingers to get an idea for how they would lie.

"I hope you don't mind me coming in like this. Aggie has been on my case for me to come meet you. I'm hoping she'll back off now that I have." His eyes sparkled. "Dare I admit, she was right? You are a very pretty lady."

Heat filled my cheeks. Seriously? Me? Blushing? I didn't think it was possible. "Thank you, Pastor… Pastor Robert. Preacher?"

He laughed. "I'm just Bobby."

I snipped and clipped, watching the shining locks as they glided through my comb. He talked and asked questions. Where did I come from in Minnesota? How did I like living in North Carolina? Did I like working in this salon? Thankfully, he didn't ask too much about my religious background. I was nervous about telling him I had none.

His hair was nice. With lots of body and a slight wave, it lay well and had the spicy scent of American Crew products. He was pleasant and uncomplicated, and I found myself enjoying this brief encounter. The cut didn't take very long, and when I finished, he turned his head back and forth with that peaceful, easy smile returning to his face. I wasn't sure it ever left.

"This is so much better than the barbershop. You're very talented."

"Thanks." Another blush. *What is wrong with me?*

He handed me two twenties at the counter and told me to keep the change. My déjà vu sense buzzed, remembering the last time a man handed me that exact amount. Weatherman. *God… uh… gosh, why did he crop up now?*

"…coffee soon?"

I caught the tail end of Robert's inquiry but clued in

enough to determine that he'd asked me out for coffee. "Um... I don't have a lot of free time, but we'll see."

His smile deepened. "Aggie told me you're widowed and have a little girl. I'm sorry for your loss, and please bring her along if that's easier for you."

He didn't mind that I had a kid. "Okay."

He extended his hand to me. "Well, Miss Opal, I hope I'll be seeing you soon."

I took his hand. Warm. Dry. Firm but not squeezing.

I rang up his cut, tucked my tip in my back jeans pocket, and did my best to ignore the speculative looks from the waiting area. I wanted to tell them it was just a cut, but it didn't matter if I did or not. Salon gossip would never be suppressed.

I just hoped it would turn from me to something else as soon as possible.

CHAPTER 11

Weatherman passed cleanly over the turning T and, at the precise moment, flipped to kick off in the other direction. He stretched his arms in a simple freestyle stroke as he glided easily through the water. Other swimmers filled the lanes this early morning, some in training for competition and some simply to work out.

He loved the rhythm of this stroke. Three flutter kicks to each arm recovery.

One-two-three.

One-two-three.

One-two-three.

Steady, smooth movements and easy, controlled breathing, his whole body working to cut through the water with as little drag as possible.

Even though the pool was filled with other people, he still considered himself sealed off from the world for a bit. The water muffled sounds, and his sight was limited by the goggles he wore. He could think here as he moved in this comfortable pattern.

This was his main stroke while he was in competitive swimming. He did the 100m, 200m, and 400m races as well as relays. A few times, he swam the 100 IM (individual medley) where he used all four racing strokes, but his butterfly wasn't as fast, as he didn't have the long arms and torso needed for that particular one.

He hit the T and flipped again. His mom came to every race day at the Y when he was a child, and later at the university. She did the chaperone thing, brought snacks and water for the team, and helped with all the fundraising necessary to support the league. He remembered getting out of the pool to see her big smile no matter if he placed or not. She never minded the wet hugs.

There were the occasional dates, but no one special. There was one man who she dated for a few months, but it didn't work out. He didn't like the guy very much, and when he asked his mom why they broke up, she gave him her serene smile and told him she didn't think he was a good fit for them.

"It takes a strong man to be a stepfather, Bryce," she'd said. "Not every man has the mettle for it. I'd rather be single than settle for someone who isn't up for the job."

How much of her life had she given up to be his mom?

Opal came to his mind as he flipped and started another lap. He could see a lot of his mom in her. Hard-working and totally dedicated to her child. To his knowledge, she wasn't dating anyone, and if he was correct, she wouldn't consider anyone who took her time away from Pearl.

"It takes a strong man to be a stepfather."

His thoughts had thrown his timing off, and he almost missed the T. Whatever madness had him thinking about Opal had to stop. He needed to concentrate on the mess that was his job and the mess that was his mom's health. Dating? Something more? Not in the cards.

He hit the wall and pulled himself out in one movement. Water sluiced from his Speedo-clad body as he lifted his goggles to rest on the latex swim cap over his hair.

He caught the young female lifeguard watching him instead of the swimmers. Portia was her name, if he remembered correctly, and she was a college student. He bet if he asked her out, she would jump at the chance. Perhaps a date with an attractive woman was just what he needed to get Opal off his mind.

He slopped over to her, feeling the weight of his body as the pool's buoyancy faded. "Portia, right?"

She beamed at him. "Yeah, that's right. And you're Bryce Turner. You have a nice stroke."

No doubt this would easy. No cajoling or talking her into bed if he wanted to go that route.

"I'd rather be single than settle for someone who isn't up for the job."

He sighed and smiled at the girl. "Thanks. Have a nice day."

CHAPTER 12

THE LAIR WAS NOT WHAT I WAS EXPECTING. THE PLACE resembled a mountain resort retreat rather than a clubhouse. A massive two-story building with numerous outbuildings and small one-room camping cabins scattered about. Everything was clean, neat, and inviting.

I debated for a moment but then pulled out the stroller from the trunk. I had Pearl and a package with me for Betsey and only two arms. The roar of a motorcycle caught my ear, and my first response was to stiffen up, ready for battle, until I recognized the person riding. It was none other than Eva MacAteer, Stud's old lady and wife. I'd met her a couple times when she came to the salon with her daughters—five, to be exact. She'd told me that Stud still wanted a boy but had made noises about giving up on that fantasy.

"Serves him right for being such a manwhore in his younger days."

I had to laugh at her blunt humor.

Stud pulled up in a minivan. Only he could make the stodgy vehicle look cool.

"Hey, girl. How are you?" Eva greeted me as she whipped the helmet from her head. Two shakes of her head and her auburn curls fluffed and settled. I loved working with it when she came to my chair.

"I'm good," I answered as I strapped Pearl into the bright yellow contraption. The sun had just sunk below the horizon, and the night sky sparkled overhead. Normally, I'd be home at this hour, spending the evening with my daughter, but I'd had a late client who put me over hours. Lori was kind enough to feed and watch Pearl for me so I could finish up. I'd also had to make a trip to the grocery store, as I was desperate for just about everything. I kept a cooler in my car for perishables in case my getting home was ever delayed. The reason for this side trip to the Lair was the box that arrived at the salon this afternoon. It was the wig I'd special ordered for Betsey. When I called her, she'd sounded out of breath and a little frantic.

"Lord have mercy, we've had a time lately. There's some stuff happenin' over to the bistro that we're tryin' to get sorted, and I been runnin' around like a chicken with my head cut off. Can you help me out and bring it up here to the Lair for me? I wanna see it real bad, and I'd really appreciate it."

When the local queen asked for a favor, it was generally a good idea to grant it.

The night air was warm, dry, and heavy. By now the weather in Minnesota would be cool, heading toward cold, while here the temperatures were still in the mid-eighties. I turned to Eva as I loaded the box in the stroller basket. "Is it always this hot this time of year?"

Eva puffed out a breath and shook her head. "It's not unheard of, but it has been a lot drier this year than most, and summer doesn't seem to want to leave. Hard to believe it's October now. How's business?"

"Good. I've got a good roster of clients now, and I think people in general like my work."

Eva grinned as five blondes ranging from ten to two exited the van. Stud and Eva's girls must have spent hours at this place, as they made a beeline for the door. Eva called out after them, "Don't get too comfortable. It's a school night, and we're not staying long!"

Light spilled out from the door as they entered, along with music and voices. *Lots* of voices.

My first instinct was to push the stroller back to the car, load up, and escape. Eva kept me from doing that by linking her arm in mine and hitching her youngest on her hip. "It's about time you made a visit. Betsey's been wanting to get you and your little one here for a while. If you haven't guessed, she collects people. Loves to be grandma to the world."

"I feel weird. This is more than I thought," I admitted.

"Yeah, it can be a little overwhelming. Hell, the whole club can be that way, but I swear on a stack of Bibles, no one will mess with you here. You get nervous about anyone or anything, give me or Stud the high sign, and we'll take care of it."

I had no doubts. Eva was a strong woman, physically as well as in spirit.

She pulled me into what amounted to a giant rec room. *This is a biker house?* It looked more like what I thought a country club would than a biker dive. The high vaulted ceilings were beamed and made me think of a castle. Several members were playing video games on a huge flat screen. Others were shooting pool or standing around with beer bottles and conversing. Molly was sitting on the armrest of the sofa with her hand over the shoulder of an older man. I guessed that was her husband, Cutter. I recognized Psalm and her two stepchildren from her salon visits.

One big family gathering. My belly churned from anxiety.

"Oooh, gimme that baby." Betsey appeared in all her booted glory, but she lacked her usual energy.

Pearl's eyes widened as the colorful woman picked her up, but my little girl never met anyone she didn't like. Her big grin and "Ha-da" greeting had Betsey chortling and playing back. "Who's a pretty girl? Who's my pretty Pearl?"

She spoke to me while she focused on my child. "Lord, it's been a zoo around here lately. I been down at the bistro helpin' out and jus' got here. Fauna's been havin' a time. You heard about the drama with that mess, right? Thank you so much for comin' by. Means somethin' special you goin' out of your way."

From the bits of gossip I'd picked up at the salon, apparently there was an incident at the restaurant where one of the waitresses got roofied. A few of the details had floated around, but I understood the police were investigating. I expected the Dragon Runners were also looking into it too.

My eyes bounced over to the all-knowing Eva, and I repeated her words in my head.

"Loves to be grandma to the world."

I'd lost touch with my mother years ago. I had no idea where she was or if she was still alive. Pearl would miss out on that important relationship unless someone stepped in. I wasn't real happy about the role being played by a biker's wife, but this place was so much more than what I'd thought. In my previous life, very few people would have stopped to help me with my flat tire. Most would just drive away and not look.

I should have been nicer to Weatherman.

"There's plenty of food over there in that little alcove. There's kid-friendly food, too, like mac 'n' cheese and nuggets. Got some deviled eggs we can cut up into little pieces too. She allergic? Go get'cha somethin', and I'll keep her for you." Betsey popped open a beer with one hand and gave it to a biker.

Did I want to leave my daughter with Betsey? Not particularly, but Pearl was grinning and giggling as the woman played and talked to her. I trusted Lori, and she was a biker's wife. It was probably time for me to trust someone else.

Get over yourself, Opal. These are good people. Stop judging them by a crooked stick.

"Thanks, I'll be right back."

The food table was full of Crock-Pots. Chilis, stews, dips, and anything else that could be put in a slow cooker and made ahead of time. Chicken nuggets and mac 'n' cheese filled two pots put aside for the kids. A big green salad sat in the middle of the bubbling ceramic garden. It seemed to be the odd man out, considering the fat and calories of the other foods.

"Betsey is still tryin' to get Brick to lay off the salt and eat more greens. It's an ongoing battle."

I turned to see a blond man who resembled what I would call an all-American football linebacker. Tall, broad, muscular, and beyond handsome. His gorgeous blue eyes narrowed and crinkled up as he frowned at the salad.

"It's a noble cause for sure, but I have to agree with Brick's opinion about kale. Cooked in soups and such, it ain't bad, but straight up like this?" He shook his head. "Not so much." He stuck out his hand. "I'm Dodge."

I took his hand and murmured my name back to him. So, this was Dodge, the custom car guy I'd heard about. I hadn't seen him in the salon, but his girlfriend, Fauna, had come in a few times. I wanted to get my hands on her tight curly hair so badly, but so far, she'd stuck with Tambre doing her braids.

"You're the new girl over at Tambre's place. Weatherman said you're a good stylist." He reached up and fingered his short locks. "Got any room for me next week?"

"Um… I don't have my calendar with me, but I'm

sure I can find a spot." *Weatherman had complimented me? Even after I was so nasty to him? Really?*

He grinned. "That would be great."

"Doesn't anyone use the barbershop?" I hadn't realized I'd spoken out loud until Dodge burst out laughing.

"If you want clipper fuzz only, he's your man. Most of us want to keep a little more on our heads. Plus, it's nice to support our people's businesses."

"*Support our people's businesses.*" To me, that concept sounded like a radical idea. To the Dragon Runners, it was normal.

Betsey held court at the bar, and Pearl was the princess. She sat on the queen's hip, grinning and babbling at everyone. She looked so pleased with herself, I had to take a quick one-handed picture with my phone and text it to Mama J. I got an immediate reply.

> Mama J: Oh, my girl looks so happy!
> Glad you both found a family.

Family. My girl had a family.

The thought of what that meant for my child made my eyes fill. Me? I would survive on less as I had always done, but this could mean Pearl had people who would always care for her and make sure her needs were covered. That possibility was more precious than all the gold in the world.

"*They've got your back, too, sweetheart.*"

I sniffled as the voice in my head spoke to me. *But they're bikers,* I silently told him.

"Family is family, baby. Sometimes you get a good one, sometimes you get a bad one. You can tell the difference."

What if I'm wrong?

"You're not."

Tears formed at the rims of my lids, and I resisted the urge to dash them away and draw attention to myself.

Out of the corner of my eye, I spotted someone I hadn't seen very often but remembered well.

Donna.

She stood out from the crowd, and yet no one noticed her. She was dressed in short-shorts and a too-tight tank top that glittered and showed off her ample chest, but the men she was around barely paid her any attention. She tried, though, arching her back and rubbing her breasts against one man's arm while pouting and flirting.

I glanced around at the other people in the room. I saw wives and girlfriends in casual wear, but they weren't showing off as much skin. Betsey had on her standard jeans, boots, and cut, and most of the other women wore similar outfits. They formed their own little group, and Donna was most definitely on the outside of it.

I watched her as I filled my plate and added some finger foods for Pearl.

Her body wasn't bad, but she didn't have the same vigor I imagined she had when she was younger. She looked tired and worn out. Her breasts hung low, and her prominent belly jiggled when she strutted on her spiky heels. Her makeup was thick and over the top to hide the wrinkles at her eyes and around her mouth. The overprocessed hair didn't help. She appeared to be a woman desperately hanging on to her youth in a world that left her behind long ago.

The reasons were pretty obvious. The older Dragon Runners around her age were all married with children. They were family men now, and the only single ones left were the younger prospects in their early twenties or so. The men Donna flirted with weren't mean to her, but they pretty much ignored her advances. They just weren't interested in being with someone a decade or more older than them.

She finally gave up and moved to another group to repeat the same gestures with a big come-hither smile and blatant invitation. They treated her the same way: polite but uninterested. Her mouth turned down, and it seemed her whole body drooped with the rejection. She turned to collect a few used plates and beer bottles and dump them into several large gray trash cans.

My hands tightened, and I had to concentrate on not dropping my plate. My heartbeat picked up. I might be an outsider to the Dragon Runners MC, but I recognized what role Donna played.

Sweet-butt. Easy-lay. House-mouse. All terms used for women who were essentially sex workers in some form. They were a convenient lay for members and provided maid services. The trade-off was money or gifts, or a place to stay.

This clashed with everything I'd seen so far about the Dragon Runners. They didn't keep a stable of women for casual use. Donna appeared to be the only one, and an aging one at that. The other women at this gathering were either old ladies, wives, or girlfriends.

In some ways, this impressed me. A motorcycle club that was more like a clan of households that supported and had one another's backs in times of trouble. This was something hard to achieve with or without bikes. I'd come from a place where people regularly tore each other apart. The only example I'd ever had of something different was Mama J, and even she had struggled mightily against the tide of life.

The smiling faces, the laughter, the happy vibe that floated around the cavernous room—this was clearly one big extended family. Brothers under one roof, all here to be a part of something big and solid.

Envy and desire hit my heart while hurt and anger started in my head.

Donna stood alone, a forgotten woman with no place and nowhere to go. What she fought to keep no longer existed for her and left her picking up scraps of whatever affection still remained. Outside. Always outside.

It made me want to cry and scream with outrage at the same time.

"Don't let the past dictate the future, sweetheart."

"You okay?" a random person asked.

I shook myself and sniffed to hide the emotions churning inside my gut. "You bet. Thanks."

Betsey stayed behind the bar, Pearl on her hip and the wig box next to her. She fumbled at the package, trying to open it while my daughter squirmed and played.

A man in a light brown uniform appeared next to them. Weatherman. He must have just arrived. His uniform was plain, but he wore it well, fitted around his incredible body. If he had one of those fancy hats with the tassels, I didn't see it. His hair wasn't flattened, and the waves lay perfectly across his skull. Waves I'd cut and styled.

He said something to Betsey and opened his arms to take Pearl from her. Betsey beamed in excitement and handed my little girl over to him. She reached and giggled as he scooped her up, fingering the shiny badge on his chest before putting her head on his shoulder.

A dull ache started in my belly and radiated throughout my body. This feeling inside me burned bad enough that I couldn't breathe. I watched as Weatherman held my little girl. Safe. Secure. She must have sensed that, as her tiny arms came up to grip his shirt and her eyes closed.

"It's okay to let your heart beat again."

Betsey opened the box and pulled another one out with a familiar logo on the side. She lifted a tangled hairpiece from it and held it up. Her mouth turned down. Tambre looked interested, but the others had doubtful expressions. I put on my game face and hurried over.

"Nice color at least. What do you think?" Betsey held the mess out to me, and I handed my plate off to someone.

I examined the wig, pulling at the strands and checking the web of the cap. This was a really fine piece. Tightly woven, full hair, soft netting with an extra layer of padding for long wear. "This will be great once it's styled."

"Oh, thank the Lord!" she breathed in relief. "I thought somethin' was wrong with it."

"Nothing a little brushing and heat won't fix. I can do most of that on a head form at the salon, but it would be best if I could do it for the person wearing it."

Betsey's eyes moved to the man who was now standing next to me. "Let me know when your mama's up to a visit. I wanna see how she likes it."

He nodded. "Okay."

I noticed Weatherman's usually smooth voice sounded rough. I glanced at him. His eyes were wet and his mouth tight. He held my daughter and my plate as if it was natural to him to wait for me. That burn in my chest ignited again as my sleeping daughter snuggled close.

Betsey popped open a beer and handed it to Dodge before getting distracted by a new arrival. She moved from behind the bar in a tizzy. "Lord in heaven, Katie Grace! What are you doing here, child?"

I was left alone with Weatherman, who was still

holding my daughter and my plate. Emotions churned in my belly like acid, and so many feels crowded my head, but first and foremost was escape.

"Let's go sit over there." He gestured with his chin. "I'll hold her until you're finished."

My instincts told me to forget the food, grab Pearl, and run.

"Stay."

For once, I ignored the voice. "No, thanks. I need to get her home and to bed."

"You can take a few minutes to sit and eat."

I spotted Donna as she sidled up to another biker. He was polite, but she was rebuffed. Again. "She's tired."

"And she's sleeping." He swayed back and forth while holding my little girl.

My heart twisted under a massive pressure to escape. My breaths came in little gasps, and I thought my chest might burst open if I didn't get out soon. "That's nice of you, but I have to go."

"I don't mind. I like kids."

I ignored him and tossed the paper plate with all its uneaten food into the nearest trash can. In my head, I recognized that I was being unreasonable, but I couldn't help it. "I don't care what you like or don't like." I bit back the rest of the words I wanted to spew. I had to live here and get along with the club that ultimately paid my bills, but I didn't have to be a member of their world. I couldn't do that. Not ever.

Not again.

I snatched Pearl from his arms, and she woke up enough to fuss at me. My feet were practically running as I hurried to the door and the parking area outside the massive cabin. My only focus was to get out of there and get home before any other voices started talking to me. I needed the sanctuary of my little apartment and the safe haven I'd made it.

I reached my car and fumbled for my keys when I realized I'd left both my jacket and Pearl's with the stroller inside the building.

Stupid! Stupid! Stuuuuupid!

I stifled a sob as I fought back a total breakdown in the dark against my car. My gut wanted to puke, and my brain was going to explode. Cravings I had long conquered churned and rose in my throat, and if it weren't for the baby in my arms, I would have run crazily down the long mountain road, screaming my head off.

"Weak. Soooo weak."

I'd hoped never to hear that sinister whisper again, but there it was, still coiled in my belly, waiting to strike when I was at my lowest point. I clung to my child, selfishly using her as an anchor to keep me sane and grounded.

The familiar rattle hit my ears, and someone called my name. "Opal, wait up a minute."

Weatherman had followed me and brought the stroller and jackets. "What the hell is your fuckin' prob —shit."

The stroller stopped next to me. Two seconds later,

Pearl and I were both taken into a warm and secure embrace. "I don't know what's going on, but I got you."

"I got you. I got you. Hang on, sweetness. Stay with me."

Words from my past echoed in my head and heart. "I'm… I'm… I can't…."

"You don't have to. Just breathe, sweetheart. Breathe with me. You can do this."

More words from my past. More emotions rolling in my belly ready to spill out. I couldn't get enough air into my lungs. I was going to pass out or go mad. Maybe both.

"Hang on, sweetness and listen to him."

The voice broke through my haziness, and I listened to it. I matched Weatherman's deep breaths and got control of myself. It seemed to take forever, but I finally settled enough to stand on my own. I pulled back enough to see those hazel eyes of his staring back at me, close and full of concern, like he actually gave a shit.

A memory flashed in my brain. A parking lot outside a church. Dark night. Me, desperately trying to keep it together and not fall back into the hell I'd fought to escape. Wild cravings about to consume me, and then a pair of hazel eyes appearing to rescue me from the abyss.

Only this time, it was a different pair of eyes that stared into mine. A different man. A different time. One second, we were acquaintances who rubbed each other the wrong way, and the next we were somehow bonded. A shared moment when everything in me was totally exposed. Somehow without words, he recognized the demons that had sprouted in my belly.

And he didn't look away.

His gaze dropped to my mouth, and I stopped breathing.

He was going to kiss me. I knew it. He knew it. Like it was the most natural step to take.

Even more shocking?

I wanted it.

I wanted it badly.

He swayed toward me, and I readied myself for his touch.

At the last second, I turned my head. I might be okay for now, but anxiety still bubbled below the surface. I'd been here before, on the brink of losing my shit entirely, more times than I'd care to remember.

Pearl grunted and shifted on my shoulder, breaking this weird trance we were trapped in. He stepped back and cleared his throat. "I'm sorry. I... I... keys?"

"My jacket pocket."

The opportunity closed, but there was still a residual sense of connection. One that would be with me for quite a while. Only time would tell what that union would mean, but for now, I had to retreat behind the walls I'd put up so carefully.

He beeped the locks. "Text me when you get home so I know you're safe."

I watched as he loaded the stroller into the trunk and then shut it with a firm click before turning to me with somber eyes. "I'm serious. Text me."

"The Dragon Runners have a code when it comes to taking care of the women in this town. You see a man wearing this emblem, you can trust that he won't leave you on the side of the road until you're safe."

Weatherman's words came back to me in a rush. Safe. I was safe with him. Only one other time had I ever felt this cared for and protected. It was taken from me, but that one taste left me with a desire to find something like it a second time—and also scared as hell of what it would do to me to lose it once more.

"It's okay to let your heart beat again."

I wanted to. I wanted that connection, but was it too much to ask to have it twice in a lifetime? Was I being greedy?

"You bet," I squeaked out before getting in my car. The engine started, and I backed out carefully, hearing the gravel crunch under the tires. The outside lights barely made a dent in the dark, but I still saw his figure watching me as I drove away.

CHAPTER 13

The station loomed ahead as Weatherman pulled into the worn lot. He blew on his hands to warm them, as he'd forgotten his thick biking gloves, and the mornings were finally getting colder. The Dragon Runners would be on the road until ice covered them. The way the dry fall had delayed winter, he expected they'd still be on bikes in December.

This morning, his head wasn't on his job, or the club, or even his mother. It was on Opal and had been the past few days. The scene outside the Lair sat with vivid colors in the forefront of his mind, and he doubted he would ever forget the sight of her nearly collapsed on the ground in a full-fledged panic attack. He'd grabbed the abandoned jackets and stroller, then rushed out to the parking area with the intent of ripping her a new asshole. Instead, what he found was a woman on the verge of a total breakdown, and he had an epiphany.

She wasn't a stuck-up bitch.

She wasn't a snob when it came to his beloved club.

She wasn't a man-hater.

She was broken.

Something in her life, her past, had *shattered* her, and she was here in Bryson City to pick up the pieces. His first thought was drugs and that being around the club triggered her. He wasn't sure why, though, as Betsey didn't allow that kind of shit in her house. A few members snuck out to the giant garage or the camping cabins to smoke a little weed, but no one dared bring it to the main house. That was a prime way to have your patch taken. Still, some event or words or scene at the Lair had brought out a bad memory of something that had shaped her into the person she was now. His newsman curiosity wanted to investigate. His Dragon Runners code was to protect. His male instinct…

Fuck! Get your head outta your ass! What is wrong with you?

His self-admonishment continued as he tucked his helmet under his arm and entered the squat building.

Two of the officers rushed around their desks, nearly running into him. Their normal speed was slow to moseying, so he immediately knew that something was wrong.

"Another dump site's been found. Same as the last one. Chief is mad as hell," Ranger Fine informed him.

Weatherman didn't have time to comment, as Chief Wilson came barreling out of his office. "You talk to Brick yet?"

"I was planning on bringing it up at the next church meeting."

"Call him now and meet us there. This one is only a few miles from his campground. It was his people there who called it in."

An hour later, Weatherman stood with the chief and Fine, along with Brick, Mute, and Bruiser as they took in the sight before them. The scene was almost an exact repeat of the last one. The difference was, there were more dead bears this time.

"How many?" Brick's low, calm tone was lethal.

"Hard to tell." Weatherman covered his nose, the smell overwhelming. He pointed his phone and snapped pictures with one hand. Skinned carcasses that appeared dumped in a haphazard pile. Bloody stumps where paws used to be. Mutilated heads missing jaws and ears. Open bellies with tangles of intestines draped across the ground. It was both horrifying and sorrowful.

Rage added itself to the mix. An emotion so present that it was palpable in the air.

Weatherman glanced over at Brick. The man's face was like granite—hard, unyielding, and completely void of expression. Anyone who knew Brick would realize the level of fury in the tough biker was off the charts.

"They weren't killed here. We ain't seen bears around the campground in decades. Too many people around, and we put out vinegar bags around the place to keep them away," he stated in an icy voice.

"Someone hunted 'em, cut 'em up somewhere else, and dumped 'em here like trash."

Chief Wilson let out a long sigh. "We got shit to go on."

Brick turned to Bruiser. "You remember them hunters from last week down at the River's Edge? The ones from Ohio?"

Bruiser shifted his bulk from side to side, clearly uncomfortable. "Yeah, there were three of 'em. They was askin' about where to go to get bigger game. I told 'em ain't nothing open right now. Deer season started in September, archery first, then black powder. Bear season starts later this year after Halloween and has limited permits because of the current population. They laughed like I'd said a joke and left the bar."

"They say anything else?"

"Not to me, but I did hear one say he knew a guy who knew a guy." Bruiser sniffed and lightly coughed. "Said the name Gus-Gus on his way out the door."

The chief took off his hat and ran a hand over the thin strands of gray hair combed over his sweating bald head. "Clem Gustler has been mentioned a few times in connection with this shit, but there's no proof and no way to get any."

"If there's evidence, it will be found." Brick stood tall and decisive. "I ain't givin' no orders to a ranger, but I can to a Dragon Runner. Weatherman and Mute need to go pay a visit to Clem's place. You can ask about the lawn tractor he's got for sale. I could send Dodge with Mute, but he's got his plate full with his dad and that other shit at his girlfriend's restaurant. Go sometime tomorrow in the early afternoon, but don't call him. Catch him off guard. Weatherman, be sure to wear your colors."

Weatherman had no problem with this plan. He'd had no dealings with Clem and wouldn't be recognized as a ranger.

Mute made a growling sound, which indicated his agreement. The large silent biker was intimidating enough as the River's Edge bouncer, but when he was riled up, someone usually got hurt. No one ever wanted to see him truly angry, and right now, he was truly angry.

"I'll text you later with a time and some details. Dodge is covered up at the garage, and we gotta get back there." Brick turned to Wilson one last time. "I'll let you know if we find anything, but I ain't makin' no promises about staying out of it. This is *my* campground and *my* backyard. I'm gonna protect what's mine."

The chief sighed again. "I didn't expect you to stand down. Just please don't do something that's gonna make me regret callin' you."

The three bikers left on a roaring note, leaving the three rangers to finish processing the scene. Fine was turning green again, and Weatherman fully expected him to start hurling when his phone rang. The caller ID sent shards into his stomach. "Shit, it's my mom."

Wilson gestured for him to take the call, and Weatherman moved away from the bloody scene to answer.

"I'm so sorry to call, honey, but I need some help." She sounded weak and in pain.

Alarm flashed through him like a heat wave. "What happened?"

"Well, Emma was supposed to come, but her daughter called, and the grandbaby is sick. I thought I'd be fine by myself, but I fell, and I'm having trouble getting up."

Weatherman swallowed as a helplessness washed over him. His mind ran through a dozen possibilities, but none of them would work. He'd ridden with the chief and Fine in the department Jeep and was stuck miles away in the woods with no immediate way back to town. The bikers had already left, and the cleanup crew was on the way.

"Can you call an ambulance?"

"Absolutely not. It's too expensive."

"Insurance will pay for it or else I will."

"I don't want them people here making a fuss. All they're gonna do is get me up and leave. No sense in spending money for that. I'll just wait for someone else."

Weatherman gritted his teeth in frustration. He'd never won an argument with the woman and recognized that he wouldn't now either. Who was available? Betsey? She was at the hospital with Table, as Lori had gone into labor that afternoon. Molly? Asleep from working the night shift at the sheriff's office. Tambre? Maybe she could get away from the shop. He dialed the hair salon and waited for someone to pick up.

The line rang twice before someone answered.

"Salon, what can I do for you?" a grating voice smacking on a piece of gum asked.

"Hey, it's Weatherman… uh… Bryce Turner. Is Tambre around?"

"No, it's been slow today, so she went over to Dillsboro for some supplies."

Shit! He thought about calling Opal, but he felt awkward after their near kiss the last time he saw her, and he didn't know quite how to handle being around her yet.

He bit his lip. *Suck it up. Your mom is in pain.* "Is Opal around?"

"Nope, it's her day off."

Good news that might make her more available. "Thanks anyway."

He hung up and scrolled to the most recent number added in his contacts. His mind raced through other possibilities, but this was the only one that worked. Before he could talk himself out of it, he hit Call and held the phone to his ear.

CHAPTER 14

No doubt this would be more fodder for the salon gossip mill. At least three of my regular clients came in the coffee shop this morning and spotted Pastor Robert and me sitting together. I couldn't call him Bobby or Brother Bobby or whatever. It was too familiar, and I wasn't ready for that yet.

He'd called the salon yesterday afternoon and asked if I'd join him for a cup and to talk a bit. Today was my day off, but I had some errands I wanted to get done, so I still left Pearl for a few hours at Lori's daycare with one of the other mothers who ran it. She'd told me Lori was in labor, and I hoped it would go well.

"I have a staff meeting later and a prayer group this afternoon," he stated while dumping three packets of sugar into his coffee. "Wednesday is my longest day with all the youth activities, but today I just have the two tasks. I take off Fridays and Saturdays as my weekend, since my work week starts at eight o'clock Sunday morning."

He was a nice man, good-looking, and stable. Some women would give their eyeteeth to be at a table across from him. I wasn't sure I was the right one for this.

My head was still full of my panic attack and encounter with Weatherman a few nights ago.

How did this happen? I thought I was immune to bad boys.

But is Weatherman a bad boy just because he wears biker colors?

"What made you decide to cut hair?"

Robert's question broke into my musings, and I quickly took a sip of my coffee to cover my inattention.

"I always liked doing hair and makeup when I was a teenager. I guess it just made sense to become a stylist." There was more to my story, but he didn't need to know that.

He stirred the sweet brew and sampled it. His mouth turned down, and he added another sugar packet. "What makes hair and makeup appealing? I've never understood why women have this need to adorn themselves like that."

I hesitated before speaking, not sure how to take that statement. Was he saying he didn't like different hairstyles or colors or all the different ways makeup could be applied?

He looked up from his cup as if realizing how his words sounded. "I don't mean that in a bad way. I think all women are beautiful the way they are. They have no need for anything but themselves."

"Some women want a little extra, I guess."

He cleared his throat. "I'm sorry if I offended you. I haven't been on a date in a while."

This is a date? "No worries. I haven't either."

"Let's not get into the heavy stuff for now. You like movies?"

"I don't go out much. Most of my nights are spent at home with my little girl. I've never taken her to a movie theater."

"But what do you do for fun?"

That was a tough question, considering everything I did now centered around my daughter. "Not a lot, I suppose. I take Pearl shopping on my day off, or we go to the park. We read a lot of books and play with her toys."

He smiled and leaned forward. "That sounds wonderful, but what do *you* do for fun?"

Again, I didn't know how to respond. Thankfully, a loud voice interrupted us.

"What do you mean, you don't have banana nut muffins? Everyone has banana nut muffins!"

Burna Jones made her presence known, and with her volume, everyone in the coffee shop had become unwilling witnesses to her complaints.

The poor man behind the pastry counter turned red. "We ran out earlier this morning. We have blueberry or cinn—"

"If I wanted blueberry, I would have asked for blueberry. With what you charge for a cup of coffee, you ought to be serving it in gold cups. Deplorable service!"

I glanced from the show at the counter back to Pastor Robert, wondering if he would get up and de-escalate the angry woman. He seemed indifferent.

My phone rang, interrupting my thoughts, and I didn't bother to check the ID before answering.

"Hello?"

"Hey, Opal, it's Weatherman. Are you off today?"

"I… well… yes. Why?"

"My mom fell. I'm too far away to get to her, and I don't have any other people around. Would you mind going by and checking on her for me?"

I was so going to hell, as my first thought was what a perfect excuse this would be to end this… um… date. "You bet. Text me the address. I'll go there now."

"Thanks. Please call me when you see her, would you?"

"Got it." I hung up and smiled. "A… friend of mine is in trouble and needs my help. I'm sorry, but I need to go."

Concern filled Pastor Robert's expression. "Anything I can do?"

"I don't think so, but thanks for offering."

He handed me his business card. "Here, take my number."

I took the white rectangle and stood up to go.

"I'd like to see you again," he started as he scooted

back his chair. The squeal was loud enough to drown out Burna's tirade, and I wondered if he did it deliberately. "Please call me when you can so I'll have your number too. If you need me, let me know." His boyish grin was kind of cute. "Maybe we can go to the Halloween festival together, and I can meet your little girl."

I nodded, figuring agreeing might get me out of there faster. "You bet."

As I left, I heard a big exclamation of "Pastor Bobby!" come from the irate woman. It almost made me want to go rescue him, but Natalie needed me more.

The drive wasn't long, as she lived only a few miles away. I pulled up to a small, quaint house in an older neighborhood that had seen better days but was still cute. The front yard was full of garden boxes that hadn't been tended in a while. I wasn't much on growing plants and stuff, but even I could tell these needed weeding.

I knocked on the front door, and a weak voice called out to enter.

The first time I got to lay eyes on Natalie Turner was when I found her on the floor of her living room. She was in a zipped-up navy blue robe with thick socks and fuzzy slippers on her feet. Her skin was sallow, and she had a floral-patterned scarf tied around her hairless head.

"Bryce called me and said he sent you over here. Sorry for the trouble."

My heart bled a little. "No trouble, ma'am."

She huffed a shallow laugh. "Land sakes, I ain't been called ma'am in a long time. I'm Natalie. Nice to meet'cha."

She extended her hand from her position on the floor. "Can you help me up and get me to my chair? I'm usually not this poorly, but I started the chemo again yesterday, and it took more out of me than usual."

I reached down and took the woman's frail hand to assist her in standing up. She weighed next to nothing, but it still took almost all my strength to lift her, as she had none. It was a real challenge, because I didn't want to accidentally hurt her either. "Nice to meet you too. I'm Opal. Weather—Bryce is a client of mine." *I guess I can say that, right?*

She sat in her chair, breathing hard from the effort of getting off the floor, and worked the remote to put it into a reclining position. "Lord in heaven, this sucks. I'm guessin' Bryce done told you I got cancer. It's kicking me hard, but I'm not gonna let it win. I want to see my grandbabies grow up. That's when I get me some."

I didn't know how to respond to that. "Uh, I have a daughter. She just turned two and discovered the joys of running circles in the apartment, but she still prefers for me to carry her most of the time."

Natalie attempted to laugh, but it ended with a coughing fit. Alarm raced through me along with a feeling of helplessness. There was nothing I could do but wait and listen. Eventually, the woman cleared her throat, her voice rough when she spoke again. "Would you mind gettin' me a glass of water? I got one a' them fancy fridges with the spigot in the door."

I found the glasses and filled one halfway with crushed ice and water. Natalie drank most of it as she reclined in the plush chair. The piece of furniture dwarfed her. "Thank you, dear. So, you have a little girl? I was hoping for more children, but my husband and I divorced before that could happen. In some ways, that was a good thing. I cain't imagine being a single mom with more than one child."

Mama J came to my mind. "I have a friend back in Minnesota who has six kids and is a single mom. Well, not anymore. She met a man who loves her and big families. They're planning on getting married soon."

Natalie's eyes opened wide, and she let out a low whistle. "Six kids and one mama? That woman deserves combat pay. Are you going up for the weddin'?"

I shook my head. "They're keeping it simple and just going to the courthouse."

Natalie pursed her lips and nodded. "That's usually best in my opinion. Lord knows all that shit gets real expensive. My friend Emma told me one of her daughters spent almost five thousand dollars on her weddin' dress. Five thousand dollars! Can you imagine such?"

I perched on the sofa near the chair, as it seemed I would be there for a while. Truthfully, it was kinda cool hearing the woman talk with her thick accent. It made me wonder how Weatherman didn't have one like his mom. "No, I can't. I have a lot of things I'd rather spend that kind of money on than a dress I'd only get to wear once."

She winked at me, and I clearly saw her son in her. "I like your way of thinkin'. You got any pictures of your little girl on that phone of yours?"

I smiled. "Oh, you bet." I pulled up the album file I'd amassed of Pearl and handed the phone to Natalie. Delight showed on her face as she scrolled through the images. Pearl as a newborn baby, curled up on my chest. Pearl meeting her favorite alligator toy for the first time. Pearl with her toothless grin, sitting in a sandbox. Pearl laughing and clapping her hands.

Natalie stopped at the video I took when Pearl was learning to walk and taking tentative steps before plopping onto her bottom. She looked at the camera, gave a frustrated "Gah!" and tried standing again. The older woman's eyes grew wet.

"I remember Bryce just after he started walking. He did it early. Lord, he was a pistol. Smart as a whip and beat the development curve every time. I'd take him to the playground in the apartment complex, and he'd climb up on everythin' he could. No fear, that boy. I didn't have to worry 'bout him runnin' off, though. He'd get up on top of whatever he was conquerin' and turn around to make sure I was still there on the bench. Mama's boy for sure, but in the best way."

What do I say to that? "He is a nice man."

"Yep, my boy has turned into a fine one." Natalie paused as she dashed at her eyes. "I know he's all for being there for me, but sometimes I feel like I'm such a burden to him. I begged him to keep that job in Tennessee at the TV station, but he's got a stubborn streak wider than the Mississippi."

I leaned forward. "I don't know Bryce that well, but I think if he really wanted to stay there, he would have found a way to do that and take care of you. I don't think you should feel guilty or bad for letting your son help you. It's what he wants to do, and anything different would make *him* feel guilty or bad."

Natalie sighed. "I reckon you're right, but I still don't like it much." She slapped her hands on the arms of the recliner. "Well, time's a-wastin' while I'm sittin' here. I was fixin' to put on a Crock-Pot of root vegetables and sausage for supper tonight. Want to help me with that? We can make enough for you and your little girl if y'all stop by later. Least I could do. Ever cut up a butternut squash?"

"A what?"

She laughed. "Help me to the kitchen. I'll sit at the table and show you."

I held her arm as she shuffled slowly into the eat-in kitchen, which was easily the largest room in the house. I noticed she had a duck theme going on. Duck curtains, duck salt and pepper shakers, duck dish towels, duck canisters, and other duck-ware were scattered across the long counter.

She sat with a grunt in one of the wood chairs at the round table. "Oh, Lord in heaven, I'm so sick of not havin' any energy. Cain't do my gardens, cain't do my house, cain't keep up with nothin'." Her faded eyes came to mine, and she grinned. "It sucks big donkey balls."

I slapped a hand over my mouth to keep from laughing out loud. I'd never expected a frail older woman to say something like that. "I'm sorry you're going through this. I wish there was something else I could do."

She lifted her hand and waved me off. "Thank you for your kind thought, but this is somethin' I gotta do alone. Yeah, there's people in my corner—my beautiful Bryce, Betsey and all her crew with the club, my church people—but you know somethin'? When it comes down to brass tacks, it's me who's gotta walk this path an' see where it goes. Some things in life you gotta face by yourself. Childbirth is one of 'em too. There may be a bunch of people around you, but when it happens, it's just you and your baby. Know what I mean?"

My mind flew back to when I was in the hospital in Minnesota, in hard labor and pushing my child into the world. I'd called Pearl's father repeatedly, but he never answered. Never came to see me or his daughter. That was the beginning of my new life as a single mom. "Yes, I know exactly what you mean."

She sighed. "Bryce says I'm gettin' too maudlin these days. I apologize for being such a bad hostess, but I'm not gonna apologize for asking you to get me a soda from the fridge and takin' out the vegetables. Got turnips, butternut squash, parsnips, and carrots. I like to roast 'em in the Crock-Pot all day with some garlic and onions and a little olive oil. Throw some browned sausage in there later, that's good eatin'."

For the next half hour, Natalie instructed me on how to cut up and prepare these unfamiliar foods. It was kind of therapeutic in a way, the peeling and chopping. After the last vegetable went in the big black Crock, she placed her hands on the table. "You did all the work, but I'm pooped. Can you help me back to the livin' room? I might just take me a nap. You probably got things you gotta do too."

I helped her stand up. "I'm gonna get my little girl and go to the grocery store. I'm not sure what I'll do later. If you need me, I'll leave my number here."

"That'd be nice. I'd love to meet your baby. Please come by for some food later, even if you only pick it up and take it home. Cuttin' up them vegetables takes a lotta time, so you should get the reward, right?"

I smiled as Natalie settled into her big recliner and leaned back. "You bet."

She tucked a colorful crocheted afghan around her legs and gave a big sigh as she closed her eyes. "Nice to know my boy has friends like you. Thank you for taking care of me and him."

Friends? When did that happen?

I hadn't really thought about it, but something had definitely changed between Weatherman and me. Any anger or hatred I had toward him wasn't there anymore, but I couldn't call us friends. Acquaintances? That didn't sound right either. I didn't have a word to describe the relationship between us and couldn't really define it.

I put it out of my mind, as I had things to do. I'd started my day with coffee and Robert, did a favor for Weatherman, met Natalie and helped her for a while, and still had my errands to run. "No problem. You have a nice day, and I'll see you soon."

CHAPTER 15

Clem's gas station was so old, it still had dial pumps rather than the more modern digital ones. Not surprising, as the machines hadn't pumped a single gallon of gas for decades. The whole place exuded an air of neglect and wear.

Mute and Weatherman rode up on their bikes, the noise only briefly masking the tinny radio crackling out an old country station. Weatherman took note of his companion's curled lip and expression of distaste. He understood that completely. Years of collected junk and refuse lay in piles all around the dilapidated building. Rusted oil cans, crumbling cardboard boxes, engine parts in plastic crates, random car parts—the entire scene was one of misery and abandonment.

Clem Gustler appeared from behind the old station, wiping his hands on a dirty shop cloth. He was somewhere in his midforties and built like a Ford truck: lean, tough, and ready to fight. His eyes darted to the rockers on their cuts, and his wariness ramped up. "Help you two?"

"Brick sent us over to ask about a lawn tractor he heard you had for sale. Still got it?" Weatherman asked.

Clem grinned and shoved his thumbs in his jeans belt loops. His faded T-shirt showed a few grease stains over a faded Coors Light bottle. He wasn't a bad-looking man, but his demeanor gave off an air of caution.

He moved the wad of chewing tobacco from one side of his mouth to the other and scratched the gray scraggle on his chin. "Yeah, I still got it." A ropy muscled forearm with a blurred Navy tattoo jerked a thumb behind him. "'S'out back. Make you deal for cash money."

"We need to look at it first."

"Sure, sure. Come on, I'll show it to you."

The tractor was pristine, totally opposite of the shack it was housed in.

"Ain't been used a lot. Got it off some stupid fucker over in Whittier. Owes me money, but he's broke, so he gave me this instead."

Weatherman was sure the mower was stolen, but he kept that thought to himself. "Blades need sharpening, but otherwise, it appears to be in good shape."

"I 'spect so. Sellin' as is, though."

Mute walked around the building. Clem eyed him before spitting a stream of brown on the ground. "You boys lookin' for something?"

"Mute likes to scout around wherever he is. It's in his nature as a bouncer. You know, to prevent trouble before it happens."

"Not sure I like him scoutin' my place."

"You got something to hide?"

The grin came back, showing Clem's stained teeth. "Not at all. Brick ain't someone to cross. Folks 'round here know better'n to tangle with him or his boys. My trailer is over yonder down in the holler. My cousin's down there too. Bet he got some 'shine for sale. Might give you some if you wanna buy that tractor and all."

Clem seemed too sure of himself, as if he had one up on the Dragon Runners in his yard. Weatherman didn't trust him at all. Going down that narrow dirt path might lead to the clues they wanted or bullets in the back. These mountains could swallow a person whole, and no one would ever find the body.

Mute came from around the other side of the building and approached the two men. He ignored Clem and twirled his finger in the air in a "let's ride" gesture.

Weatherman took the cue. "I think I've seen enough. Mute doesn't drink, and he's ready to go. We'll tell Brick about the tractor and let you know what he decides."

"Don't take too long. Buck Melford is interested too."

Both Dragon Runners mounted their bikes and took off with Mute in the lead. The scenery flashed by, mostly bare trees as the drought had taken effect. The normal vibrant colors were dull, and the leaves fell quickly this season. The big Halloween party was happening this weekend, and the campground where it was held had already shed down to bare.

Weatherman followed Mute as he pulled off at an overlook. Both men took off their helmets and gloves. Weatherman could tell Mute was upset and probably wanted to get back to his pregnant wife, as she could pop anytime now. If this business weren't so serious, he'd be home right now enjoying being a father. Instead he was out dealing with garbage like Clem Gustler.

"What did you see?"

Mute gave Weatherman a dirty look and pulled at his beard before whipping out his phone.

Mute: 10 oil drums. Clean. Holes.

Oil drums themselves were nothing, but with cutouts in the sides? That meant possible bear baiting. Food was stuffed and sealed into the containers and then put out along known bear paths. The purpose was to attract as many animals as possible in one area for easy hunting. Illegal as hell in North Carolina. Add some heavy-duty horse sedatives and it was like shooting fish in a barrel.

Weatherman hated the pun.

Mute: Lot of bags of cheap dog food.
No dogs around.

Bingo. If it looked like a duck, walked like a duck, and quacked like a duck, it had to be a duck. The problem was, the drums and dog food were circumstantial, and they would be hard-pressed to get a search warrant. Weatherman had the impression from Clem that even if they did get a deeper dive at the place, there wouldn't be any hard evidence to convict.

He inhaled sharply. "We need more. This isn't enough to go on yet."

> Mute: The guy who owns the tackle shop by the lake talked about his favorite hunting spot once. Real private and hard to get to, so he didn't go there often, but he always saw a lot of deer and bears. Somewhere between Peachtree Creek and Andreas Branch.

The mountains were full of backcountry campsites, trails, and other hidden spots. The idea of a secret place for hunting was not some wild theory—these forests were huge and thick with areas no one had ever seen before.

> Mute: We need to get this to Brick. Nothing else we can do now. Stay alert at the Halloween ride.

A grimly pressed mouth sat on Mute's face, echoing his bad mood. Hopefully, getting home to his woman and children would soothe the silent beast.

"I'm with you. I'll share with Chief Wilson, but his hands are tied for now."

His phone buzzed with a text, and he was surprised to see it was from Opal. She'd come by the house the same night after helping with his mom and brought Pearl with her. The sausage stew was one of his favorites from his childhood, and most of the root vegetables came from his mom's gardens. Served with homemade biscuits or cornbread, it was simple and filling. Natalie usually made homemade biscuits, but for this night, they came out of a Pilsbury can. She mentioned that Opal had been the one to fix the tasty meal and was delighted the younger woman came by with her daughter. His mom insisted they stay for dinner, and for the first time in a very long while, the house had laughter in it. The little girl completely charmed his mother as she giggled and played with her stuffed alligator.

> Opal: I don't want to bother you, but Betsey is champing at the bit for me to get the wig fitted for your mom. When would that be convenient for you and her?

Dead mutilated bears. Evidence of illegal baiting. His mother's cancer. The Halloween event. So many problems piling up. He wasn't in the mood for company, but something about seeing Opal and Pearl held some appeal. Even with all the shit swirling around, there was a simple peace that came over him when watching the pretty hairdresser and the obvious love and care she had for her child.

Weatherman: Would you be willing to come to my place on your day off this Sunday? I don't know what she's got planned for dinner, but bring an appetite. I'm sure she'll want to feed you and Pearl again.

Opal: She doesn't need to worry about us. We're fine.

Weatherman huffed a laugh before answering.

Weatherman: I'm sure you are, but I learned a long time ago not to argue with my mom. It also means something to her to give you a meal for your trouble. Please just let her do it.

For a few seconds, he thought Opal wouldn't reply, but then a final text came through.

Opal: Okay. I'll be there around 5:00. Does that work?

Weatherman: Perfect. See you then.

He smiled and slipped the phone back into his pocket. As he turned toward his bike, he caught the speculative expression on Mute's face. Almost like the big man knew a female had been texting him.

"Mind your own business, Mute."

He grunted in a strange, garbled laugh as he strapped on his helmet. Even though the huge man couldn't talk, that didn't mean he couldn't communicate. Weatherman expected by noon the next day, it would be all over the club that he was showing some interest in a woman.

CHAPTER 16

I HUNG UP AS I SNEEZED AGAIN AND WIPED THE SWEAT from my brow. Never in my life had I dealt with allergies. Now, for the first time ever, I'd learned of something called ragweed and that the season would last until the first real frost, which so far hadn't appeared. Apparently, it was a big thing around here, and many people suffered from it with stuffy heads and watering eyes. This morning was the worst, and I felt like crap, but if I didn't work, I didn't get paid. I stopped at the drugstore on the way to the salon and armed myself with some generic allergy medications, hoping I would last through the day.

My head hurt as I walked from my car to the salon.

"Uff-da," I muttered as I took stock of my station and what I needed to replenish. I didn't have any color jobs for a change and only two appointments this afternoon, but walk-ins were plentiful, so I was sure my chair would be full today.

I was tired. Pearl had been fussy last night and again this morning when I'd dropped her off at Lori's place. Cutting molars now? I didn't know this time, but this was her usual pattern for growth spurts, teething, or both.

Somehow, we'd get through the day. Though dinner might be a drive-through tonight, as I didn't have the energy for much more than work and home.

I didn't make any plans for Kimmie. She seldom stayed home long enough for any conversation or dinner. Where she spent her evenings was a mystery, but when she came home, the smell of booze and pot came with her. She'd been late to work several times, and I'd watched our serene, gentle boss go from concerned to annoyed.

"What people do on their own time is their business, but when it starts affecting my business, we have a problem," Tambre said the last time it happened.

I was worried about my friend and tried to talk to her about it, but Kimmie brushed it off as me being overprotective.

"Stop being such a mother. You forgot how to party since we moved here."

I loaded my styling gels and checked my stacks of towels as another sneeze tickled my nose. I snatched up a tissue just in time for me to let loose into it.

Tambre approached me as I was wiping up and sniffing. "You okay?"

I dumped the tissue in the trash can. "You bet. Just

getting used to the concept of allergies. I've never had them before."

She nodded and made a humming sound in her throat. "'Tis the season for it. You should see the pollen in the spring. It gets so thick sometimes, the cars turn dusty yellow. I wish we would get a good rain to wash some of it away instead of these little sprinkles once in a while. We really need a good dousing."

The bell rang.

"Hey, y'all," Molly called out. "I brought some coffee and donuts from Pam's place. Good golly, you should see the lines! I saw Blue talkin' to some lady with four kids and a dog. Well, he was talkin' and she was flirtin'. Guess she don't know about Psalm or decided to ignore that big-ass ring on his finger." She set down a paper bag and a cardboard carrier with four tall cups. "Cream and sugar are in the bag. Where's Kimmie?"

I kept my mouth shut as I accepted a coffee. It was hot despite the protective sleeve, and I almost dropped it.

Tambre's eyes narrowed with irritation. "She was scheduled to open."

I sniffed and confessed, "I don't know where she is."

Tambre shook her head. "It's not your problem or responsibility, and I'm not asking you to get in the middle. Kimmie is a grown woman, and she'll have to handle her own choices, good and bad. I don't want her to be in trouble, but she's turning out to be unreliable, and I can't have that here. I'll be glad to help her if she asks for it, but unless she straightens up, I may have to let her go."

I hated that. Kimmie and I had been through a lot together, and I thought we'd both come out the other side, but the demons of our past were slipping back into her life. They would come for me, too, if I didn't stay wary.

A half hour later, Kimmie still hadn't shown up, and Molly left in a huff. Not good to stand up a Dragon Runners woman, especially one of Molly's status.

It was late morning, while I sat in my chair cradling my aching head, when Kimmie finally made an appearance.

"Omigod! I was so sick this morning, I could hardly move."

Hangovers will do that to you. "You missed Molly's appointment. Should have called."

The pink-haired woman chuffed as she moved to her station and plopped her big shoulder bag down. "My phone is dead, and I didn't have my charger."

I bit my lip. I'd been through this scenario many times with her since we moved here. Always an excuse. Always a reason. Always someone or something else's fault. I usually had an abundance of patience because I'd been that person at one time in my life, but I just didn't feel up to dealing with my friend today. "Well, you'd better make it right with Tambre. She's not happy about it."

Kimmie rolled her eyes in irritation. "Tambre's never happy. She crawled up my ass last week over being late. It was only a few minutes, and she acted like the world collapsed."

I found that hard to believe. Tambre didn't throw fits or get in people's faces. I'd seen her handle clients like Burna Jones with ease and distraction. That didn't make her a pushover, though. She had the talent of making people listen without shouting or putting on a big show. It was kind of impressive watching her defuse a nasty situation.

My tendency was to let things with Kimmie go, as I had enough to handle in my own life, but my patience drained away like my sinuses.

"You still need to get here on time, Kimmie. It's part of the job."

She rolled her eyes at me and flounced to the break room to grab a Mountain Dew. Tambre was also in the back, and I expected she and Kimmie would have a few words. I stayed out front and planned the deaths of the little men with jackhammers at my temples. I'd never had this kind of headache in my life.

"You look like shit, girlfriend," Deandra commented as she walked by my station. "We don't gotta lot goin' on here. Who you got comin'?"

"Joanna Porter and someone new. Marsha?"

Deandra flipped a hand of artistic nails at me. "I know Joanna pretty good. I think that Marsha person is a tourist, so anyone can take her. I'll work them in so you can go on home and keep your germs to yourself."

"Everyone says it's allergies."

"Mm-hmm. You ain't had no allergies before, and

there's a nasty flu bug goin' 'round the schools. Take the day. Maybe tomorrow too."

I decided not to argue. A phone call and quick drive later, I was picking up a very irritated Pearl. My normally cheerful girl was not happy and letting the world know it. She threw a fit when I put her in her car seat, then another one when I took her out. I sat her in her high chair, where she wailed until I lifted her on my lap. Not even her favorite McDonald's fries made her want to eat.

My girl was sick. Had to be. Kids got ear infections, right? She wasn't pulling at her ears, though, and they didn't look red. Her gums were fine, so she wasn't teething. Growing pains? It was a thing. Maybe she had a fever. It was hard to tell, as I was flushed myself.

I dosed her with baby Tylenol and sat in the rocker, hoping the familiar rhythmic movement would get her to sleep for a nap. The pediatrician was still open, and I needed to call and see if they had time to see her this afternoon. I prayed I would make it until then. My head was about to explode, and I wanted to cry with absolute frustration. I understood why some parents had to walk away from screaming, crying children. It was the biggest experience of helplessness, yet you still had to take care of your kid regardless of their behavior. No one ever warns parents that there will be times of such exasperation, you wonder if you're cut out to be one. My patience was growing thinner and thinner as my head pounded away.

No, that was the door. Someone was knocking at my door.

My heart jumped. Surprise visitors were usually not the good kind. I hadn't had good experiences with the police, and I couldn't think of anyone else who would show up at my apartment.

Is it about Kimmie?

The knocking persisted, and I hauled myself up from the chair with a crying Pearl to answer the door.

The person was wearing a uniform, though not the one I was expecting. A brown shirt with a shiny badge showed in front of my peephole. Weatherman.

I sat Pearl on my hip and moved to open the door. That single bit of effort had me sweating and ready to drop. I saw a familiar box in his hand.

He smiled sheepishly. "I hope you don't mind the girls at the salon telling me where you live. You forgot the wig up at the Lair, and Betsey asked me to bring it to you so you could do whatever before Sunday. I tried the salon first, but they told me you went home sick. Looks like they were right."

I groaned and stepped back. I wasn't happy with him being here, but at the moment, I wasn't up to arguing over it. "Just leave the wig on the counter. I'll see to it as soon as I can."

Pearl let out a squeal and twisted like a pretzel in my arms. I yelped as I almost dropped her.

Weatherman caught her from me, and she immediately stopped crying. She sniffled a few times before curling into his shoulder and popping a thumb in her mouth.

The room spun a bit as I looked up at him. "I'm okay. I've just never had allergies before. Pearl is the one who's sick. She's been fussy all day."

He placed the back of his hand on her forehead with a frown. "No fever. You sure she's sick?"

My head felt like it was ready to blow, along with my patience. "Yes, she's sick. I've given her Tylenol, but it's not working. Uff-da, can't you tell?"

He glanced down at the quiet baby resting on his chest. "Got a thermometer somewhere?"

I had one of the zapper types that you placed on the forehead for a reading but hadn't used it yet. Mostly because the effort of going to the bathroom to get it was more than I could manage. "Top shelf in the bathroom cabinet."

He sauntered into the tiny tiled room to get the thermometer while I staggered to the sofa. A moment later, he placed the white instrument against my head and pressed the button.

"Fuck. You're topping at 103.1. Allergies my ass. You have the flu, babe. Pearl isn't sick. You are."

"But I gave her Tylenol." I didn't even try to stop the whining sound of my voice.

"Do you have the adult version?"

"I don't think so."

"Luckily, the convenience store down the street does." He put a now-content Pearl down in her playpen and handed her alligator to her. She grabbed her *gay-toh* and hugged it close. "I'll be back in a few."

I lay on the sofa and groaned as the world tilted the wrong way. I'd never been sick before, at least not like this. Whatever this was had hit me like a ton of bricks. The little energy I had drained away as I got up to get a glass of water. My mouth was dry, and my muscles ached; the short walk to the kitchen was almost more than I could handle. Pearl was occupied and appeared a lot calmer than she was earlier. Perhaps she'd been feeding off my bad mood all day, and I'd just assumed she was sick.

The icemaker didn't spit out the cubes from the door anymore, so I had to open the freezer to get them. I plunked several in a plastic cup and filled it with water. I gulped down one full glass, then went for another. The next moment, I found myself on the floor with no idea how I got there, watching the water from my spilled glass spread across the cheap linoleum.

River. I left one in Minnesota. I found one here. Flowing water. Where does it go now?

I didn't know where those thoughts came from. My head pounded so hard that I figured it had shaken something loose inside.

Pearl let out a "Wa-da-wa-da-wa-da" and pointed at the door. I turned my unfocused gaze to a figure approaching me. A man. It took a moment for me to recognize him, and when I did, my heart burned with sudden emotion and my eyes filled, tears spilling out uncontrolled over my lashes.

"Camo," I sobbed. "You're here."

His beautiful hazel eyes shimmered as he smiled at me, and I saw his overlapped tooth in front.

"Hang on, sweetness. I got you."

How many times had he said that to me? "I'm trying so hard, and I miss you so much."

"Here, babe. Take these." Weatherman handed me two white pills.

"No, I don't take drugs anymore. I left that life behind when I got pregnant with Pearl. I won't go back to that."

"It will help, babe. Trust me."

"It's only Tylenol. It's safe."

Weatherman brought a fresh glass of water to my lips and encouraged me to swallow. The pills went down easily. He made me finish the cool liquid, tilting the plastic cup until I'd drained it all. Then he pulled out his cell phone.

"That's good, sweetness."

"Bad fever. One of the highest I've seen."

"You have a good place here."

"Cold compresses where? Are you sure that'll work?"

"You got this."

"If it doesn't break in a couple hours, I'll call for an ambulance. Thanks, Emma. And thanks for staying the night. I'll see you tomorrow."

Weatherman appeared before me again. "Let's get you up." He lifted and carried me, not to the sofa but to my bedroom, setting me down gently on top of the comforter.

"You need to take better care of yourself, sweetness."

"I'm so sorry, Camo. It's all my fault." The tears kept coming, and I couldn't stop them.

"Don't be sorry, Opal. You didn't do anything wrong."

"Raise up. I'm gonna put some ice bags under your arms and neck. Mom's nurse said it's the fastest way to reduce a fever. Just bear with it a minute."

I hissed as Weatherman pushed cloth-covered ice under my shirt and in my armpits. Another cloth was draped across my neck. "That's cold."

"That's what ice does."

A shiver ran through my body. "I need to take care of my girl."

"I got her."

"I got her."

The two voices blended together, and for whatever reason, those sound waves assured me that Pearl was okay. Her babbled words and happy giggle drifted to my ears. "Maybe I'll just rest my eyes for a moment."

"You do that. I'll be here."

"You do that. I'll be here."

I WOKE UP TO A DARK ROOM WITH MY SKIN COVERED IN A sour sweat. My head ached, and my body was weak, but I was alert. Panic set in when I noticed Pearl was not in her crib. She was ready to move from that to a toddler bed soon, but I hadn't gotten one for her yet.

Shit, where is my daughter?

Visions of her wandering around the apartment and getting outside by herself sent me into a frenzy. I jumped out of my bed and almost fell to the floor from the dizzy black spots that appeared in my vision.

Focus, Opal. Slow down and focus.

A low male voice came to me from the living area. I peeked out and spotted Weatherman on the sofa with Pearl next to him. Her *gay-toh* sat smushed between them while she jabbered and pointed to the pictures in the book he was reading to her.

"Yes, that's the blue fish. Can you show me the red one?"

She blew bubbles and slapped at the page. "Bissssssssh!"

I held back a laugh, but it came out anyway.

"A-ma!" My little girl grinned at me but kept her position next to Weatherman. He raised his eyes to me, and for a moment, I got lost in their hazel hue.

"I reheated the fries and nuggets a little while ago. She ate well, and I cleaned up her face and hands but that was it. If she needs changing or bathing, I can do that, but I thought it would be a little too personal right now." Weatherman rose from the rocking chair and carried Pearl to me. He must have moved it when I was out of my head. His hand reached out to check my forehead. "I talked to Emma, Mom's caregiver. She said the bug going around is a bad one. It hits hard and fast but leaves just as quickly. I think Pearl avoided it this round, and you shouldn't be contagious anymore."

A frisson of alarm hit me. "Uff-da, I hope you didn't catch it!"

He shook his head. "I got a flu shot so I could be around my mom. In her state, she can't afford to catch anything. Just to be safe, I'll spend a couple days in my place at the Lair so I'm sure not to take anything home to her." He looked at me with contemplation. "You should probably stay home tomorrow too. I imagine you feel pretty weak right now. Your roommate around?"

I glanced at the wall clock. If she wasn't home by now, she probably wouldn't be. "I haven't seen her since work."

He pressed his lips together. "I'll stick around until you eat something."

"You don't have to do that. I can handle it."

His eyes got very soft. "Opal, there's nothing in this world you can't handle, but you are allowed to have some help from time to time. Think you're up for a shower?"

That sounded heavenly. "If you're okay with watching Pearl?"

His eyes cut to me with an are-you-serious-right-now look in them.

I sighed. "Okay. Let me change her first, and then I'll go."

It took more energy than it should have to take the old Pampers off my daughter and put a new one on.

She wasn't a squirmer, but that simple task still took a lot out of me. I went into the bathroom, carefully removed my clothes so I didn't fall over, then stepped under the hot spray. The shower was great but exhausting. I'd never been like this, and I hoped I never would again. It sapped what little energy I had, and all I wanted to do after drying off was crawl into bed and not move the rest of the night. As a single mother, that wasn't an option, but having Weatherman here was a big help. I came out of the bathroom in my warmest pj's and slippers to a sight that sent a thousand mixed emotions racing through me.

Weatherman sat in my rocker with Pearl on his lap. The chair's soft creaking from his movements was the only sound in the room. She was asleep, curled into his firm body.

Safe.

Secure.

Trusting.

My throat clogged, and I had to swallow several times as my eyes filled with water.

"Love has no limits, sweetness. You're allowed to do it more than once."

"Is that true?" I asked the universe.

Of course, it was silent.

Weatherman looked up from his seated position, and his eyes met mine.

No. No, I was not ready for this.

Not ready at all.

CHAPTER 17

Weatherman had to turn away as the soft wig slipped over his mom's hairless scalp.

The leftovers were still on the table—a simple meal of baked ziti and cheese with garlic bread and salad. Pearl had crammed fistfuls of the stuff in her messy mouth and smeared sauce all over her face. No one minded. In fact, his mom had watched the little girl with complete fascination and remarked on how smart she was. A smile stayed on her face for the entire meal.

He sat on the couch with the freshly cleaned toddler and played with her as Opal worked with his mom. It took a few days for the woman to bounce back from the bout of flu, but luckily Pearl didn't catch it. Opal hadn't remembered anything from the few fever dream hours, or at least she hadn't asked about it. He was curious about the name Camo but decided not to bring it up unless she did.

"There we are," Opal said as she adjusted the snug netting. "How does that feel?"

"It's a lot more comfortable than I thought it would be. It's like I'm wearing a really nice stocking cap." Natalie shifted to sit straighter in her recliner, currently in its upright position. It was awkward, but Opal worked around the cumbersome chair.

He bit his lip to keep it still.

"Let me style it around your face a little." Opal's voice held a tender note to it that burned into his memory. "You can do this yourself on the form I brought you before you put it on. With a little care, you'll get about a year out of it before you'll want a new one."

God willing, Mom will be here in a year, he thought as he swiveled back to see Opal lift part of the wig in a fat curling iron. Her face was soft, and his breath caught.

He turned away to keep the knot in his throat from getting any bigger. Betsey wanted to come and see the results, but then she got the call that Katrina was now in labor and went to the hospital to welcome the next Dragon Runners addition. Weatherman sent out a few prayers for a successful and safe delivery, as well as a thanks that Opal was okay enough to be here.

"Your little girl is cute as a button. Two years old, right?" Natalie asked with shining eyes.

"Yes, and thank you. It's hard to keep up with her now."

"Did your husband move with you?"

Opal's hand jumped. "Um… he died."

That had Weatherman's attention. He hadn't really thought about Opal's past much, as many other problems occupied his mind. Because of her young age, he'd assumed she was either divorced or had Pearl out of wedlock. Burying a husband and then moving across the country to a new place? That took a lot of guts. Was that the reason she had the panic attack at the Lair? The mystery behind those blue eyes was deep and made him even more curious about her.

"I remember when Bryce started crawlin'. Seems it weren't too long before he was walkin' and runnin'. I read to him every night." Natalie reached up to touch the ends of her new hair as she reminisced.

"I read to Pearl too. It'll be interesting to hear what accent she learns." Opal flicked the iron off the hair piece and picked up another section.

"You said before that you're from Minnesota. Gets real cold there, don't it?"

Another flick. "Winter can be pretty bad some years, but I guess we're used to it. This will be my first winter anywhere else."

"You got people up there?"

"Just the friend I told you about already, Mama J."

Natalie gave a short laugh. "Yeah, the one with the six children. Lord ha' mercy, that's a lot of work."

Opal laughed as she picked up a brush. "I can't even keep up with one some days. Janice is her name, but everyone up there calls her Mama J. I'm so grateful that she took me and Pearl in when she did. It was a rough time in my life. I don't think I could have handled it without her."

Weatherman digested that information and filed it away. Was that when she'd lost her husband? Pearl's father, he assumed. No family? Pregnant and alone? He leaned closer for more. Pearl blew a wet raspberry and pulled open the pocket of his shirt to peer inside.

"Sounds like you had quite the life. So, what do you think of our little town?" Natalie sat still as Opal moved around and brushed out the wig.

"It's a lot at times. The accent is different, and there are some words I don't quite understand, but I'm learning." The plastic bristles glided through the locks, and Opal smoothed her hand over them. "I've never had a lot of people around me like this before. I had some friends in Minnesota, but nothing like it is here. I used to… hang out with a motorcycle club up there that was very different from this one."

Another piece of the puzzle fit in place, and Weatherman acknowledged it with a small nod. It made sense. She'd had a bad experience with bikers that left her scarred. One bad enough to relocate to a strange town in a state vastly different from the life she once had. Not every club resembled the Dragon Runners MC. At one time, they were heavily into illegal businesses, but Brick had reinvented the club into what it was today. There were still some questionable activities, but for the most part, they stayed on the right side of the law. Anything else was kept under wraps by Brick alone.

His instincts ramped up. What did Opal go through?

"There we go. How's this?" Opal held up a hand mirror.

"Well, now, ain't that something. I look twenty years younger. What do you think, Bryce?"

Weatherman gazed at his mom, distracted for the moment. For the first time in weeks, she had a healthy color to her skin. Her genuine grin was framed by a pretty bob reminiscent of his teenage years. Yes, she did resemble an earlier version of herself, a pretty woman before the cancer and the poisonous treatments that dripped into her veins every week. "It's beautiful, Mom. Just like you."

Opal packed up her kit. "Let me know when you need me again. I'll be glad to make a house call anytime."

"Oh, you're so sweet. I'd love for you to meet Emma. Come by tomorrow when you can, and I'll introduce you." Natalie's thin hand patted Opal's leg, and Weatherman noticed the prominent blue veins on the back.

His voice was thick when he spoke. "I'll walk you out."

Pearl put her head onto his shoulder and cuddled close. Whatever Opal's life had been like in the northern state didn't seem to touch the happy, content child. It was a testament to a mother's love and dedication. There were good parents who devoted their lives to raising their children and protecting them from all the harm the world possessed. And there were bad ones who barely acknowledged that they had kids. He'd been blessed with the former and wondered about Opal's upbringing.

Night fell quickly this time of year, and with clear mountain skies, the stars shone like glitter across a sea of midnight blue. He gazed up and pointed at a trio of lights. "Look there, Pearl. See that? That's Orion's belt. The hunter."

She gazed up for a few moments but lost interest quickly and flopped back into her resting position.

"It's getting close to bedtime." Opal smiled gently as she loaded her bag of tools into the car. "I bet she'll be out before we get home. Let me take her from you."

"I got it. Just open the door for me, and I'll get her settled."

Pearl made a slight mew of protest as he buckled her into the heavy car seat, but she settled when he handed her the well-loved alligator toy. A pink blanket lay on the seat next to her, so he tucked it around the little girl as her eyes blinked slowly up and down. "I don't think you'll make it out of the driveway." He turned to Opal and took a deep breath, the cooler air stinging his nostrils and bringing him a bit of focus. "I admit that this is not the Sunday afternoon I wanted to have with you, but I thank you for taking care of my mom."

She smiled and waved off his words. "Oh no, Betsey bought it for her."

"But you picked it out. Styled it. Made it look really

nice. She loves it, and I expect she'll be wearing it all the time. It means a lot to her and—"

He stopped talking as emotions threatened to overwhelm him, swallowing the lump in his throat before he continued. The simple change in Natalie's appearance was such a confidence booster, and he hadn't seen his mother smile with genuine happiness in quite some time. It killed him a little. "When I was growing up, she always took pride in her hair. I remember people's compliments on her style, the shine, the lack of grays. Mom considered her hair to be her best feature. It's gone now, and the doctor said it might be different when it comes back. *If* it comes back."

He nearly broke as he paused again. Steamy air sliced in and out of his nostrils as he fought to keep it together. "Opal, you have no clue what that wig means to her. The happiness in her eyes… I can't—"

Her arms came around him, and he was pulled into a soft, warm body.

"It's okay. I got you."

It wasn't a light half hug. This was full contact and solid. Her head rested on his shoulder as Pearl loved to do, and she fit to his body perfectly.

Like she was meant to be there.

He didn't think about it. If he did, his logical mind might have caught up with his emotions.

He didn't hesitate. If he paused, it wouldn't have happened.

He didn't stop. Not this time.

His hand slid up to her neck, tilting her head back so he could cover her mouth with his.

There were no fiery sparks, no flash of lightning, no roar of heated flames. This was a kiss of comfort. Not sexual, but one that allowed him to lean on someone else for a moment and let go of some of the pain in his heart. She opened to him and allowed him access. He took it.

The kiss lasted longer than he expected and shorter than he wanted. He lifted his head but kept his mouth close enough to feel her trembling lips under his. It wasn't hard to tell that she hadn't been kissed in a long time.

It had also been a long time since his body had reacted this way. Even though this was not a prelude for sex, there was a shared intimacy between them that transcended the physical action.

His gaze met hers, and he noticed the wetness at the corners of her eyes.

"I'm not apologizing for kissing you," he whispered. "I've been having a really rough time with life lately. Not as rough as my mom, but it's still taking a toll on me. Work is stressful as hell. Home is too. I'll consider this to be between friends, yeah? We can talk about it later or not, but right now, I can't. I'm gonna let you go home. Thank you again for taking care of my mom."

Every instinct he possessed drove him to kiss her again and take the soothing relief she offered, but he forced himself to let her go and step away. She was shaky but silent as she got in the car, and he held himself back not to go to her. The shell-shocked look on her face made him want to know what was in her head and heart.

Was this the beginning of something, or was it doomed before it started? He had no clue, but one thing for certain stood out: the future had changed.

He waited for the taillights to fade before entering the house. His mother sat in her lift chair. "I like your girl."

He groaned and ran a hand over his face. "I don't think you can call her 'my girl,' Mom. We don't know each other very well, and if the truth be known, we started off pretty bad."

The amused curl of Natalie's mouth told him he was in trouble. It was the same look she got when she'd caught him making out with his high school girlfriend. "It didn't look too bad to me from that kiss y'all were sharing. Reckon you're almost done with the gettin'-to-know-you stage."

Weatherman felt his cheeks flare up. It had been years since his mom managed to embarrass him. She used to make a point of it when he'd acted out as a teenager. "Don't think I won't make a scene in front of your friends if I need to!"

That fiery statement came from a strong woman in her prime, not from someone fighting for their life. That didn't stop his cheeks from reddening, though. "I didn't know you could see us through the window."

She chuckled. "Don't you remember? I got eyes in the back of my head. Even when I'm not here anymore,

I still plan to watch over you, so be careful what you say and do."

Pain brushed over his chest. "Mom, I can't."

Natalie sighed, and the corners of her mouth turned down. "I realize you don't want to talk about it, but the whole of it is, I may not be here much longer. It's not up to you or me to make that call, but we still gotta deal with it. I done told you where all the papers are, and I called down to the funeral home to make sure all the plans are in order just in case."

"Mom—"

She raised a bony hand. "Now hush, sweetheart. Ain't no sense denying it. I've always been a practical person, and I raised a practical boy. I hope I can be here a long time, but I might not. I've given you the best gift I can now in that all my arrangements are decided and paid for. That's one less thing you gotta deal with when the time comes, whether it be next month or twenty years from now."

She coughed lightly before continuing, her voice growing raspier as she spoke. "Ain't nothing more to say 'bout that. Only part I got left is what happens to you. I don't want you to be lonely or by yourself. That's why I like your girl. I think she'd be a good one to keep after."

"She's older than me and has a child."

"If you think that matters, you ain't the boy I raised up."

No, it didn't matter to him. Not the small age difference, nor the fact that she had a little girl. Motherhood had never been a turnoff to him, perhaps because of his own experience growing up. If anything, he found her more attractive because of her dedication to Pearl. Still, a relationship was not in the cards between him and Opal. "It's not good timing, Mom."

"If you're waitin' on a sign or for the right time, you might miss out on somethin' real good. Sometimes you gotta adapt. You hear me?"

"I'm listening."

"I know that, but do you *hear* me?"

He inhaled sharply. "I'm trying, Mom. I really am."

<hr>

PEARL STAYED ASLEEP AS I MOVED HER FROM THE CAR TO her crib. Kimmie was out wherever she went these days, and for once, I was grateful that she was gone. I needed to sort my head in a bad way. It was hard, and as I lay back in my bed, I was full to the brim with thoughts of Weatherman.

I'd learned from the talk at the salon that he'd given up his career to come home and take care of his mother. Natalie had confirmed it when I met her the first time. How many children would do that for their parents? Even if I knew where my mother was, I doubt I would consider making that kind of sacrifice for her.

I still didn't know what possessed me. Some weird demon who liked to play practical jokes, maybe? What drove me to wrap my arms around the man and hug him to me?

"It's okay," I'd whispered to him. "I got you."

I got you. Those words were spoken to me once when I struggled at rock bottom. Someone offered me a hand to lift me out of the quagmire my life had become. I'd grabbed it with desperation and found more joy than I'd ever deserved.

That hand had paid the ultimate price for me.

"I got you," I repeated with tears filling my eyes. "I got you. I got you."

He'd leaned his head down to my shoulder and pressed his forehead to the side of my neck. I'd stroked over the planes of his back, repeating the same three words. We were pressed tight as we shared our mutual sorrows. Weatherman was strong and smart, but even he became helpless when facing insurmountable odds.

Life didn't guarantee happy endings to everyone. Some of us had to work and bleed for the chance.

Then he kissed me.

And I let him!

I tried to find my anger and hate.

It was gone. Like smoke from a fire, all the negatives I'd strained to keep had dissipated under his kiss. I wanted to burrow into him as I'd seen my daughter do, have those strong arms around me again, and surround myself in his heat.

That unrelenting desire terrified me beyond any fear I'd ever experienced.

I stared at the cracked ceiling and asked out loud, "What's happening to me?"

"I keep telling you, there are good people in this world, sweetness. All you have to do is let them in."

I wanted to ignore the annoying voice, but it was impossible. This time I talked back.

"I don't know what to do, Camo. I'm so confused."

"I get that, baby. I can't tell you why or how, and I can't tell you that it's gonna be easy, but please trust me. It'll be okay."

My throat had closed up after speaking the name I hadn't uttered in so long. Tears flowed down my cheeks, and I let them go unchecked.

"I miss you so much."

"You're stronger than you think, baby."

CHAPTER 18

CLEM GUSTLER PULLED HIS FIST BACK AND PUNCHED HIS cousin in the face. "What the fuck were you thinkin'?" His voice was cool but tight with tension.

Walt dropped to the ground, spitting blood, and fingered his split lip. "What's your fuckin' problem?"

Clem couldn't believe his ears. "The bears, dumbass. What made you think dumpin' them near the Dragon Runners' campground was a good idea?"

The man on the floor scratched his greasy head. "Dunno. I thought it funny to play a trick like 'at on Brick."

"Funny." Clem's single word came out bitterly sarcastic. "I got a real interestin' visit from some new guy named Weatherman and Mute. Fuckin' Mute. Last thing we need right now is fuckin' Brick and his boys pokin' into our business. That rich Canadian fella is comin' soon to hunt cougars. Paying us ten grand if he gets one."

"We ain't got no cougars left 'round here."

"Page Harper over in Tennessee is gonna trap one and bring it over for them to shoot."

Walt grunted as he stood up. "That's right. I forgot."

Clem shot a stream of tobacco juice between his teeth at the wood floor. "Stupid shit for brains."

The old cabin was completely off grid. No electricity, no running water, no phone lines, nothing but the raw single-room structure. He had no idea who built it or who the land belonged to. He and his brothers had found it on a hunting trip years ago and used it whenever they needed to hide. Usually, it was from the game warden or forest rangers. Today, it was the Dragon Runners MC.

The temptation to leave Walt here teased Clem's mind. The only way to access this remote place was on four-wheelers, and even then it was tricky, with no real path or road. This was where they brought the hides and other parts they harvested from the bears and other animals. Four bear skins were stretched on racks next to six red foxes and three coyotes. A dozen more assorted ones were in curing barrels. Walter fucked up the last bunch by not salting them quick enough in the field, and by the time they'd made it to the cabin, the hair was starting to fall out. The leather was still usable, but the hunters usually wanted a full-hair hide of their kill for a rug. Clem made sure he had backup hides to send them when that happened. Not one of them could tell the difference between the animal they shot and a substituted one.

Clem figured it was a win-win. Some bored rich guy wanted to go hunting but not get his precious hands dirty, so Clem would supply the animal they wanted to shoot. He got paid for the "hunt" and then paid more to do the skinning and tanning. The big targets were the bears, but foxes, coyotes, and turkey buzzards were scavengers, and he'd picked off a few of them when they came to investigate the remains. Everything was for sale if you had the money.

It was simple: put out bait barrels loaded with dog food and horse tranquilizer, then wait for a bear to find it and get drunk. Hibernation for pregnant bears should be starting by November, and he'd already tagged a bunch of dens for quick kills when the time came. Males would still be out and about all the way up until December, and with the extra-warm fall, it might be even longer before they settled down. It was rare, but when winters were too warm, there were some bears that didn't hibernate at all.

Easy pickings. Easy money.

Ethics be damned.

Yeah, he was supposed to get a hunting license for only one bear and turn in the tooth for population study, but when did he ever follow the rules? Too much hassle, plus that shit was expensive.

"Hey, Clem? Them livers and such is all dried out now. What's that fella want 'em for?"

Clem's lips rose in an irritated snarl. There was also a contact they'd made in Canada who bought the livers, gallbladders, and other unwanted parts. From what

Clem could tell, the guy ground up the dried-out organs, mixed it with other shit, and sold it as magic medicine.

"How the fuck should I know? Probably makes your dick hard or somethin'."

"Oh."

My genius cousin, Clem thought with a mental eye roll. "I don't give a shit if some jackass wants to snort powdered shit up his nose so he can fuck his wife on Saturday night. We're makin' money, and that's all that matters. But we ain't gonna make any more money if you keep fuckin' around with the Dragon Runners."

Walt gave his cousin an acidic look and fingered his split lip again. "Who the fuck put you in charge?"

"You got the connections up north?"

"No."

"Then shut the fuck up. Page said he'd text as soon as he gets a cougar trapped. I don't want nothin' goin' wrong with this shit, so keep your damn mouth closed until we get our money. You understand me, mother-fucker? Keep away from the fucking Dragon Runners."

CHAPTER 19

Halloween was a surprise. It seemed that the entire town closed up and headed over to the campground owned by the Dragon Runners MC for a big all-day barbecue festival. They had vendors, crafters, games, piles of food, kids in costumes, candy, and rides on the road nicknamed the Tail.

Short for the Tail of the Dragon, anyone who hung around bikers learned about this legendary piece of asphalt, and how they dreamed of its eleven-mile stretch. It also had the reputation of eating unskilled or arrogant riders, and many had lost their lives to its appetite.

Today was also my first official date with Pastor Robert—at least, I thought so. He'd called me yesterday to confirm us going to the festival together. Truthfully, I'd forgotten about his invitation, but I didn't like the idea of ditching him. He'd been nothing but kind and polite to me, so in the end, I decided to go out with him.

I told him I would meet him here instead of transferring the car seat and stroller. He was okay with that, and we set a time.

He was in fitted jeans and a patterned dress shirt. His neat hair, glasses, and general appearance made me think of a young business professional or banker or something like that, not necessarily a preacher. He looked really nice.

Pearl had a blast and was full of happy giggles for everyone. She stared mesmerized at the spinning lights and stuffed herself with treats. She walked a little but preferred to be pushed around. The stroller had a back that laid down flat, so when she was sleepy, I could put her down for a nap.

The rides held no interest for me, but I tried some of the games. Ring toss, water guns, Plinko disk drop, even a booth with ax throwing. I didn't win anything, but the vendors handed out old slap bracelets and ugly keychains as consolation prizes.

Robert won a stuffed lion and presented it to me with a gleaming smile. He wasn't pushy and didn't try to hold my hand or anything like that, but he did stay attentive to me and Pearl. Occasionally, he would push the stroller as we wandered through the crowds and talked to each other.

"It must be tough being a widowed mother at your age."

I hesitated but didn't have the need to correct him. "I manage."

"You're very admirable and brave. Many women

wouldn't have picked up and moved so far away from home. What does your family think about it?"

"I didn't have a lot of family. Just one or two very close friends."

"Your mother?"

Again I hesitated. How was I supposed to tell him that she gave birth to me but wasn't really a mother "She's... gone."

"I'm sorry to hear that. You've had a very tough life. It's amazing that you've come this far and been so successful. Many women would have crumpled under that much weight."

I saw what made him a good pastor. His attitude for listening and paying attention was phenomenal. He didn't spout fire and brimstone, doom and gloom, or anything I'd always associated with church people like the ones I'd seen in movies. I couldn't really see myself with a preacher or someone like that, but he exuded such kindness, it did have me wondering what it would be like. It also had me feeling guilty, as I'd kissed Weatherman, and his touch still occupied my thoughts.

It bothered me that he hadn't called or texted, but most men I'd dealt with in the past seldom kept their word. When he said we'd talk later or not, I guess he meant the "not" part more.

My past struggles left scars, deep ones, and so far, I hadn't been around anyone who I thought could under-stand them and where they left me. Some of the ladies at the salon regularly spouted off Bible verses and talked about forgiveness and love for all. Was that a real thing or just words?

The campground bathroom facilities weren't enough to accommodate the need of the crowd, so a row of porta-johns had been set up on the far end near the tree line. Pearl was napping, and I was about to burst. Robert also confessed his need with a grin, and we decided to take turns. The porta-johns were not my first choice, but the long lines at the regular restroom building had me turning the stroller in that direction anyway.

I went first and braved the plastic booth. It had me thinking about toilet training for Pearl. I was glad she was still in diapers for now, as bringing a potty-training toddler in here would not be one of my top ten wanted experiences. I washed my hands as much as I could, thankful that I'd learned the joys of keeping pocket-sized hand sanitizer with me at all times. I emerged to see Robert holding the stroller and staring between the booths with a curled lip of disgust.

One glimpse told me all I needed to know.

Through the sliver of space, I saw Kimmie on her knees sucking off one man while another smoked a blunt, watching and waiting for his turn. The faint sweet and earthy smell of pot wafted to my nostrils, and I tensed. Both men had on dirty shirts that declared them to be carnies in charge of the traveling rides. Kimmie finished the first man and took the twenty-dollar bill he handed to her before starting on the other.

"We should go. I think you said you wanted to look at the soap tent, right?"

Robert's voice had a forced sound to it, as if he smelled a pile of shit and had to pretend it was roses. It bothered me, both the sight of Kimmie on her knees and the contempt I was sure Robert had for her. The same contempt he might have for any woman on her knees for money.

I snatched the stroller handle from him and started moving away. Pearl woke up and fussed at me, but I kept moving. Robert caught up to us a few moments later.

"I'm so sorry you had to see that."

Back to the gentle Pastor Bobby whose love and concern rained over everyone. How would he feel if I told him Kimmie was my roommate? How would he react if he found out that I'd seen plenty of public blow jobs before? What would he think of me if I ever told him about my past and what I'd done to survive?

Memories swirled in my head. Ones I wished I could erase like chalk from a blackboard. Instead, they piled on, higher and higher, and my belly burned with the need to purge. My focus was so intense, I didn't realize where I'd gone until I heard my name called in a friendly greeting.

"Opal! Over here!"

I turned to see two people near me, one in a wheelchair and the other behind it. Weatherman and his mom. Natalie didn't have on the wig I'd styled for her. Instead, she was wearing a tall, elaborately braided contraption and a thick white robe like a Roman goddess. The wheelchair was disguised as a chariot, and the woman in it smiled with delight.

"It was Bryce's idea. What do ya' think?"

"It's amazing. You look wonderful."

She did look wonderful. Vibrancy shone from her face, and her energy level was higher than I expected a cancer patient would have. Tambre had mentioned that she was done with treatments, and things seemed to be going in the right direction.

My attention turned to the man behind the wheelchair, and I stopped dead in my tracks.

He was breathtaking in his biker regalia. The club colors were on full display, and something about them radiated an aura of dominance. Alpha male in every sense. It tingled my nerves, and I became hyperaware of him.

Right now, he was staring at me—or rather, at the man next to me—and the memory of our shared moment outside his house came to mind. He'd said it was between friends, but I felt weird with him seeing me out with another man.

"Pastor Bobby." Weatherman gave a short nod as he growled the greeting.

"Bryce, nice to see you again, son."

"Son"? I was confused. Weatherman was a few years younger than me and Robert, but not that much to be called "son." Maybe it was a pastor thing?

I got even more uncomfortable when Robert put his arm around my shoulders and pulled me in close.

"Nice day for the festival. Your people did real good this year."

"Your people." Why did that sound like an insult?

Apparently, Weatherman thought it did too. His back straightened, and tension filled the air.

Thankfully, Pearl broke the awkward stand-off. She woke up and squealed with delight seeing two familiar people in front of her.

"Eh-da!" she exclaimed and stretched out her arms.

Weatherman relaxed and grinned at my little girl. He bent over and lifted her from the stroller without asking permission. "How's my little peanut?"

When did my daughter become his "little peanut"?

Robert's back stiffened, and his arm tightened around me. "Opal, do you know this man?"

I felt a little like a chew toy being pulled between two dogs. "Yes, I cut his hair, same as I do yours. I styled Natalie's wig, although this isn't the one I did."

Natalie seemed unaware of the thick testosterone floating in the air. She smiled and reached up a thin hand to touch her towering hairdo. "I decided that while I'm still here on earth, I'm gonna have as much fun as I can. It's been years since I dressed up for Halloween."

Robert chuckled. "Amen, sister. We'll leave you to your celebrating. Perhaps we'll see you in church on Sunday."

The use of "we" threw me. Was he implying that I'd be in church on Sunday with him? A quick vision of me standing in a choir loft, wearing a plain conservative dress to my knees with a high frilly collar and my hair tied up in a tight bun, almost had me laughing. My eyes darted to Weatherman and his fierce frown.

"I believe in the Almighty, but I'm already in one club, preacher. Don't need to join another one."

Natalie gave an indignant huff. "Bryce Turner! Church is church, not a club."

"It's a club when you have membership requirements. Church is supposed to have wide-open doors to anyone and no judgments, right?" He placed Pearl back in the stroller, and my girl squalled in protest. "We need to get going, Mom. I told Dodge I'd watch his booth while he grabs some food."

Natalie pursed her lips. "Orneriness. Pure orneriness."

He turned away and didn't look at me again. I had the sense that I'd done something wrong.

But I couldn't think about that now, as the heat rolling off Robert was enough to broil a steak.

As fast as he'd turned it on, it was off again, and he was back to sweet Pastor Bobby. "Food sounds like a good idea. Shall we head over to the barbecue tent?"

CHAPTER 20

THE END-OF-THE-DAY RIDE WAS A BIG DEAL AND MARKED the end of the festival. The crowd watched as the entirety of the Dragon Runners MC, in full costume, mounted their bikes for a final Tail run. Brick was in the lead as a big red devil with Betsey behind him as an angel in white. The other bikers were similarly outfitted. Mute was menacing in all black like a paladin knight. Normally, Katrina would be on the back with him, but she was at home with their first child and the newborn. Stud and Eva were both dressed as Viking warriors. Molly and Cutter were Mario and Princess Peach. Taz and Tambre did a Western theme, and it was easy to see Tambre's heritage. She looked like a Native American queen. Dodge wore coveralls splattered with paint, and Fauna was in a chef's uniform. I wasn't sure if those were actual costumes or work clothes they simply had on hand. Table came, but he had his three children with him, so he couldn't ride. Lori was at home.

The bikes lined up in front of the crowd of people to massive applause. Brick and Betsey nodded in acknowledgment. Bike revs and roars increased the volume of the crowd, and Pearl's eyes widened at the sounds. She didn't cry, though, just had a curious and fascinated expression on her tiny face.

"I don't know why they have to show off like this. All this noise and swagger. It's a little much, wouldn't you say?"

I smiled at Robert's words, but I didn't think the run was over the top or bad. I didn't see bragging or boasting or gaudiness. I saw a united front of people joined together as one. It made me a little envious.

I glanced around, wondering if Kimmie was here or still behind the porta-johns. I hoped she'd simply left and gone home.

Brick made his bike roar a few times to work up the crowd before taking off. The club circled the campground before starting the Tail run. I noticed Weatherman at the back, by himself still, with no costume. Several women waved and gestured to him, volunteering to ride with him. His helmet shield was up, and even though his face was kinda squished, he smiled as he turned them down. He pulled up to his mom and Emma, who now stood behind the wheelchair, and dismounted, then lifted his mother's hand to his mouth and kissed her knuckles.

Mother and son. I had no words to describe the

emotion that flooded my heart at the sight. I was sure if Natalie had the strength to ride, she'd be on the back of that bike, and no one would question it. There was no way, though. Not in her frail condition.

He got back on his motorcycle to rejoin the group of riders. I fully expected Weatherman to pick up some random woman to fill the space behind him, but his next move shocked the hell out of me.

Donna stood by herself on the periphery of the campground. Alone. Outsider. Leftover. Weatherman stopped his bike next to her and tapped the seat behind him. Donna placed a hand over her mouth before nodding and taking the helmet he handed her. She strapped it on and mounted the bike, settling herself easily. Two revs later, Weatherman took off, following the group of bikers already well down the twisting road.

He took Donna. He took the outcast woman on the Tail ride to include her in the group. I didn't get the impression that it was an attempt for some action later. It seemed more like what a little brother would do for his big sister.

"No judgment." He'd said those words to Robert during our run-in earlier. The condemning tone in the pastor's voice when he'd talked about Kimmie was far different from the actions of Weatherman. True, seeing Kimmie on her knees was an appalling sight and not one I'd expected here, but Robert showed disgust instead of wondering why she needed money so badly to give out blow jobs behind a row of smelly porta-

johns. I guessed he would view Donna the same way. Her and anyone else who lived a life like hers.

After the bikes took off for the Tail run, people started making their way to cars and trucks. It was a bit of a relief that my date was over and I could go home to relax. Pearl was snoozing hard when I loaded her into the car. Robert stood behind me as I buckled her in and tucked her pink blanket around her. The night sky wasn't completely dark, but I was ready to find my home and my bed. I once again wondered where Kimmie was.

Robert tried to fold and load the stroller, but the mechanism was too much for him to figure out. I raised the lock to collapse the yellow contraption in a few seconds, and he graciously lifted it into the trunk.

"Thank you," I murmured awkwardly. How did I end this? Tell him thanks for a wonderful time? Shake his hand? Get in my car and wave goodbye?

He decided for me as he stepped in close. I had less than one second of warning before he placed his mouth on mine. Soft, closed lips. Full press. It was sweet and innocent, but as surprising as it was unexpected.

I jumped a little at the contact. He misinterpreted the reaction as something else as he pulled back a little. His hand came up to stroke my hair in a familiar way as he smiled down at me. "I had a great time today. I hope to see you again soon. Maybe you could come to my church service tomorrow morning?"

My brain short-circuited. "I don't know. Um… what time?"

"Starts at eleven. We have a nursery for the little ones, but so far, there aren't many of them. Pearl would have a person all to herself."

"I've never really been to church before."

"No problem. I'll meet you at ten forty-five out front and get you seated. Wear a nice dress or nice pants, and I'll take you out to lunch afterward. Okay?"

Does this mean I have a second date with Robert? What am I getting myself into? And what about Bryce? The voice in my head decided to stay quiet when I really needed some answers.

Sunday was one of two days off I had during the workweek, and my normal mode was house cleaning and a trip to the laundromat near the train museum. I supposed I could delay those joyous tasks for a few hours. "I guess I can be there."

His smile deepened with pleasure. "Wonderful. I look forward to it." He leaned in and kissed me a second time, this one a little longer, and he fitted his lips more against mine. Still sweet and caring. Not like the one I shared with Weatherman where it seemed like he wanted to take me into himself.

Was it wrong of me to feel guilty about it? I needed to escape.

"I'll see you tomorrow morning."

Yeah, it was a lame thing to say, but all I could think about was getting home and processing what was happening.

Weatherman steadied his bike as Donna dismounted. He only took a short ride on the Tail, as he didn't want to leave his mother at the campground too long. Emma would drive her home so he could take this time to ride with his brothers, but he still planned to go back to the house and not to the Lair tonight. Natalie had been in good spirits all day, but Weatherman's premonition was that she would crash soon and hard. As much as he would like to go hang with his brothers, his mother might need him more tonight.

Donna had cried when he offered to take her behind him. He did it to be nice to the woman, but also because she had no illusions about him and where they stood. She still made the offer, and he politely declined.

She nodded in understanding. "I get it. I'm probly old enough to be your mama."

"Not quite her age, but that's not the big reason I won't sleep with you. When I take a woman to bed, it needs to be for the right reasons."

"You gotta be in love or somethin'?"

Weatherman paused. "Yeah, something. Something more than scratching an itch."

Donna rolled her bottom lip between her teeth, and he noticed her eyes getting wet. "I used to love gettin' invited up to the Lair when I was younger. Made me think I was special 'cause not every girl got to go. I'd party with lots of men up there and loved every minute. Me 'n' my best friend, Nikki? We used to think we were big stuff. Nikki's gone, and now it's just me. Sometimes girls still come to party, but it ain't the same."

She inhaled with resolve. "Got me a job at Ingles, so I have to wear a uniform. Not my thing, but I thought maybe people would look at me different. But they don't. I'm still the town slut in their minds."

Weatherman regarded the woman. "I had a friend in college. Nadia Camston. She was a student during the day, and at night she worked at the Silver Stock Gentlemen's Club as a stripper, exotic dancer, whatever you want to call it. Some of the guys thought she would be an easy lay. There were girls who looked down their noses at her about what she did for a living."

He smiled as a memory came up. "I was sitting in the cafeteria when one of them said something nasty. I can't think of the words, but I will never forget Nadia's reaction. She stood up tall, right in the middle of the lunch rush, and said as loud as she could, 'Live my life and walk in my shoes a few days before you judge me.' I think that's powerful."

Donna cocked her head to the side and grinned. "I guess it is. You never really know what people are going through or why they do stuff, right? Even if it's a mistake."

Weatherman gave a short laugh. "I think that's the point she was trying to make. Wanna know the truth?" He leaned in as if imparting a big secret. "She was a virgin. She'd taken years of dance lessons as a kid and used those skills to put herself through school so she could graduate without a lot of debt. Her focus was on getting a business degree in marketing with an emphasis on social media applications. Last time I talked to her, she was heading to Japan with a team for some sort of expo thing. Still single but dating some sort of investment banker dude."

"That's kinda awesome."

"Yes, it is. I'm really happy for her success."

"I guess I need to go home. I gotta be at work tomorrow morning." Donna frowned. "I really hate wearing that stupid shirt."

Weatherman laughed. "We all do what we have to do. Good luck with your day."

"Thanks again for the ride. I really mean that," Donna said as she waved and then turned to find her car in the nearly empty lot.

He didn't mind taking the woman with him on the ride. He'd wanted to ask Opal, but she was clearly with Pastor Bobby. A date? She had no obligations to him or anyone else, yet it pissed him off big-time to see her with another man. The moment they'd shared in front of his mother's house was branded in his memory. He'd done his best not to relive those few moments over and over, but they regularly crept into his thoughts. It was impulsive to kiss her, but it was also right. He didn't know why; it just was.

On the far side of the lot, he spotted her getting Pearl into her car seat with Bobby looking on. A slight chuckle of satisfaction passed his lips when he saw the preacher having trouble folding up the stroller, but it disappeared when he watched the man lean in and kiss Opal. It wasn't a serious kiss in his estimation, as he saw Opal react with surprise, but she didn't pull away.

His chest tightened, and he had the urge to go punch the guy in the face. He had no right to do that, but he wanted to.

The possessiveness in his gut should have surprised him, but it didn't. He didn't know when or how, but somewhere during his brief meetings with the pretty hairdresser, she became important to him. Important enough that the green jealousy gremlin sat on his shoulder.

He kept his eyes on the two of them and noted with some relief that Opal got in her car and drove away. Bobby waved them off before finding his way to his own vehicle and driving off in the opposite direction. So, they didn't ride together? That made him somewhat happier.

He waited until the red taillights of Bobby's car disappeared, then took off in the direction of Opal's place. Nothing bad about doing a drive-by to make sure she got home okay. The reassurance that she was alone with Pearl? Just a minor bonus.

CHAPTER 21

"Ingles has a big sale on turkeys this week. Getting ready for Thanksgivin', I reckon."

"I found this coupon app. All you do is scan it, and it comes off the bill."

"I can't stand them places that only got self-checkout. I'd rather have a person than a machine."

The salon chatter surrounded me with everyday fluff. Groceries, whose kid was dating who, school events, church bazaars, and other news.

The more I worked here, the less isolated I felt. I learned many of the local women's names and found out much about their lives. Tammy Belle's youngest child was battling leukemia. Charlotte Dane's husband was retiring next year. Marilyn Walker's son won a football scholarship to UNC-Chapel Hill and would head there next year. Every day I learned the news of their lives—both good and bad. It didn't matter if they had big houses or rented small apartments. It didn't matter if they drove sporty convertibles or minivans. It didn't matter if they dressed in designer fashion or from the Goodwill store. Their concerns were the same.

"Heard about Katie Grace? Someone told me she got drugged over at that new restaurant a while back."

"Yeah, I heard about it. Supposed to be some serial wannabe rapist or some such shit."

That got my attention. I hadn't met Katie Grace, but then again, I didn't get out much. My life consisted of work and home. The necessary outings to the laundromat and grocery store were the highlight of my week. Walmart wasn't my favorite place to go, but it was one-stop shopping that got me food, cabinet hardware, baby clothes, and a new coffee maker to replace the one that died. I only had to pull out the stroller once instead of four or five times at different stores.

This new dramatic discussion had the whole salon wagging their tongues with relish in one big group.

"Blanche told me it was a sex trafficking ring. They's out for new blood to send overseas to their brothels and to sell to European royalty."

"You really think some Spanish or French prince is gonna want a hometown girl from the mountains of North Carolina? Puh-leeze."

"It could happen."

"Only in the movies or a romance book."

"I read an article…"

I let the gossip fade to white noise around me. The topic wasn't one I wanted to hear anything about. I hoped this Katie Grace person was okay. Thankfully,

Courtney was in my chair getting a touch-up and cut. She dropped the subject, but then she started in on a new one that wasn't very comfortable either.

Courtney grinned at me from her reflection in the mirror. "Rumor has it that you paid a visit to Pastor Bobby's church and sat in the front row. And this is after spending a whole day with him at the Halloween barbecue. Does that mean you're datin' him now?"

"I'm… I'm…" *How do I answer her?* I paused to think about my first real experience with religion.

Yes, I did end up going to his church, as I couldn't think of a way to get out of it. I didn't know what to expect from a church service, but what I got was far different from anything I'd imagined. I'd seen movies where preachers yelled out dire warnings about sins and the pits of hell. A "repent or burn" sort of thing that always scared me. The sermon Robert calmly spoke was about kindness, forgiveness, and acceptance. His gentle demeanor fit the image of him behind the pulpit, and several times, he smiled at me as if sharing a special moment. Burna Jones had been in the three-member choir singing loud and "amening" every time she got a chance. I spotted Hilda next to her as she stayed in her grandmother's shadow.

After the service, while Robert was shaking hands and chatting with his congregation, she approached me shyly. "Can I ask you something?"

Burna was regaling someone with tales of woe from a recent trip to the grocery store, so I turned to the timid girl. "What's wrong?"

Hilda had looked around nervously before she whispered, "I've been asked to the Winter Snowball Dance at school. Andy Melford. He's on the football team. I still can't believe he knows who I am. I..."

She bit her lip and stopped speaking for a moment, dropping her gaze to the floor.

I placed a hand on her shoulder to give her a little encouragement. "What is it?"

"Can I make an appointment for you to do my hair and maybe give me some makeup pointers? You always look so pretty, and I'm not, so I thought you could... you know..."

She'd asked for my help, so how could I turn her down? Hair and makeup? This was something I could do—and wanted to.

Hilda kept her voice low. "My grandma doesn't know Andy asked me. If she did, she won't let me go. I told her I wanted to go with Kania and Joy so she'd be okay with it." She inhaled quickly, and her voice grew earnest. "I can pay from my babysitting money. I just... I just..." The air leaked out of her in a long sigh. "I just want to look pretty for him."

I remembered giving her a slight squeeze on her shoulder to get her eyes back up to mine. "Hey, Hilda. You don't need to get pretty for anyone. You do that for yourself, not some boy. The hair and makeup? I can take that and make it into something special. I'm glad to help you do up right for your dance, but you need to make sure it's okay with your grandma. Salon policy about working on minors. Give me a call next week and we'll set it up, okay?"

Burna had cornered Robert and started in about something. He glanced up and grinned at me with boyish charm as if asking *"What else can I do?"* In some ways, he was like Brick of the Dragon Runners in that he had responsibilities to care for his people. He listened, advised, and helped them solve problems, all while keeping them together in one big family unit.

Perhaps this wasn't such a scary place after all. The Lair wasn't as bad as I'd made it out to be either.

I'd begged off going out for lunch after the service and did a drive-through on my way to do our laundry. Pearl loved scarfing down McDonald's fries almost as much as she loved her toy *gay-toh.*

And I had a lot to think about.

I should have expected the glances and inquiries at the salon. Eventually, all news made its way here.

Courtney was still expecting an answer, and I only had one to give. "We're just friends."

Yeah, it sounded lame even to my ears, but it was all I had.

She giggled with sparkling eyes. "He's quite a catch. Handsome, secure, and soooo nice. You could do a lot worse."

It was true. Pastor Robert was a catch. He ticked all the boxes for being a good man, and a good companion. He treated me well and was good with Pearl. He'd kissed me, and even though there weren't a lot of sparks, I did like him. Would feelings develop over time? Slow-burn love? Was that enough, and did I want to go there?

Weatherman's face cropped up in my confused thoughts. We had a rocky start, mostly due to me not wanting to be around a biker club. Over the past few months, I'd learned more about him, how he gave up his career to take care of his mother, how he treated his friends, the support he had for the people in the club.

My biggest bother was that both men had kissed me.

One was sweet and tender.

One was reverent.

One warmed me.

One awakened me.

If both men walked into the salon at the same time and wanted to see me, which one would I choose?

Weatherman's hazel eyes floated in my mind as I finished Courtney's hairstyle and rang her out at the register. I had no other appointments for the day and was about to see if there were any walk-ins I could take. Then, as fate would have it, the bell jangled over the door, and the object of my thoughts came in.

"You got time for a trim?" Weatherman growled with a frown.

The salon women tittered, and I could only imagine the wild stories their fertile minds developed.

Not really. "You bet. Just give me a minute."

I ran to the break room and grabbed a full-sugar soda from the fridge, downing it until my throat burned.

I cut hair. It's my job. Women, men, and children. Weath-

erman is no different. Just a client. That's it, so stop with the weird guilty shit about hanging out with another man for a day.

Why the hell did I need to stop and give myself a scolding pep talk before touching Weatherman's hair?

I walked back to my station where he stood. His face was stony and his jaw tight. Yeah, he did need a trim, and he came to me to do it.

"You dating Pastor Bobby for real?" he asked as I approached.

I swear there was an audible shift as all the ears in the place pointed in my direction and strained to hear my answer. Why did I suddenly feel like I was treading on thin ice? "He's not my boyfriend, if that's what you're asking. We hung out, and I visited his church, but that's it. We're just friends."

"Good." He turned and sat in my chair as I flipped the drape over him. "I want to take you for a ride on the Tail sometime."

I almost dropped my scissors. A ride on the Tail meant a ride on the back of his bike. A ride on the back of his bike meant….

I sprayed his hair with my mister and picked up my comb and scissors. "Okay."

Shit! Why did I answer like that?

I dropped the subject, and so did he. His back was straight, and he sat still and silent as I worked. So many little pieces I noticed as I combed and threaded the waves through my fingers. How his hair lay, its texture, the variety of strand colors. The shape of his ears. One had an emerald stud in the lobe. Thick eyelashes. He had a few flaws as well, if you could call them that. A mole just under his hairline at the back of his neck. A small thin scar just under his left eye. He smelled good. Not like the perfume of commercial products but a clean scent. I wondered if he used the soaps that Psalm made.

Pheromones. Hormones. Something was making my head flutter in hyperawareness of the man in my chair. Simple haircuts were not an intimate act, but this one felt like it. I shouldn't have drunk an entire sugar-filled soda. It was making me sweat.

At the register, he paid me as usual with a generous tip. "When is your next day off?"

"Technically, it's this Sunday."

He frowned. "You going to Bobby's church again?"

"I wasn't planning on it, but I'll have Pearl with me. I can't ride with a baby."

"No, but we'll do something together. Think about it."

His stare grew intense, and my belly flip-flopped. He stood so close to me that I felt the heat from his body. The world faded a bit until the only person I saw was him.

Only him.

The bell jangled harshly, throwing us both into chaos. We jumped apart as if burned, and my head buzzed with adrenaline and relief.

Or was it regret?

"I done told you not to put that shit on your head!

When God was handin' out sense, you missed the line."
A large woman walked in with three girls in tow. "Is there anyone here who can fix this mess? My daughter and her friends decided to make TikToks last night about dyeing their hair, and this is the result."

Three heads of dry, overprocessed, streaked, patchy hair in various shades of blue, purple, and pink presented themselves.

My mouth dropped open. This was going to be a rough call. "Oh wow. That's… wow."

Weatherman backed away and cleared his throat. "I gotta run, and you need to get back to work. I'll catch up with you later, yeah?"

Catch up with me later? Damn, I need to stop repeating his words! "Sure, you bet."

He nodded once and left. I turned back to the trio of teary teenagers. "Let's start with a good clarifying shampoo and deep treatment to see what we have to work with. Who's first?"

CHAPTER 22

"Do you want popcorn?" Robert asked as he held open the door for me.

The movie theater was an older one, family owned and operated. I didn't know how long it had been around, but it was a fixture in this town, much like the Dragon Runners MC. Melissa Wall sat behind a sheet of plexiglass, taking money and handing out paper tickets. She was mainly Bex's client but had sat in my chair once about a month ago. Cute short layers with blonde highlights that were easy to maintain, as she had little time to herself while running the family business. Right now her pretty blue eyes were fixed on me and Robert.

It didn't feel right to call him Bobby as he'd told me to do. I don't know why, but it just didn't.

I hadn't planned to go out with him this evening but got pushed into it more or less by the ladies at the salon. Perhaps they wanted to participate in a real-life soap opera starring the preacher, the biker, and the stylist.

Robert came in as a walk-in trim this afternoon and waited for my chair to be open. Then he asked me about seeing a movie tonight, and I swear the whole place perked up with excitement. I tried to put him off by saying I had Pearl to take care of, but Deandra blew up that excuse by volunteering to watch her for me.

Other people greeted us as we entered the theater and found seats. All smiles and speculative glances at seeing the local young, single pastor out on a date. There was an unease that settled in my stomach, but Robert hadn't done or said anything wrong, nor did he treat me badly. He didn't try to kiss me or claim me. Not even hold my hand. He opened the doors for me and was attentive without being pushy or hovering, just as he'd been at the Halloween festival. He was overall pleasant and kind as always, and I really had no reason to be so antsy.

I couldn't figure out exactly what the movie we watched was supposed to be—action, comedy, or drama. It was entirely forgettable, but maybe that was because I couldn't get into the story. My thoughts kept drifting to Weatherman and what he would say if he spotted me and Robert here together. Tendrils of guilt ate at my brain, and I had to concentrate not to fidget.

Robert was innocent. I was not.

Both men were attractive in their own way. Both men were educated. Both were successful in their chosen fields. Both seemed to want to be with me, but that was where the similarities ended.

Robert's scholarly appearance was much different

from Weatherman's athletic ruggedness. Robert had this ethereal aura of kindness around him, while Weatherman gave off a vibe of raw power. Robert flowed like a calm steady river. Weatherman moved like whitewater rapids, fast and potentially overwhelming.

If I had to choose, who would I go with? The safe bet or the one who drove me a little crazy?

After the credits rolled, we got up to leave.

"I hope you enjoyed the movie." He smiled and pushed his glasses up on his nose.

"Yes, it was nice." I guessed it was. I had no clue.

"I enjoyed the company more."

It didn't take an expert to recognize the flirty tone. What did I do now? Say thanks? Indicate that I wanted another date? *Did* I want another date? I was so lost.

Thankfully, someone interrupted my musings as we entered the lobby.

"Pastor Bobby. Nice to see you."

Of *course*, it had to be Table of all people. His sons hung off either arm, and Angel stood next to him. They had apparently just seen the latest Disney movie based on their excited chatter.

Robert stiffened next to me, and his easy manner changed. "James, nice to see you too. I hear you have another child?"

Table smiled, unaffected by the pastor's cold tone. He curled his colorful biceps in tandem to lift both giggling kids. "I do. Lori is at home taking some 'me' time, and I've got hooligan duty."

"What's a hooligan?" one of the boys asked.

"A kid who never cleans up his room." Table grinned down.

"I'm a hooligan too!" crowed the other one.

Table let out a chuckle and turned his unreadable eyes to me. "Opal, I hope you're having a good night."

How am I supposed to handle this? "Yes, I am. I hope Lori's well. If she wants a home visit for a haircut, just let me know, and I'll be glad to take care of her."

Table nodded sharply. "I'll do that. Have a good night."

The family walked away with the kids singing the latest Disney song. I smiled, thinking it wouldn't be long before I started taking Pearl to kids' movies and buying whatever princess toys came with them. Maybe I'd save up enough money to go to the mother ship itself—Disney World, with all its pretty pictures.

As a kid, I'd always wanted to go but never got the chance. It was just some fantasy that would never happen. Now, that dream was actually within reach and was one I could fulfill for both myself as well as my daughter.

"Penny for your thoughts?" Robert asked as we walked to his car.

I shook myself as visions of the most famous mouse in the world faded. "I was just thinking about taking Pearl to Disney World someday. Like for her fifth or sixth birthday. I want her to be old enough to remember it."

"Maybe we can do that together."

His serene face gave nothing away, but his words

sent a jolt through my body. Did he plan on being with me that long?

He leaned in and placed his lips on mine. Soft. Gentle. Warm. Just a simple kiss with no pressure or depth.

He took my hand and held it between us. "I really like spending time with you, and I'd like to do more of it. I think we fit together well with our personalities and our lives. I like you. A lot. I hope we're on the same page. What do you say?"

The bottom dropped from my belly, and I was stunned. My words came out cautiously. "I don't know what to say. Are you… are you asking me to be your… your girlfriend?"

His smile showed nothing but gentle benevolence. "Yes, Opal, that's what I'm asking. I know it's a little much, but I hope you'll give me a chance."

"I'm… I'm…" *I'm out of my league!* "I'm not ready for anything serious right now."

"No problem, my dear. I can wait. In fact, I'm heading off on a mission trip for a few weeks. I won't be able to see you or call you much, as I'll be working most of the time. When I get back, maybe you'll be ready by then. Unless… you have someone else you're interested in?"

Weatherman's face popped into my head. "Nope. I'm just not into… um… dating right now. I want to focus on my job and my daughter, you know?"

"I understand. We can keep going out casually like this, but you understand that people talk, right? If we're seen in public together enough times, everyone will assume we're a couple."

I was very familiar with the salon gossip machine. "I can't help what other people think about me."

"This is very true. I just don't want to see you uncomfortable or hurt. People can be very cruel. If I may, I think it would be best for you to stay away from those bikers. They're a rough crowd, and I wouldn't want anyone to get the wrong impression of you."

Something about the way he said those words made my ears perk up. "What do you mean, 'the wrong impression'?"

He took a breath as if reaching for infinite patience. "Women who hang with bikers have a certain reputation. You don't want that in your life or Pearl's life."

I paused. Not a single member of the Dragon Runners had ever been disrespectful to me or treated me as less. I worked for a DRMC business. One of their people took care of my child. I'd been to their headquarters and did a favor for the queen. Pearl had been welcomed into their fold, and Betsey had more or less added her into her flock of "grandchildren." The last time I had my oil changed, Dodge did the work and bartered a haircut in exchange. I got the better deal. In fact, the only person who had ever said anything bad about the MC was the man standing next to me.

Robert made me wonder if some people's prejudices ran so deep, they would never look outside their own little bubble world. If so, it didn't matter how hard someone tried to change or improve their lives, they would always be judged by a crooked stick.

I straightened up. "My reputation here is based on my ability to cut and style hair. If anyone wants to criticize me, they are welcome to do so. As I said to you before, I can't help what other people think about me. I can only do my best to find my own peace."

I was sure he would bring up going to church with him, but he left that alone.

"You're right. You can't decide for other people. I'm sorry if I stepped over the line. I'm just really concerned about you. And Pearl."

His tone didn't sound as condescending as his words, so maybe he was genuinely concerned for me. Still, that same caution flag popped up again, just as it had every time I'd been out with him. How would he treat me if he really knew me? He wanted me to be his girlfriend officially. Would I have to hide myself and act a part to make that happen? Did I want to take it that far?

The universe had no answers for me. My heart sped up, and my belly churned with anxiety. Two thoughts came to the forefront of my mind. One was escape, and the other was talking to Weatherman as soon as possible.

"Thank you for that. Speaking of my daughter, I need to get back to her and let Deandra get home."

"I'll walk you to your car."

I really wished he didn't insist on that, but I was stuck. At least I got him to drive separately again.

When we reached my vehicle, he leaned down to kiss me again, but the sudden roar of a powerful engine and a flash of headlights startled us both. I spotted Table in his giant extended truck with his kids waving from the windows.

"We're in the hooligan club!"

A small muscle twitched in Robert's jaw, and then it was gone again. "I'll see you soon, okay?"

I nodded, hoping the relief didn't show on my face. "You bet. And thanks again for the movie."

CHAPTER 23

As I combed out another section of a new client's hair, Tambre came up to me with her mouth in a thin line. "I'm trying hard not to involve you, but I need to know if Kimmie is coming in. Her shift started two hours ago, and I had to call in Deandra to take her appointments. I can't keep giving her passes."

My stomach bubbled with pressure. There was a weird vibe in the air, and I couldn't put my finger on what it was that caused it. My worry over Weatherman and Robert was bad enough, and adding in Kimmie's problems made me want to go hide somewhere. It didn't matter, as I still had a child to prioritize and a career I needed to nurture. I picked up the length of blonde and point-snipped the ends. "I don't know where she is. She didn't come home last night."

I hated saying that. I didn't want to throw my friend under the bus, but it was true. She didn't come home last night. Again. She'd stumbled in once last week about 4:00 a.m., so drunk that I wondered how she got home without wrecking her car. She'd spent hours in our one bathroom, vomiting and stinking up the apartment. The extra-heavy makeup didn't hide the acne outbreak, and her hair needed some serious treatment. I mentioned her condition, and she went off about how lame I was and how I used to be fun.

If that's what fun looks like, no thank you.

Tambre inhaled through her nose as if reaching for patience. "Okay, then. I'll ask Dee to stay for the day. I can't have my business affected this way. You're here, and you do your job very well, but I'm going to have to let Kimmie go. I hope you'll stay."

Kimmie and I didn't have a long history, but we did move from Minnesota to North Carolina together. We had plans and dreams of outrunning our pasts, but it had caught up with her, and now she had to pay the price for that. I hated watching her spiral downward, knowing there was nothing I could do about it. This feeling of helplessness wasn't new to me, but as much as I wanted to help my friend, I had a daughter to think about. I couldn't give up a job that I liked a lot and paid me well. The last time rent was due, I paid it all myself, as Kimmie said she had no money. The claim was lack of clients, but that was a lie. There were lots of women who wanted their nails done, and when tourists were thick on the ground, many of them came in for vacation specials. They also tipped the most.

"I'm not planning on going anywhere." Saying the words out loud made me feel like I was backstabbing my roommate; however, I had my own life to live and my own responsibilities. If Kimmie wanted help and asked for it, I would give it to her, but if I had to make a choice between her and my child? There was only one answer I had for that question.

"Good to know, 'cause you got a fully booked day and another one tomorrow." Tambre smiled. "You've earned quite the reputation. People are starting to call and specifically ask for you."

I was stunned and a bit intimidated. Flattery wasn't something I had experienced very often, and the talents I used to be known for weren't ones I wanted to pursue again. "Thank you. I'll do my best."

"I can't ask for more. I'll let you get back to it." Tambre left me to go greet a couple of women who'd just walked in.

"She's right, you know," my client, Eden, chimed in while she examined her fresh cut. "You're really good at what you do. Word of mouth goes a long way in this town. Courtney told me how great your work is, and I have to say, she was right."

I fluffed her hair forward to check the fall and make sure the length was even. "All done. I just do hair and dab a little color. It's not that special."

She let out a little chuckle. "Girlfriend, not everyone can do what you do. Don't ever cut yourself short."

I didn't know what to say as I finished up. "I appreciate that."

"Oh, I'm sure. Even Burna Jones recommends you,

and you know if she says anything nice about someone…."

The bell tinkled, and the subject of our discussion walked in.

"Speak of the devil and she appears," Eden muttered.

Tambre met my eyes and pressed her lips together to keep from laughing. I did the same.

"My granddaughter said she has an appointment," the sour woman announced.

Tambre cleared her throat. "Yes, she does, but it's not for another half hour."

She harrumphed. "She's got some dance she's going to and decided she wanted her hair done. I told her she'd have to pay for it herself, out of her babysittin' money, but I was going to supervise. Lord knows what she'd do to herself otherwise. Get some crazy dye job to make her look like a peacock. Foolishness. I don't see what the fuss is over. I trim up the ends at home and it don't cost nothin', but she's got her mind made up that she wants a fancy style for this dang dance."

Hilda stood shyly behind her grandmother. Her long hair was tied up in a ponytail holder, all one length with no discernible style, uneven split ends, and a bunch of flyaways decorating the strands. On the upside, it was clean and thick. Plenty to work with.

My heart went out to her. She was thin and a little gangly. Her clothes were clean but not stylish or fitted very well. I remembered the story of her parents' death on the Tail and thought about how much of a shock that was. It was hard to imagine her life up to now and what kind of future she might have. I couldn't fix everything for her, but I could do this much.

"Hi, Hilda. Nice to see you again. Let me ring Eden up, and we'll go get you shampooed."

Eden followed me to the register to pay for her services and said she'd call to schedule her next appointment. Once she was gone, I went back to Hilda.

"So, do you have an idea of what you want?"

Brown eyes glanced up, and she mumbled something.

Burna snapped sharply, "Speak up, girl. No one's gonna pay any mind to you if you don't."

The teenager seemed to shrink into herself. It wasn't hard to see why. Burna's presence and sour attitude sucked the life out of everything around her. I imagined the poor girl struggled daily to find anything positive or good. I identified with her and recognized a kindred spirit. It wasn't easy to survive when you were stuck and had very few choices to get out.

I lifted a tangle. "Let's get you shampooed and conditioned. Then we'll talk about what you want to do."

Burna sniffed. "That costs extra, don't it? Just spray it down with water first. I have things to do."

I spotted Tambre burring up for a confrontation and stepped in the gap to avoid it—and hopefully give Hilda a break. "It's going to be hard to give your granddaughter a nice style without some conditioning treatment first. How 'bout you leave her here while you go run your errands? I'll take good care of her, and no wild colors. Okay?"

Burna opened her mouth to protest, but then a miracle occurred, and she backed down. "All right, then. I guess conditioning isn't a bad idea."

I turned to Hilda and smiled warmly. "You really do have nice hair. It's got nice body and the perfect amount of curl. Do you straighten it at all?"

Hilda hazarded a quick glance at her grandmother. It was an awkward and stiff move. She didn't really act scared of Burna, more like she was trying not to trigger her or start a ruckus. Living with the older woman had to be tough. "I don't have a flat iron."

"I hope you never do. There are so many women who would love to have hair like this."

Her eyes came back to me. "Really? I always thought it was plain. Dull."

Her unspoken *"like me"* echoed silently, and I wanted to hug her so badly.

Tambre noticed it, too, and we exchanged a quick glance. She gave me a "go ahead" nod and spoke to Burna in her soothing voice. "I understand there's a new fabric store that opened recently. Have you been there? What's it like?"

The older woman turned and pounced like a tiger smelling fresh meat. "The service was terrible…"

I let her fade to white noise and sat Hilda in my chair. "What did you have in mind?"

The girl squirmed. "I was thinking, like, layers

and… um… bangs? I don't want it real short, but not so long and maybe not so heavy?"

I nodded with the surety she needed at the moment. "How about some simple long layers just below your shoulders and some shorter ones around your face? Takes out some of the volume and makes styling easier if you want to add more curl or framing. I can do side-sweep bangs but keep them longer also to blend. Wanna try?"

"Whatever you think is best."

Uff-da, this girl! "No, sweetheart. This is your hair and your call to make. I can make suggestions, but there's no right or wrong here. Whatever you want is what's best."

Hilda took a deep breath. I didn't think she'd ever had this opportunity before. "Yes, let's try."

Burna raged over the "outrageous price of fleece" as I shampooed Hilda's long tresses. "I'm going to use a colored conditioning rinse to bring out more of the chocolaty tones. It won't dye your hair, just enhance what you already have. Okay with you?"

The girl relaxed a little. "Sounds good."

I wrapped her up in a conditioning treatment and left her to sit while I prepped the rest of my station for the makeover. Burna finished with her critique of the fabric store and moved on to grocery store prices as Hilda left the wash sinks to sit in my chair. I combed through the mass, then clipped up several twisted clumps on top of her head. The cut was a simple one and didn't take a long time. I took off about six inches of the length and point-snipped the ends. As I worked, I talked to the girl.

"What color is your dress?"

"Kind of a teal. I found it at the Goodwill store. Might have been a bridesmaid dress at one time, but I took off all the ruffle-y parts and hemmed it some to just above the knee. I didn't want to throw away the leftover material, so I made a flutter drape around the shoulders."

"Wow, that's impressive. I bet it looks great. Think you'll go to college after you graduate? You could go into fashion design or something."

The girl jumped as if shocked anyone would ask such a thing. "Um, probably not. We don't have money for that."

"I can relate." I let down one clip of hair and threaded it through my fingers. "There are loans and scholarships available, though."

"Gramma says it's all a waste of time."

The click of my scissors got louder and sharper as I worked. "There are other opportunities that don't take a four-year degree. It depends on your interests or hobbies. I liked hair and makeup, so here I am, doing something I love. You have time to figure out what you want to do. It's kind of exciting, don'cha know?"

"I… don't really have any real hobbies. I read a lot. Clean the house. Sew a little bit and babysit."

I laughed as I combed her bangs forward over her eyes. "Makes you sound like the perfect housewife."

"Gramma says I'm too plain to get a man."

My scissors grew silent for a moment. I had to take a breath before I ruined this girl's cut. Memories assailed me of my time in high school. Sure, I had some good times, but also ones that weren't pleasant. I had my own demons with my mother and the past, and it made me want to hurl that this young girl—no, young *lady*—might be exposed to that kind of meanness.

"You're not plain, Hilda. You're like a caterpillar. One day you'll come out of that cocoon and set the world on fire. Sometimes it takes longer to get there, but you will. Just please remember to take your time. There's a whole life ahead of you, and the best part is, you get to decide where it goes."

Hilda kept her eyes down. "I don't know if I'll ever leave this town. Gramma says I have to get a job as soon as I graduate from high school or move out. Probably both."

I opened my set of heated ceramic rollers and began winding her hair around them. "I used to feel stuck where I lived. Same town, same people, same streets. Everyone around me either worked at the shoe factory or for a business that supported it. I never thought I'd have a life outside Red Wing, but here I am. Living in a different state and doing something I love. I had a lot of challenges, and it took me a long time to find myself, but I'm glad I did. As hard as it was at times, I would do it again just so I could appreciate and be grateful for what I have now. Let's do your makeup while the curlers do their thing, yeah?"

I didn't go heavy-handed with an oily foundation,

just some mineral powder to even out her skin tone. Neutral palette with some light contouring on her cheekbones and highlights under her eyes. Her eyebrows were already thick, and I tweezed and trimmed them a bit to give them a more defined shape. Subtle was the best style for her eye makeup with a touch of sultry. I chose shimmering golds and browns with a teal accent to match her dress color. Dark chocolate eyeliner with blended flicks at the corners emphasized the blue color of her eyes. The mascara added its own volume, but her lashes were so thick, she didn't need a lot of it. Neutral lip color and a touch of gloss, as anything too dark or heavy would look over the top.

The bell rang as someone came in, but I was too focused on Hilda to take much notice. The rollers came out, and I ran a wide-tooth comb through her hair to smooth and blend the curling layers. "Almost done, honey. Just a little spritzing and you're ready. Take a look."

I spun the chair around to let her see her reflection. Hilda's mouth dropped open. Soft bangs draped across her forehead, tapering to a swept-back frame with the ends gently curling under her jaw. The look emphasized her heart-shaped face. Long, wavy layers flowed down the back when she moved her head. Highlights from the conditioner shone bright under the lights. The makeup was understated, but her eyes still popped with color. There was so much potential and beauty in this girl ready to come out if only she had some encouragement and a kind word. I hoped I got to watch her grow into it.

"I-I like it. Maybe…."

Her inflection made me think she had more words but didn't want to risk saying them out loud. My heart clenched a bit as I filled in the blank. *"Maybe I can be pretty?"*

Wetness shimmered in Hilda's eyes, and mine started to fill as well. I would damn well work my ass off to make sure this girl got to be a diamond one day.

We both stared at her reflection, and I spoke to her with as much passion in my voice as I could find. "Don't ever put limits on yourself, girlfriend. Whenever you're ready, all you have to do is ask, and I'll make you shine."

I grinned at the teenager as I took the cape off her neck and shook the odd hairs to the floor. Hilda ducked her head, but she couldn't hide her smile.

Burna stopped her new tirade about low-thread-count sheets and looked at her granddaughter. Her face relaxed for the first time since I'd met the woman, and her mouth closed. Her thin lips pressed together, and I was afraid of what might come out of her mouth next. I prepared myself to jump in and defend my protégé, but then I saw Burna's chin quiver. It was a tiny movement, almost imperceptible, but the only emotion I'd ever seen from this woman before was disdain or contempt. That little shake told me that, for all the bluster she spouted, Burna Jones loved her granddaughter. Perhaps she didn't know how to show it, but it was there.

"It will do," she finally said as she sniffed and yanked a tissue from the box on the counter. "Tambre, you should do something about the dust in the air. It's making my eyes water."

Tambre and I exchanged amused glances before I turned back to Hilda and snapped a picture. "You're beautiful, and don't think for one minute you're not. Have a great time tonight, and make good choices, yeah?"

Hilda smiled, and I could see the woman inside her ready to be born. So much potential. All she needed was a little support and a spark to ignite the flame.

I had to turn away before I lost myself. The figure in front of me caught my attention, and I locked eyes with Weatherman. He was staring at me with an expression I couldn't read exactly, but it didn't turn me off.

In fact, it started a now-familiar heat in my own belly, and I took a breath to relax the sudden flood.

"Got time for a trim?" His voice was low and a little rough.

"Yes, I'll make time for you."

Weatherman seated himself in my chair, and I spritzed water over his head. "That was Hilda Jones, wasn't it?"

I combed through his hair. "Yes, it was. She's going to the winter dance with a boy named Andy Melford."

Weatherman kept his head still for me but grunted an affirmation. "I know his father. Good family. You made her look stunning tonight."

"I didn't do much."

He shifted his hand from under the cape and brushed the small hairs to the floor. "I think you changed her life tonight. I've never seen that girl radiate joy like she did when I came in this building. She's walking a little prouder, a little more confident. You made that happen, babe."

I flushed at his compliment. "It's really not that big a deal."

"It is to a teenage girl who needs someone to assure her of her worth." He circled his face with an open hand. "You did all that just for her. That's a special talent."

Warm fuzzies bloomed in my belly. He was right in that Hilda did indeed appear to stand straighter and taller when she left the salon. There was so much potential in her future as long as she had people behind her to push her on to greater things. I sent a message to the universe and asked it to watch over my girl tonight and lead her on the path to a wonderful life, wherever that might be.

"Mom wanted me to ask what you're doing for Thanksgiving."

The question was such an abrupt change of topic that it threw me off a bit. "I don't know. I usually don't do a lot of holidays, but since I have Pearl, I need to think about that more."

"Mom's not up for cooking, and I'm a disaster in the kitchen, so we're planning on going up to the Lair for the big spread Betsey's planning this year. Would you and Pearl like to come with us?"

I didn't hesitate. "You bet."

"Good."

I combed through his hair to check the lay and make sure I didn't miss any flyaways. The hairs flipped through the teeth to settle in their perfect waves. I loved working with him. "All done."

He paid at the front and stopped to turn to me directly. "I meant what I said earlier. You changed that girl's life tonight. I expect you've changed a lot of lives, and you don't have a clue how much that means to some of them. What you told Hilda, you need to tell yourself. Don't ever put limits on yourself. You are beautiful, and don't think for one minute that you're not."

CHAPTER 24

Night fell early this time of year. The Lair's outside lights made welcoming halos on the ground as we parked close to the entrance. Pearl babbled from her car seat, excited to be someplace different.

Weatherman's headlights flashed across the front of the building. I'd been here only one other time, but there was a sense of familiarity to it. Weatherman drove his mom's big white Chevy Traverse so we could put her fancy walker and the stroller in the back. Natalie had stopped using the wheelchair and was gaining strength again. Pearl was walking pretty well now, but she still had moments when I had to carry her and needed the yellow contraption.

Weatherman took Pearl out of the car and gave her raspberries on her cheek, making her giggle.

"Am-mah-dah!" she declared as he put her down and helped his mom.

Betsey was the first person we saw. The few times I'd been around her, she'd made a beeline for Pearl. Tonight, Pearl stumbled up to her and babbled her baby words.

"Hey, cutie britches!" The woman scooped up my daughter and set her on her expert hip. "How's my little precious Pearl? How's my baby?"

The rest of us became afterthoughts as she turned and carried my little girl into the building.

The place was the same as the last time I came. People played video games, shot pool, talked, drank, and ate. Stud conversed with Dodge and had one arm around his oldest daughter with another one pulling at his leg. I didn't see Eva or Fauna. Table waved from where he stood with a pool cue in his hand. I caught a glimpse of Lori herding her brood to a kids' spot with plates. One pointed look from her had Table leaving the game to help her. Tambre sat on one sofa with a baby on her lap, who I guessed was Lori's newborn.

Betsey had taken over Pearl and played with her while strolling around the large room. She stuck a finger in her mouth and stared at the deer head over the giant mantel that sported a springy turkey headband. She pointed at it and dropped her alligator on the floor. Mute scooped it up and handed it to her. She gave him a drooly grin, no fear of the giant.

Maybe it was because she was in the arms of someone she trusted to keep her safe.

I trusted Betsey too. I trusted all of them.

A buffet was set up along one wall and was covered with every imaginable Thanksgiving food item. Platters of turkey, ham, and venison sat alongside an army of vegetable casseroles and a mountain of mashed potatoes. Another table had just as many dessert offerings, with pies, cakes, cookies and some sort of fluffy chocolate stuff that made my mouth water. No excuses for anyone to go hungry here tonight.

"Let's grab some food, babe," Weatherman said.

Babe. The title made me feel things I'd thought were gone. I still had a ways to go, but this was the beginning. The start of something new. Something good.

I filled a plate with just a spoonful of everything and still ended up with a huge pile. I also made a smaller one for Pearl. Weatherman did the same for him and his mother, sticking by my side as we made our way down the long table.

"Try the sweet potatoes. They'll change your life." He plopped a helping onto my plate before adding to Pearl's and his.

Betsey "fed" Pearl, which consisted of letting my daughter smear potatoes and gravy all over her shirt.

"I'm sorry for the mess."

Betsey laughed and let out a "Pshhht" while clicking her nails at me. "Don't you worry 'bout it. This here is my mama cut. It's been spit up on, chewed on, and peed on more than once. I wouldn't trade it for all the tea in China."

Grandma to the world indeed.

I spotted Katrina coming in the front door wearing her nurse's scrubs. She had a baby carrier in one hand, a big bag over the opposite shoulder, and a tired smile. Mute hurried over to her and leaned down to kiss her before taking the baby. I watched as the huge man picked up the squirming bundle and cradled his child. Mute always struck me as the most brutal and fearsome biker of the Dragon Runners, but the tenderness and care on his face blurred out any thought of that. His child would never be harmed.

It was breathtaking.

A father's love. A true father. Not some sperm donor who couldn't be bothered to even meet his child.

I had to look away before I lost it, but it was hard. Everywhere my eyes landed, there was evidence of deep care. Table smiled and ruffled the hair of one child. Natalie sat on a sofa with a plate of food in her lap and talked with Psalm, more than likely about some sort of fiber craft. Eva arrived with the rest of her clan, and Stud greeted her with a big kiss that made their oldest daughter roll her eyes. Brick stood talking to several of his men, but when Betsey strolled up to him still carrying Pearl, he raised his arm around her shoulders, acknowledging her status in his life.

Everyone had a place and purpose in this club, and I found myself wanting my own spot in it.

Weatherman and I sat in an alcove with floor-to-ceiling windows that looked out on the massive pool deck. The pool itself was huge and currently covered for the season, but there was a hot tub still open and bubbling away in a screened-off area. Several people were making their way to it, and I wondered if they had on bathing suits under their fluffy robes.

"Betsey doesn't allow skinny-dipping, but it still happens from time to time," Weatherman remarked.

"How do you know?" I asked as I lifted a forkful of the sweet potatoes.

He dipped his chin and gave me a mischievous look.

"Oh. Never mind." I had to grin. "During the winter in Minnesota, the lakes and rivers freeze up enough that we put out ice fishing shacks like little neighborhoods. Some of them are just tents, and some are real little houses with beds and kitchens for longer stays. We have these long augers to drill through the ice so we can put lines in for fishing. I don't think it gets cold enough to do that here."

"It's rare that we get a freeze like that, but we've had a few hard winters when the ice and snow build up like crazy. Then again, we also get really mild winters like this one, where we're lucky if we see three flakes drift down." He paused to take a bite of food. "I'm serious about the sweet potatoes, babe. Try 'em."

I put the fork in my mouth, and heaven exploded on my tastebuds. "Uff-da, this is good."

He smirked. "Told you."

We ate in silence for a few minutes, and then he asked, "So, how does life here in North Carolina compare with Minnesota?"

I paused to think of the right response. "It's different and the same. I mean, like the weather and the way people talk are big ones, but people are still people no matter where they live. Minnesota mothers deal with the same things North Carolina mothers do. Schools, kids' sports, households, money—everyone talks about it all the time at the salon, all the challenges they have on a daily basis."

He made an amused grunt. "I'm thinking you're like a bartender/counselor, expected to dole out advice while rolling perm rods."

"Sometimes. Tambre's better at it than me. She's one of the few who can handle Burna Jones."

"So, what did you do before you became a stylist?"

My stomach churned. "Um… nothing interesting. How about you? What did you do before you became… well… a weatherman?"

He smiled as he wiped his mouth. "Most people call us meteorologists now. I spent a lot of time on the swim team and later as a lifeguard. I met Table and Lori my senior year, just before I won a swimming scholarship. It took care of most of my college tuition. That, my savings, and guilt money from my father put me through school, and I was able to graduate debt-free and with a little extra left over. I'm one of the few students who lived at home and commuted for classes. Saved a lot of money that way."

He stacked my empty plate on his and stood. "Go grab us some drinks, would you? I'll get rid of these, and then we can take a walk outside for a bit."

Walking with Weatherman? It sounded like a children's book title, and I had to suppress a giggle. "You bet."

I got him a beer from the cooler and myself a Diet Coke. He twisted off the tops of both bottles before handing me my soda. "I guess the temperature outside isn't that cold to you, right?"

"Well, I'm not planning on wearing shorts, but it's not like Minnesota cold, if that's what you're asking."

He reached out his hand. "Pearl is safe with Betsey, and my mom will also keep an eye out. Come with me."

The weird flutters in my belly came back. "Why?"

His eyes caught mine, and the intensity kept me from moving. "I want to know more about you."

I wanted to ask, "Why?" again, but the word stuck in my throat. Instead, I took his hand and let him lead me outside.

The air wasn't really cold, but there was a crispness to it. I wondered for a moment how Pearl would be about winters here. A northern Midwest baby now in the South?

We strolled along the pool deck and out onto a gravel-covered path. Motion sensor lights followed us, winking on as we approached and turning off as we left their area. I spotted several large buildings on the property and a bunch of short square ones. I also noticed that he didn't let go of my hand.

"Over there is the private garage and workshop. Behind it is maintenance and storage. What you see through here are camping cabins that are used in the summer for overflow guests or when the members want more privacy."

"I thought everyone had their own rooms in the Lair?"

"Most of us do, but occasionally we need more space. A few of us smoke a little weed now and then, and out of respect for Betsey, we don't do that in her home."

I smirked. "Smoke a little weed, eh?"

He laughed out loud. "Well, I'm not without sin. Not like your Pastor Bobby."

I laughed this time as well. "Robert isn't my anything. He's nice, and we've gone out a few times, but that's all." I paused before making the observation. "You don't like him much."

Weatherman stopped at a plain wood bench. The light gave off a bluish hue as it shone down on us. "It's not that I don't like him. I just don't agree with him."

"You don't believe in God?"

He sighed and sat, pulling me down with him and keeping our hands linked. "I believe in God, just not the version he spouts from the pulpit. My mom and I used to attend a church when I was little, but we stopped when the pastor started ranting over gay people going to hell. I had a hard time understanding how that could come from a God who claimed to love everyone."

He shifted, leaning back to gaze at the stars, and pointed to the sky. "See those stars there? The ones that form a big square? How 'bout the diamond shape on the left above it and the arch on the right? That's the constellation Pegasus."

It took me a minute to see what he was showing me, but I finally spotted the shape. "Wow, I see it! That's pretty neat."

He moved his finger to another spot. "See the one below, another square, and the three above? People commonly call that one the Little Dipper, but the real name is Little Bear or Ursa Minor. The Big Dipper, or Ursa Major, is below it and more upright."

It was pretty exciting to recognize the star shapes. "Yes, I see them too. What else is up there?"

"Over there is Orion. I showed him to Pearl once. He's real easy to recognize because of the three stars that make his belt."

Weatherman spent several more minutes showing me other constellations and groupings of stars.

"How did you learn all of this?" I asked.

"One of my closest friends over in Tennessee was gay. I met him during a stargazing event with a local astronomy club. Even though he was older than me, we still hit it off as really good buddies. He never hit on me or did any of the things that pastor said he would. He wasn't evil. He wasn't perverse. In fact, he was a Christian, baptized and everything. Tim was a music teacher and worked at one of those last-chance schools where they put kids who are considered delinquent. The pay was shit and the conditions worse, yet he went to work every day with middle schoolers who'd fallen through the cracks. His side job was playing the piano in a church band. One that never pointed fingers at him. He died last year from a heart condition, and I attended his funeral. Standing room only. There's no telling how many people that man helped to a better place while he was on this earth for such a brief moment. How can a gay Christian go to hell, especially one who sings praises and works hard to better other people's lives? Doesn't make much sense to me."

He had a point. It was a question that I certainly had no answer for.

"The estimate is that there are around a hundred billion stars in our galaxy, and the visible ones form these constellations."

My brain could think in hundreds more than billions. "That's… well… a lot."

He smiled. "Wanna blow your mind more? There are between two hundred billion and two trillion galaxies in the universe, and that's only the ones we can see. Counting that many stars?" He put his other hand next to his head and flared his fingers while making an explosion sound. "Bottom line is, the universe is pretty damn big. I can't believe a God whose power created all of that would be limited to a small group of people on a tiny planet that's insignificant in comparison to everything around it."

"I've never really thought about it. It's kind of…."

"Overwhelming?" he supplied.

"Yeah, that's it. Overwhelming."

We sat in a comfortable silence, looking up at the sky and listening to random night sounds. I felt at ease, like there was nothing I needed to say or do. I could just be in the moment and let everything go. The worries and the fears all disappeared, and I was fine—truly fine—with my place in the world. Weatherman brought me a sense of peace where Pastor Robert, even with all his kind words and gentle spirit, did not.

I finally broke the quiet. "When I went to his church that one time, Robert preached forgiveness of sins. Is that something real?"

He turned to face me. "I don't see why not, but it's not up to me. I believe my job is to love and take care of my family and others as best as I can. That's it. That's one big reason why I joined the Dragon Runners. You won't find judgment here. Not from Betsey. Not from Brick. Not from any of my brothers or their women."

His fingers were cold as they traced my jaw and pulled me to him. "Not from me."

There was a split second when I felt his breath against my lips before he covered them with his. Soft, dry, sweet. He didn't open them. He didn't bite at me or force his tongue into my mouth. It was a gentle contact that lasted a long time.

When Robert kissed me, it was nice and sweet, but nothing more than that. When Weatherman kissed me, all I could focus on was him. The shape of his lips, the texture of his skin, the movement of his hand as it cradled my chin—all of it combined into an intimacy I wasn't prepared for.

He lifted his head just enough to break contact but

stayed close. So close that his breath puffed warmly against my mouth.

Then he shifted me to straddle his lap before he pulled me to him again, this time firmer, wetter, and just *more*. I opened in invitation, and he accepted, giving me his full taste as he explored mine.

My heart jumped once. Twice. The heat in my chest grew with intensity as that organ came alive and made its presence painfully known. I was sure he could tell it was pounding away in tandem with his.

I was completely torn. Half of me wanted to run away in fear, and the other half wanted to burrow deep into his body and find all his mysteries. Confusion filled my head, but there was one thing that was crystal clear.

I was falling in love with Weatherman—with Bryce Turner.

He ended the kiss, pulled back, and kept holding my waist. His grip tightened around my hips as he spoke with as much conviction as I'd ever heard. "I can't tell you what to do, but I will say this. I don't want you to date Pastor Bobby anymore. I want you to date *me*."

The burn in my chest flared. "I have a child."

"You do, and I care about her too."

"I'm not well educated. I didn't go to college."

"Doesn't matter. Different people have different talents, and not all of them need four-year degrees."

"I have a lot of baggage in my past that you don't know about."

"And when you're ready to tell me, I'll listen."

Everything I said, he had an answer. Perhaps they were rehearsed, but he talked as if they came from his heart. My head was roaring with white noise as my heart melted away in my chest. I barely breathed as my whispered question came out almost inaudible. "How can you guarantee you won't leave me?"

He stopped at that and raised a hand to run through my hair, then cupped the back of my head. "I can't. Just like you can't guarantee *you* won't leave *me.* The only promise I can make is that I will always try my best to be the man you expect and need. We have a connection between us that's not going to go away. I think it's time we do something about it. Take a chance on me, babe."

I rested my head on his shoulder as I sat on his lap. His arms wrapped me up to hold me close. Cheek to chest, belly to belly, hip to hip, every part of me touched every part of him, fusing us together as if we'd become one person.

"What are you thinking, sweetheart?" he rumbled under my ear.

"I'm scared," I admitted.

"Me too."

That took me by surprise. "Why are you scared?"

"I've dated a lot of women and had a few serious relationships, but nothing so significant that I got hurt. I did the breaking up, and I'm not proud of it, 'cause I hurt some people I cared a lot about. I think this time, I'm the one at risk." He paused. "However, I don't want to miss out on *this.* If you're ready to jump off that cliff with me, we'll go together."

"What if we fall to the bottom?"

"What if we find a trampoline and bounce higher?"

I stopped talking. We could spar with what-ifs all night. It all boiled down to him and me gambling on a future. *Our* future.

Would there be one?

"It's okay to let your heart beat again."

It was. It pounded hard and fast, on fire, and so hot that I was afraid it would burst out of me to scorch everything around it to cinders.

I couldn't do this. I couldn't! I couldn't! *I couldn't!*

Could I?

"It's okay to let your heart beat again."

"I'm not ready to sleep with you."

"Sex is not a requirement for dating. I didn't go to bed with every woman I've gone out with. We'll get to that when we're both ready."

I went silent again, torn between worlds.

"It's okay to let your heart beat again."

"Let your heart beat again."

"Let your heart beat."

"Okay. Let's try."

He moved to dip his head. Easy, gently, naturally, his lips conformed to mine. I'd been kissed before as a stamp of ownership. Bryce's kiss wasn't that. It was a reverent confirmation that we were in this together and a promise that we would give it a serious go. My nerves continued to jangle warnings, but we stepped up to that precipice together, and I felt the whoosh as we leaped over the edge.

By the way his body jolted, he felt it too.

The kiss ended, and neither of us spoke for a few moments. The night sky was the only witness to this world-shaking event.

I broke the church-like silence. "We have to get back to Pearl and your mom."

The corner of his mouth tipped up, and he stroked his thumb over my bottom lip. "*We.* I like that. Let's go."

CHAPTER 25

Clem sat perched behind the blind, sighted down the barrel of the heavy rifle, and slipped his finger over the trigger. The bear was a big male, moving sluggishly and thick with fat for a long winter that didn't seem to be coming anytime soon. Clem breathed out and began to squeeze.

The gunned roar of a four-wheeler burst in the air as Walt crashed roughly through the brush. The bear spooked and ran.

Clem threw down the rifle and cursed long and loud as it bounced out of the perch and to the ground. "Goddamnit, you fucking shit for brains! I had him!"

A wild-eyed Walt ignored his cousin. "Rangers! There's rangers on the ridge!"

Shit. Clem hated to admit it, but it was a good thing after all that Walt interrupted that perfect shot. The .003 Win Mag was a loud gun, and no doubt the sound of it would bring those damn cops running. "How close are they?"

"'Bout a half mile on the other side of the creek."

Fuck.

"They done found the bait barrels we put out over yonder. What do we do?"

Clem climbed down the short distance and picked up the rifle. The barrels were plain ones with no distinctive logos to tell where they came from, but that asshole Mute might recognize them if given a chance. Clem was sure the biker had seen the ones he stored at the gas station shed. They'd been moved to the cabin, but the damage was already done. So far, Brick hadn't made any moves, which made Clem nervous.

He growled at his cousin. "What direction they headed in?"

"East."

Clem nodded in partial relief. "Away from the cabin, then." He shouldered the gun. "Get them other barrels over there emptied and scatter the food. We'll load 'em on the four-wheeler and run it low until we get farther away. The sound won't carry over the water noise."

"Things is gettin' real tight, Clem. Maybe we need to do some rethinking."

"Ain't your job to think. You just get them barrels taken care of."

Walt licked his lips as his eyes darted from the squat vehicle to the trio of dark green cylinders. "What if we get caught? What happens to us?"

"We ain't gettin' caught."

"Yeah, but what if we do?"

"I said, we ain't gettin' caught."

"Yeah, but—"

Clem's temper snapped, and he arm-barred his cousin across his throat, forcing the bigger man's back against a tree. "Did you hear me, you piece of shit? We. Ain't. Gettin'. Caught. Stop with your bullshit and get them barrels done."

"Hold up. Anyone else hear that?" Weatherman stopped moving and signaled the other two rangers to halt as well. It was hard to detect, but there was a faint sound of a four-wheeler for a brief moment before it was swallowed up by the gurgling creek.

Officer Fine stage-whispered, "Yeah, I heard it too. Comin' from over yonder."

He pointed in the opposite direction of where Weatherman thought it came from. The forest could be deceptive, and a compass was always a good companion to have. There were very few markers in this area to follow, and getting lost was always a danger. Hikers got turned around easily, and many times, search parties had to be called in to find them.

Today was not a day for finding people. It was an exploration of bear trails and possible places where poaching sites might be found. Whoever was behind the massacres had to have a central place for curing hides and preserving the parts of the animals they took.

The mountains were full of hidden places that had potential. The satellite images showed several tagged bears that used this route regularly, making this a prime target for the illegal hunting; therefore, the three-man team was sent to check it out. Drones were used when possible, but the heavy tree growth made it too difficult and inaccurate to fly them, and the chief wanted precision detailed reports.

All three rangers carried rifles and hoped they wouldn't have to use them. Any wildlife, including bears, would ignore them, run away, or potentially attack. Weatherman hoped any encounters resulted in door number one or two.

The engine sound no longer dressed the air, but Weatherman was positive that there was a vehicle up here somewhere. He checked his GPS marker and glanced at the other two officers. "Either of you know about any campsites or private land up here?"

Fine shook his head. "Nope. All national forest."

"We may have company. Be alert."

The rangers moved forward with higher caution. Weatherman sensed the restlessness in Fine's accelerated breathing. He wasn't too thrilled himself at the thought of finding a two-legged predator as well as a four-legged one.

They kept to the left of the creek as they followed close to it. Weatherman was about to tell everyone to turn back when he stepped on something soft and crunchy. He looked down to see a pile of cheap dog food nuggets under his boot.

"Bingo," he said, motioning the other two rangers forward. He pulled out his tracker and marked the spot. "I think it's safe to say we're getting close. It's getting late, and we need to head back. Tomorrow, we'll grab as many satellite images as possible of this area within a ten-mile radius. Think that's wide enough?"

"Should be. What are we looking for?"

"We'll know when we see it."

CHAPTER 26

"Coach Driscoll said he's gonna retire at the end of this school year."

"First Baptist Church is havin' their annual pancake night next Saturday."

"There's a stomach bug goin' 'round the schools. Thelma Doss said all four a' her kids got it last week."

"Didja hear about them killed bears? Someone told me awhile back 'bout a big pile of 'em shot, cut up, and left out to rot."

That got several heads to turn and another subject to chew over.

"Oh my goodness, I heard about that. I cain't remember who told me, but it was somethin' 'bout poachin' bein' on the upswing."

"Not enough rain coming down. Bears and other wildlife are coming closer to the river and lakes for food sources. There's been a lot more sightings this past year."

"They say if you pee on the trees around the camp-sites, it keeps 'em away."

I thought about Bryce. He was a ranger, and this was something he had to deal with. I didn't know much about hunting or regulations, but Tambre had mentioned poaching before, and from what I could tell, it was a big problem. I wondered how dangerous his job was.

Dating. I had no idea what that actually meant, as I'd never really dated anyone before. Now I was dating Bryce. He texted me in the mornings to wish me a good day and again at night to wish Pearl and me a good sleep. Most of our times as a couple were simple. He came by the salon to take me to lunch as often as he could. We held hands in public. Pearl and I spent several evenings at his mom's house for dinner, and we watched TV together while Pearl played and Natalie stitched. He carried Pearl or held her hand as she toddled along, sometimes swinging between the two of us.

He bought us a Christmas tree in early December and helped me decorate it. My first one ever. It was small, as befitted our apartment, but it didn't matter. I was excited, and so was Pearl.

She clapped and giggled as we draped way too many lights around the greenery. Bryce laughed at me as I meticulously placed each ornament to make them all even. Whenever we were with each other, he teased me, flirted, or touched me.

What we hadn't done was sleep together.

Something else I had to do was tell Robert I was with Bryce now. The salon gossip told me that he was back from his recent mission trip and had been for a week or so. I fully expected him to be coming to me for a trim very soon. Perhaps he'd already found out through the town's grapevine about me and Bryce?

I shook my head to clear my thoughts as Tambre came up to my station. Her mouth was tight and pinched. My boss wasn't someone to lose her temper, so just seeing her this angry sent wary shards of sharp glass through my gut.

"Kimmie was supposed to be here at ten this morning. It's going on three."

"I have no idea where she is. I haven't seen her in several days."

This was true, as Pearl and I went shopping with Natalie at the mall on Saturday and spent Sunday with her and Bryce, watching movies at their house and messing around in the kitchen. I finally saw my first cushaw and got to make it into a pie. Kimmie was nowhere to be found, and I'd stopped making any attempt to keep track of her.

Tambre shook her head. "I'm sorry for this, but I can't keep this up any longer. Kimmie no longer has a job here. I took a chance on hiring people based on a friend's recommendation, and I got burned. I won't take that risk again with my business."

I choked and jerked around as panic clawed at my throat. "Please don't fire me, Tambre!"

She gave me a serene smile and spoke in a placating

tone. "I'm not firing *you*, dearest. I need good strong people here, and you're one of the best I have. It's Kimmie who's not pulling her weight. Frankly, I kept her on longer than I should have, mostly because I wasn't sure if you'd leave with her."

My heart fluttered in relief.

Tambre continued, "If Kimmie asked me for help, I'd be glad to support that, but she's not there and may never get to that point. Some people can pull themselves out of ruts and forge new paths, and some people are happy where they are." She paused and then switched subjects. "I've been meaning to talk to you about something for a while now. I'm not getting any younger, and I've been thinking about my exit plan."

I frowned. "What do you mean?"

"Someday, I'd like to sell the place and retire. Or at least have that option. I've been toying with the idea of having an assistant manager with the thought of buying me out one day. Neither Bex nor Deandra is interested. If I go that route, think you might be?"

My brain took a hard spin. Part of me wanted to jump at the opportunity. The other part was scared shitless. "I don't.... How will that work with me being a single mom? I never went to college, just a local vo-tech."

Tambre nodded. "I get that. I'm not ready to toddle off into the sunset with my walker just yet. I'll be working here with you and helping you learn just as my mentor helped me. Think about my offer for a bit.

No rush. Like I said, I'm not retiring next week or anything, but I'd rather start making some plans now."

Wow was the only word that came to my mind. Me. An assistant manager. A full manager. A business owner. Was that even possible? It seemed that idea was more of a childhood dream, like wanting to be a princess or a pirate or some other fantasy figure. I used to measure time by the day, with no thought to any kind of real future. Now it was staring me in the face with an opportunity that had never crossed my mind.

I worked through several walk-ins in a partial daze as my brain wandered through this new idea and what it could mean for me and my little girl.

But, like always, something had to come and derail that train.

The bell rang over the door, and all eyes turned to see Kimmie arriving. She shuffled in like she was in pain. "Sorry I'm late. I think I caught that stomach thing that's been going around."

I bit my lip as the next client sat in my chair. Everyone there recognized that hangovers weren't caused by viruses. My best course was to keep quiet. Kimmie was about to get canned, and there wasn't anything I could do about it.

"Kimmie, I need to talk to you." Tambre's voice sounded sterner than a schoolteacher's.

The shop gossip had died to nothing as the entire salon waited and watched. There was a smidgeon of survivor's guilt happening in my head, but I had more important things to think about.

"I know I screwed up and I'm late again, but I was really sick this morning. I'll make up the hours. Promise."

"You don't understand. I need to talk to you privately."

Kimmie must have heard the note in Tambre's tone. "Why?"

My friend's single-word question sounded belligerent. This was not going to go well.

"I'm sure you don't want me to do this publicly."

Kimmie's face flashed red and screwed up in an ugly way. "You're gonna fire me, aren't you? Well, then, I fucking quit. I'm sick of this shitty town and the shitty people in it. I'm packing my shit and going back to Minnesota. So fucking boring. Nothing but a cheap tourist attraction. Dumb fucking hillbilly assholes!"

The quiet in the salon resembled a funeral home. Not one person said a word or even moved as Kimmie raged. Luckily, she didn't start throwing anything. Property damage would up the ante, and I doubted Tambre's calm, forgiving nature reached that far. Mine wouldn't.

"I'll pay you cash what you're owed," Tambre stated as she opened the register. "Then you can go anywhere you want."

"Fucking bullshit job. This place is a fucking joke." Kimmie snatched the money from Tambre's hand and stomped to the door. She shot a hard glare at me. "You coming with?"

As messed up as our friendship had become, she

and I *had* been through a tough time together. "Kimmie, I...."

"Didn't think so. Have fun with your stupid preacher. I bet he only fucks in missionary. I know you find that position boring as hell."

I froze. Panic crawled up my spine. "Kimmie, please...."

Her nose wrinkled up in a nasty sneer. "Don't fucking think you're all that, bitch. Remember, I *know* where you've been and what you've done!"

"Please don't—"

"I've seen you crawl across the floor to give a blow job for a twenty. You used to snort up with Rebel and fuck his buddies for drugs. Hell, I bet there wasn't one man in the Dutchmen MC that you didn't suck off or fuck. You'd even do two at a time right there on that dirty clubhouse floor with every man in there watching. You're a fucking club whore, same as me!"

"Get out."

A new voice, low and menacing, came from the doorway. My breath halted as Bryce stepped inside. To make matters worse, Robert was right behind him.

An invisible hand with black ugly fingers wrapped around my throat, its sharp talons digging into my skin. I couldn't breathe. My worst nightmare was taking place right here, right now as my past rushed to tear through my future. Secrets I'd planned on taking to my grave were laid out in the open for everyone to hear. Judgment the size of boulders came at me from all sides like a biblical stoning, and their weight was crushing.

Kimmie tried to bluster her way through. "Who the fuck do you think—"

"I didn't stutter."

Kimmie let it go and left, her parting shot echoing around the room. "Fuck this place, and fuck you, too, Opal. Don't ever forget you're a fucking slut, and now everyone knows it!"

"That's it. Tambre, go call Blue."

"Fuck you too!"

Kimmie roared off in her car, squealing the wheels bad enough that the smell of rubber drifted into the salon.

I was shaking hard enough that my knees threatened to buckle underneath me. I lifted my hands and saw my fingers twitching. Dizziness hit me, and I tried to breathe but nothing happened. I'd forgotten how my lungs were supposed to work. My vision was starting to gray at the edges, and I lost any sense of balance. The roaring in my ears drowned out any other sounds in the salon, and only one word hissed loud enough to be heard.

Whore! Whore! Whore!

An ugly, nasty word describing such disgusting filth that wasn't worth anyone's regard or attention.

I was on my way to the floor when two large male hands scooped under my arms and held me up. They were warm. Firm. Their grip kept me from falling.

"I got you."

Bryce. His strong voice penetrated the dark and brought me back to focus.

"Breathe, baby."

"Breathe, sweetness."

My chest opened up, and I filled my lungs slowly, counting to four in my head. I raised my eyes to meet his, and for once, that beautiful hazel shade didn't bother me. His strong presence and defensive protection were centered on me. Only me.

"Let him in, sweetness."

Camo's voice was loud in my imagination. I spoke back to him the same way. *What if this is wrong?*

"What if it's right?"

"Show's over. Let's get back to it, shall we? Who's next?" Tambre called out. "Opal, do you need a minute?"

I swear nothing fazed that woman. "I'm fine." The tears finally broke. "I'm so, so sorry, Tambre. I'm… not that person anymore."

"If we measured everyone by their past, we'd all be underground. Every person in the world has challenges, some more than others. It's not the trials that judge us but the way we rise and deal with them after."

Tambre's earthy alto floated around me like a warm hug. She couldn't physically do that, though, as I was still in Bryce's arms. My legs finally solidified enough to stand, and I took my own weight back. He still didn't let go.

I didn't either.

Tambre continued talking. "Believe me, my friend, you're in good company. All I'm saying is, if you need to take a minute or two, your chair will be here waiting for you."

My scrambled thoughts failed to order themselves, but one stood out. I wasn't fired along with my roommate. Or former roommate.

"You got a coat? Grab it and let's go."

Bryce's deep command took over, and I moved with him as he took my hand. I noticed Robert had disappeared, but I didn't think anything of it. Tambre tossed me my padded jacket, and Bryce led me from the salon.

"Where are we going?" I asked.

"Taking a ride."

"Isn't it too cold?"

"We're not going far."

He held the heavy garment as I slipped my arms into the sleeves and zipped up the front.

"Gloves?"

I pulled out the thick over-the-cuff ones I had in my pockets and put them on. He handed me a full-face helmet he'd pulled from one saddlebag. "It's my mom's from when I used to take her riding with me. I keep it in here just in case I ever need it."

I remembered seeing that same helmet handed to Donna on the night he took her on the Dragon Runners' final run of their Halloween barbecue. He placed it on my head and tightened the strap under my chin. "Fit okay?"

"Yes." I sounded hoarse.

"I'll get you a custom one later. Let's go."

I was still foggy as I mounted up behind him. It was

the heavy cruiser, and I briefly wondered if he'd brought that one specifically for this purpose. Then we took off in a muted roar.

The wind bit into my jeans, and my legs froze quickly. The last time I rode on the back of a bike was in Minnesota. It didn't take long for me to find my balance, leaning with Bryce and awakening awareness of the man in front of me. His muscles moved with the motorcycle, and I moved with him, taking cues from his position. He revved, and I braced for the surge of power from the beast underneath us. Bare trees flew by as he made his way along the road, and before I knew it, we were entering the Tail. This was where the skill of the rider became critical. Some curves were gentle, and some were so tight, the physical force made me dizzy. I trusted the man guiding the bike along the Dragon's spines to keep me out of harm's way.

As he'd stated, we didn't go far. He came to a pull-off overlooking a stand of trees covering a mountain vista.

I dismounted as he held the bike steady, tendrils of dread uncoiling in my gut. I was alone with Bryce after having all my secrets exposed in the most brutal way possible.

What happens next?

HE PULLED OFF THE ROAD AT A CLEARED STOPPING AREA with a scenic overlook. Opal dismounted and took the helmet off, handing it to him before walking away. Weatherman stowed it in the saddlebag and observed the woman's stiff posture, her back tight and her arms clutching themselves as if they were the only things holding her together. He couldn't blame her, as she was just laid open and raw by someone who was supposed to be a friend.

"You're a fucking club whore, same as me!"

Kimmie's nasty words echoed in his mind. There was a story there, and not a pretty one. He'd already made some conclusions about Opal's past based on what she'd garbled out when she was sick and delusional. He also guessed that there was more to the hairdresser from Minnesota. What he did know for certain was her dedication to her child and making a good life for the both of them.

He kicked out the stand and clicked off the engine before swinging his leg over the seat. The leather chaps squeaked as he made his way to her. He heard the sobs before he reached her, and his heart cracked. Without thinking, he stepped behind her and put his hands up on her shoulders to pull her back against him. "It's just you and me here, babe. You're safe."

She held her breath, and Weatherman held his, waiting for her to shatter like glass. Then she turned to him, buried her head in his leather cut, and let go. He kept silent as she crowned his patch with her tears.

She finally wore herself out, and the calm quiet of the woods took over. The bird sounds and buzz of insects were pretty much gone at this time of year. Only the occasional woody crackle punctuated the air as the trees changed temperature. The bears would be denning by now and had already started their winter sojourn. The Dragon never truly slept even in the winter and waited for whatever confessions Opal would make. It would take her words and hold them for her, absorbing the pain, taking it into itself, and making it disappear to be forgotten.

"Kimmie was right. I was a club whore. I slept with so many men at the Dutchmen MC compound for money or gifts. I didn't care if they were married or not. I'd let them do things to me, whatever they wanted, just so I might feel loved for a little while. I did drugs with them, whatever they fed me. My favorite was the white powder, and I got hooked on it. At that time, I thought that was where I belonged and the only life I had open to me."

His heart skipped a few beats, but he held on to her, letting her set the pace as she let out all the poison in her mind.

"I have no idea where my mom is. I turned eighteen, and she was done. I came home after my high school graduation to find the apartment empty and cold. I had a part-time job at a local chicken place, but wasn't enough to pay rent or much of anything else. The manager was aware I was alone." She gave a harsh laugh. "My mom told me once that I had to learn how to suck cock and do it well to get and keep a man. He was my first one and paid me twenty bucks afterward. I got desperate one month for rent money, and he paid me fifty for my virginity. He only wanted to pay twenty, but I held out long enough to get more."

It was hard to hear. The organ in his chest bled at each word. She tried to pull away from him, but he tightened his arms around her. No way would he let her loose while she broke herself down into pieces.

"One of my coworkers told me about the Dutchmen and how I could make some quick, desperately needed money from them. I went there one night and found a different world. I got high for the first time and liked it. It made the sex easier to get through. I was about to be evicted, and that night I earned my back rent."

Her breath hitched, and fresh tears started dripping onto his leather. She tried again to move away, and he stopped her a second time. "Stay where you are, babe."

"Why do you want to hear all this shit?"

"I just do. I also think you need to say it. Let me remind you, you're safe. We're good at listening. The Dragon, the woods, and me."

For a moment, he thought she would stop, but she took a few breaths and spilled more secrets.

"The drugs made it simple. Get high, get drunk—or both—and take the money. After a while, it wasn't so hard to do. There was a part of me that dreamed that one day one of them would love me and help get me out of that life. When I got pregnant with Pearl, I thought her father and I would be together and build the family I never had. His name was Rebel. At first, he was over the moon to be a dad, but it didn't last long. I got clean when I found out I was going to be a mother, but he didn't. The white powder was more important than me or her. He left us and died of an overdose before he ever met his daughter."

His rage ramped up with every tear that fell. Rage at the life Opal had been forced by circumstance to live and the scars it had left behind. No wonder she was so wary of bikers and biker clubs.

"The night she was born, I vowed I would change my life and give her a better one than I ever had. They called me Peebles when I was in that club. I decided never to be Peebles again and to be Opal instead. It was the easiest and, at the same time, the hardest decision I've ever made. Mama J, I've mentioned her before, took me and Pearl in while I went to school to earn my cosmetology license. I don't think I could have done it if I hadn't had her help."

"She's the one with six kids, right?"

"Yes. She has a story herself of struggle as a single mom, but she made it on the other side and is happy with a thriving business and a good man at her side."

His phone buzzed in his back pocket, and he had to let her loose to take a quick look at the screen. The message wasn't about his mom but from Mute.

Mute: Tambre called. Betsey has been activated. Getting the boys together for their help. Got your woman covered here at the Lair.

He stifled the smile of relief as he slipped the phone back into its spot. Betsey's biggest talent in this world was empathy and healing. She was good at it, and once she took someone to her heart, they stayed there.

He lifted Opal's hand and pulled her over to the high fenced railing to lean against the cold metal. He could see her face now. "I imagine it was a big struggle at times."

She barked a short laugh. "Only every single day. I attended Narcotics Anonymous meetings and fought the constant cravings. Still fight them sometimes. So many times, it would have been easy to give up and go back to the white powder, but what would happen to my little girl?" She definitively shook her head. "No. Not gonna happen. Ever."

"So, this guy Rebel is—or rather was—Pearl's father. Can you tell me who Camo is?"

She startled. "How do you know that name?"

He stroked a hand over her cheek and brushed away the wetness there. "You mentioned him the night you got so sick. You thought I was him a few times."

Her face changed, eyes closing and her mouth pressing inward as if trying to keep from bursting apart. "He… he was my first real boyfriend. I used to ride behind him. Camo was his road name." She brushed at her eyes and sniffed, then reached out to the wet spot on his chest. "Excuse me. I didn't mean to make a mess on your cut. It just catches me off guard sometimes."

"Did you love him?"

She nodded in the affirmative. "Yes. He was the only person who ever truly cared for me. He picked me up when I was at the lowest point and rescued me, and he loved me and my daughter when I was convinced no one would. Never judged me or put me down or made me feel like I was less because of some of the bad decisions I made. I thought we would have a great little life together, all three of us, a house with a fenced yard, a dog and cat. But he… he…."

Fresh tears poured down her face. Weatherman let her cry for a moment as he shifted his arms around her in a loose hug from behind, and she leaned into him. "What happened?"

Opal's voice broke. He heard the crack as she fragmented into a thousand pieces. Her words came out in a ragged gasp of air as if shards of glass tore through her throat. "He didn't just die. He… he was… killed while trying to protect me! Shot in the heart."

Weatherman inhaled, taking in the scent of the surrounding icy pine. He wasn't expecting that answer, yet he wasn't surprised. The level of pain radiating from this woman was off the scale; therefore, something tragic had to have happened. Losing someone you loved had to be the hardest situation any person dealt with. It didn't matter if it was watching them slowly die of a nasty disease or go in a matter of seconds by a bullet. Grief was grief. Pain was pain.

He wrapped his arms as tightly as he could against her body. "I'm sorry. So sorry for all the shit you've been through, babe." He had no other words of comfort or wisdom. He wished he had more to give, but all he could really do was hold her and check his reactions.

Part of him wanted to get Pearl and wrap mother and daughter up in a protective bubble until they were completely insulated from the bad stuff in the world. The other part of him wanted to drive to Minnesota and throat-punch the assholes who'd hurt his woman.

Yeah, he told himself, *she's* my *woman now.*

More sobs escaped her throat, and she visibly fought against letting them out. Weatherman didn't know if he should be impressed by her control or frustrated by her stubbornness. His chest pressed tightly against her back, and her head rested on his shoulder. He tipped his head forward and rested his chin on her hair.

"We were just getting started when it happened. I had some trouble with a bad deputy. Corrupt cop thing. He'd… stopped me a few times and demanded… favors to not give me a ticket."

Anger jolted in Weatherman's throat. He didn't have to think hard about what she meant by "favors."

"I had no power. No standing. No support until Camo gave it to me. I told the cop no more, and one night he tried to force me. Beat me up pretty bad. I thought I was gonna die, but I called Camo before I got out of the car and left my phone on so he knew where to find me. He came with some of his friends. I was on the ground bleeding and heard shots. When I woke up in the hospital, they told me… they told me…."

She whimpered, and he barely heard her hoarse whisper. "Camo gave his life to save me. I'm not worthy of that. It's my fault he died. All my fault."

Weatherman squeezed, adding his strength to hers,

holding her together. His rage mixed with sorrow and admiration at this woman's strength. To have been through such an emotional ordeal and survived was amazing. Add that to her addiction battle, and the level of power it took to overcome everything made it awe-inspiring. She had scars, deep ones, but she'd lived through it and found a way to move on. Healing took a lot of time, and he could tell she was in that process and would be for a while yet.

He didn't have to think about it long—he simply made his plans to be a part of it. "It's not your fault. I'm not going to list the reasons why, 'cause I bet you've heard them a dozen times already. You're still grieving, and you're allowed to do that as long as you need to. I'm here. My mom is here. Betsey, Brick, Table, Lori, all the Dragon Runners are here for you. I told you I'd keep you safe, and I meant it. Camo sounds like he could have been one of us. A brother. I wish I could have met him."

He pressed his face into her neck. "Also, babe, don't ever let me hear you say you're not worthy. With what you've been through and what you've had to do to get to this place, right here, right now, there's no one who deserves a chance at a good life more than you. I hope you'll get used to the idea of me being around to watch you grow and see what's next. I can't be Camo, but I can be the man in your life if you'll let me."

Opal didn't pull away from him, nor did she turn around. The woods remained still in hushed reverence at this turning point. She finally spoke in a husky tone.

"I don't know what to do. I… feel something for you, but I'm scared. So damn scared of loving again. The two men I thought I had a future with were taken from me. I don't think I can handle losing that one more time."

Something released in his chest. She wasn't rejecting him or the idea of being with him. He imagined there were some men who would hear her story and run for the hills. He wasn't that kind of man. It would take patience and perseverance to make this work, but he had never failed at any goal he'd set for himself in his life. He wouldn't fail at this one either. "I can wait. It's been a heavy day, and we don't have to make any decisions just yet. I do need to tell you something. Mute texted me, and Betsey knows what went down at the salon. She's taken it upon herself to rally the boys and get you set up at the Lair for the night. I hope you have it in you to let her do that for you."

"I don't want to be trouble."

His chuckle puffed her hair. "Trust me, babe. It'll be more trouble if you don't let her take care of you. I'd prefer to take you home with me, but I don't dare go against Betsey when she's on a mission."

"Why would she want someone like me in her home?"

He breathed in to take in the scent of her hair. Some sort of coconut-lime shampoo. "Betsey is a rarity in this world. She's the least judgmental person I've ever met and has no problem twisting herself into knots to help someone in need. The only time I've ever seen her go after anyone is when one of her people gets hurt. No one will tangle with her when she's in mama bear mode. She considers you one of us already. I promise, if you take a chance with the club and with me, you'll never be alone."

He waited as she made up her mind.

"Okay."

CHAPTER 27

I guess it's true what they say about living in a small town. A person sneezes on one side and someone across the way says, "Bless you."

We collected Pearl from Lori and headed up to the Lair. It was dinnertime when we got there. Smells of comfort cooking filled the air.

Betsey met us at the door. No questions. No disapproving stares. No condemnations. She just opened her arms and took me in, and for once, she only had four words to say.

"You're gonna be okay."

This was a statement made as if it was a factual law.

That was it. That was all it took. I clutched at her shoulders and let loose like I was dying. I'd seen a mother's love in Mama J and the DRMC old ladies, but I'd never had it for myself. Betsey might be the grandma to the world, but right now, she was the maternal figure I needed. One I hadn't realized how much I'd missed until now. "I don't know how to thank you for… all of this."

"Pshhhht, this is part of being a family. We hold each other up, and if one of us falls, we're the net that will catch you. I want you to stay here tonight, and you're welcome to stay longer if you want. I always got room. Period. Now, let me feed that baby of yours, and you take a little 'me' time. Deal with life when you're ready."

I wasn't hungry, but the tangy scent of pork barbecue enticed me to eat a little. Betsey cooed and played with Pearl as my child smeared mashed potatoes all over her face rather than use the curved toddler spoon clutched in her hand. Bryce stayed by my side at all times, as if shielding me. My shelter in the storm.

"Mute and Dodge went over to check your place. Kimmie cleared out already, and we don't know where she went. They can't tell if she took any of your stuff, but she did turn all the faucets on full blast and propped the refrigerator and freezer doors open. They took care of it, so you don't have to worry. If anything is missing, we'll replace it."

I wasn't surprised at Kimmie's pettiness. It bothered me, as I'd been paying all the rent and utilities for the past couple of months, and that act was nothing more than spiteful vengeance, but she was so far into herself that she probably didn't recognize how far she'd fallen. I hoped wherever she went, she would find her way back.

This was a typical night at the Lair. Some members came in for a quick visit before heading home. A few of the single members played a game of pool while the giant TV showed a football sports show. The deer head above the fireplace wore a Carolina Panthers ball cap, showing where the Dragon Runners' allegiance lined up.

Betsey walked around in her heeled boots with Pearl firmly on her hip. When my girl squirmed to get down, Betsey let her do that and kept an eye on her steps.

No one asked me about the details of today's event. No one pointed at me and whispered behind cupped hands. No one bothered me at all. It was refreshing to just be in the moment and not have any obligations or responsibilities.

But time doesn't stand still for anyone. Night had already fallen, and Pearl started her demands to be held. She toddled first to me to pick her up, then reached for Bryce. He lifted her and let her settle on his shoulder as we sat on the sofa side by side.

"I called Mom, and Emma is going to stay with her tonight. I don't want to leave you alone right now."

Does that mean he wants us to sleep together or just be under the same roof? I was acutely aware that we hadn't gotten physical as in sex. Yeah, we'd made out like a couple of teenagers, but nothing else. Bryce had never pushed that boundary. Did he want to touch me now, or did hearing about my past make him cringe away from that intimacy? "I'm… um… sure I'll be fine."

"I know you will be. I'm still staying." He leaned over and kissed my temple. "What's on your mind?"

"Where...?" I started. "I'm not sure where I'm supposed to be."

"Betsey has a full guest suite upstairs if you want to use it, but if you're okay with it, I'd much rather you stay with me. My room isn't the biggest one here, but it's private."

"What about Pearl?"

He glanced down at my little girl, whose eyes were drifting closed, but it was Betsey who answered. She walked up to us and deftly transferred Pearl into her arms. "Now, don't you worry 'bout this baby. I got everythin' she's gonna need upstairs with me. You okay leavin' her with me for the night? I promise I'll come get you if she won't settle, but I think she's on her way to a good sleep. I think Mama needs one too. You come on upstairs if you want, and you can bring your man with you or not. You need some time alone? I'll run his ass off and give you that. If you feel better 'bout stayin' with him in his room? You do whatever it is that makes you comfortable. Ain't no one here gonna say nothin'."

More tears built up behind my eyes. "Why are you so good to me? I'm nobody."

Betsey's voice became tight. "That's where you're wrong, darlin'. I heard what you did for Hilda Burns. You might have changed that girl's life, and that right there is something special."

"It was just a haircut."

"To you, it was just a haircut. To Hilda, it was an openin' to a whole new world."

I pondered this. I'd seen Hilda since her winter dance transformation. In fact, I'd gotten more teenage clients coming in and asking for my services. The thought had never occurred to me about what influence I had on these young girls. I had firsthand experience of how a kind word of encouragement, plus a little makeup and hair color, could boost someone's outlook on life. Betsey loved her bright red hair and heels and wore them with pride. Molly loved her colorful nails. Tambre had her thriving salon. Katrina, Eva, Psalm, Lori, Fauna—all of them had their talents.

Me? I helped all of them look and feel pretty.

"I think I'll stay with Bryce, if you're sure you can handle Pearl?"

Betsey smiled warmly. "Darlin', I've been a mama and a gramma to a lot of kids. That's my gift. Now, you go get yourself some sleep. Tomorrow is early enough to handle anything else."

Bryce guided me down a hall that led to his room. It was pretty far in the back of this rabbit warren, and he didn't lie when he said it was small. The double bed was only full-size, not queen, and took up most of the space. A small beat-up dresser and nightstand took the rest. It had its own bathroom, but only a shower stall big enough for one, a pedestal sink, and toilet. The room was very basic, but it was clean and neat. I'd stayed in worse places.

What made it great was the man standing behind me. He put his arms around my shoulders and pulled me back into his body. It must be one of his favorite ways to hug, as I'd been in this same position before. I remembered the picture Betsey showed me of him hugging his mom from behind.

This is one way he shows people he loves them.

Where that random thought came from, I had no clue, but it made sense. *We* made sense.

My belly quivered and my heart sped up as I took a breath, and my voice trembled a little as I spoke. "If I asked you to make love to me now, would you do it?"

"Yes." He pressed his lips against my temple, and I felt the word burn my skin as he said it.

His kiss answered my question, and there was no doubt that after tonight, a single path would lie in front of me. One that I would walk for eternity, and Bryce would be right beside me.

"Are you sure someone like you wants to be with someone like me?" I had to say the words in a whisper.

"Babe, stop thinking so much. If I didn't want to be here, right now, with you, I wouldn't."

"What if—"

"Stop. We can 'what if' all night and still not figure anything out. For the record? Your past does not bother me. It's your future that I'm interested in, and I plan to be a big part of it. If you're not ready for this, that's fine. We'll wait. But please recognize this fact: I'm here, and I'm not going anywhere."

I kissed him. *Me.* I moved first. It was me who made it happen.

I turned in his arms and pulled his head to mine, opening my mouth and taking his. He didn't pull back or close himself off to me; rather, he let me set the pace. Something inside my chest released, like turning a valve and letting out a pressure I hadn't known I carried. No more tension, and no more questions. This was where I should be. Where I belonged.

Here with Bryce Turner.

I pulled his cut and the shirt over his head, and he raised his arms to accommodate the action. He resumed kissing me as soon as it was off and didn't care when I dropped both articles to the floor.

"I should be taking care of you, babe."

"Please, Bryce, let me do this my way."

"Okay, sweetheart. You let me know what you need. Got it?"

I reached to undo his jeans, then pushed them down. "Got it."

He let me touch him and kiss him wherever I wanted. I ran my hands over his chest and traced the swimmer's muscles with my fingers. His nipples were flat brown circles that I discovered were sensitive. I teased him with my tongue before sucking one in my mouth and heard him groan in response. Reaching lower, I cupped him through his dark gray boxer briefs.

"Fuck, Opal!" he gasped as I stroked his hard length through the cloth. His erection grew as I followed its outline, and a bead of moisture made a spot.

In my past life, I'd have been pushed to my knees by now. Bryce didn't do anything more than stand in front of me trembling as I caressed and teased him. Now and then, he would take a sharp breath and grit his teeth. It was intoxicating to find that I had a choice and more control than I'd ever had before.

It turned me on. Big-time.

I led him to the bed and pushed him down to lie on his back. There was no headboard, so he placed his hands flat on the wall.

I hadn't dressed for seduction or pleasure but for work: jeans, a black ribbed Henley shirt, plain beige bra, and panties. I quickly added my clothes to his on the floor. He didn't move or protest as I mounted him, sliding my core along his thick shaft. It felt good, so I did it again and again.

He writhed under me as if in pain. "Baby, I'm gonna finish before you get started if you keep that up."

I lifted off him, and he breathed a sigh of relief.

"Were you that close to coming?"

His eyes met mine, but he kept his hands where they were. "Yes, I was. I've been wanting this for a long time, and I hope I don't mess it up."

"You're not going to mess up."

"I will if I come first. I really want to make this good for you, babe."

"Do you have condoms?" was my throaty answer.

He flicked a finger to the nightstand drawer. "Should be some in there, but they've been in there a while. Not a bad idea to check the expiration date."

I smiled at the Trojan Magnum box. Yes, they were old but still good. I tore one open and rolled it over his erection, noticing he had a slight curve. He bit his lip as the latex stretched down his length. He was still rock hard in my hand.

"I want to be on top for this first time. Are you okay with me doing that?"

"Yeah, baby. I'm good."

I straddled him once more, planting my knees at his hips and settling over him. He reached for my hips to help me balance as I took his length in my hand and brought it to my opening.

"You sure about this, baby? Once we do this, there's no going back."

"I'm surer about this than I've ever been about anything."

I lowered myself onto him, slowly taking him inside and stretching around him. It had been a long time for me, and he was not a small man. It took me a while to work down on him, lifting and sliding, but he didn't lunge or force me to go faster. I watched as his jaw clenched and unclenched as he fought to control himself. When he was fully seated inside me, I stopped moving and rested. He pushed himself into a sitting position so we faced each other, touching almost shoulder to shoulder.

His eyes were on mine, and the intensity in them kept me locked in that gaze. Every sense was open. I heard our breaths come together in sync. His hardness flexed inside me, and I gripped him back. My hand came to his chest to feel his heartbeat, and he did the same, placing his palm just over my breast. Our pulses aligned themselves together as they combined into one.

This connection between us was more than physical. There was a depth to this intimacy that opened up to more—so much more that I couldn't fathom how far it could go.

He flexed again, and I responded, this time with a whimper in my throat. There was no need for frantic pounding, thrusting, or pumping until one of us came. It was building slow and sure and steady.

Another flex.

Another squeeze.

Another heartbeat.

Another breath.

Another flex.

When the orgasm came, it didn't flash like lightning but rather rolled through me like thunder, booming and deep. I let out a small cry, as it was more than I could contain. Our eye contact never wavered, and his palm pressed harder into my chest as he reached his own climax. We were linked with a strong, powerful force that neither of us could control on our own, but together we could hold the world. There was a bond here that had no limits and simply would not be broken. Some would call it love, but that tiny word sounded insignificant to all I'd experienced tonight. I felt him shoot inside me, filling the condom that I admit I resented, as it was the only barrier between us.

He reached up to brush under my eyes, and only then did I realize there were tears flowing from them.

"You okay, baby?"

"Yes." I had no other words. Nothing else came to my mind to say.

He leaned in to kiss me. "I get it."

As much as I wanted to stay like this forever, we had to move sometime. My legs tingled as I shifted off him, and he stood us both up. I smoothed over the muscled planes of his chest and abs, marveling that this was mine.

"You need the bathroom while I deal with the condom? There's a toothbrush I haven't opened in the medicine cabinet. Help yourself."

Once we were both back in the bed, he wrapped us up in a dark blue comforter covered in stars. I recognized some of the constellations he showed me from our night at the Lair. It had been a long, stress-filled day, but it had ended with hope for a better place.

Sleepy words gurgled from my mouth as he took up the spot behind me and spooned into my naked body. "Will it always be like this?"

"I'll do my best to make it that way, babe."

I DON'T KNOW HOW LONG I SLEPT, BUT I WOKE UP TO A heavy darkness. Not scary or pressing, but more like the blanket I used to hide under when I was a kid.

Bryce still lay behind me, fitted exactly to my body. His breath tickled across my neck as he slept on.

Then another awareness came to me. Something almost tangible with a gentleness I'd recognize from only one source.

"Camo?" I whispered lightly, barely forming the word.

"I said before, sweetness, he's a good man. I trust him to take care of you and Pearl, and he will for this lifetime. I'm good to go, 'cause I'm leaving you in good hands."

A tiny prick pierced my heart. "Do you really have to leave?"

"Yes, my love, it's time."

Tears formed in the corners of my eyes. "You're not mad?"

"Oh, darling, I'd never be mad at you. Life always moves forward, and you have many changes ahead of you. Pearl will grow up and move on. You'll keep adding to your career, touching people's lives and changing them for the better. You may even have more children, as you have so much love to give them, and you'll do it with a strong man by your side. He's your support. A solid anchor who's not there to hold you back but to let you soar as you were meant to."

"I'm going to miss you."

"I'll always have a place in your heart, a special one that's just for me. Now, go do great things, sweetness. Never hide the love you have inside you."

A soft, cool puff of air brushed over my forehead, as if a small kiss had been placed there.

Then he was gone.

I expected a tearing grief to hit me as it had when I heard the news of Camo's death. Instead, I was filled with an almost joy that he'd found his place at last.

And I'd found mine.

Bryce shifted behind me, and his arm around my middle pressed inward. "You okay, honey?" his sleep-sated voice rumbled in my ear.

"I'm very okay."

CHAPTER 28

"Glenda Mark's golden retriever, Sadie, just had another litter of puppies. Cute as buttons!"

"School board meetin' got canceled."

"I found another long black hair growing out under my chin this morning. I swear them damn things just erupt overnight, 'cause I didn't see it yesterday."

The salon resumed its daily offerings as if nothing had happened. No one mentioned Kimmie and her outburst, or me, or anything. I was greeted at the door with the usual chorus of "Heys" I'd come to expect. I thought for sure that I'd be treated with disdain and cold glares as Donna had been, but none of that happened. I didn't know what the difference was between us other than I had left that life while she was still in it.

Tambre came from the break room with a cup of coffee in her hand. "I'm so glad you came in today. Bex called in with a sick kid and has to stay home. I've called her clients to reschedule, but if you can help with some of them, that would be great. There's an event at the high school tonight, and it seems everyone else in the county wants a fresh color job and decided to book an appointment this week."

"You bet." I walked to my station to set up for the day. I already had a full schedule of color touch-ups and several high school girls, including Hilda. Her grandmother had grumbled about it but allowed her to have her hair done professionally now. I'd worked a deal with Hilda to keep Pearl a few times in trade so she could keep her money. She would come here later today for her appointment. I'd asked her about the Melford boy when she called for a time, and I could hear the happy sigh through the phone line. Apparently, they were together now, and it was a good match.

It was midmorning when the second shoe dropped. The bell announced that someone had just entered the salon, and the room hushed quickly. I turned to see Robert in the waiting room. He was watching me with a deep frown on his normally serene face.

I had to face him sometime, and I was between clients, so now was as good a time as any. There was no reason for me to look anywhere else in the salon, as I was sure every eye was glued on the both of us.

"Can we speak outside for a minute?" His tone was tight and dry, coming from thinned lips.

He turned, and I followed him to the parking lot. If his aim was privacy, I doubted that would happen. The front windows were big and wide with no curtains. I had the absurd thought that they resembled a TV screen at the moment. All the salon ladies needed was some microwave popcorn, and they were set.

"Something funny?" he asked.

"Not really," I answered on a sigh. "I can already guess why you're here. It's about yesterday."

He nodded. "Is what that woman said true?"

I thought about Kimmie and our shared past.

I thought about Betsey and her long hug of welcome last night at the Lair.

I thought about Mute, one of the scariest men I'd ever seen, and the reverent look of love on his face as he held his newborn.

I thought about Tambre and the calm support she always gave me.

I thought about Bryce, my confession to him, and how even after I'd bared myself and every dirty secret I had, he didn't walk away.

I thought about the incredible night I spent with a man who, even though he hadn't said it yet, loved me and my daughter. He was committed to me and I to him in a way few souls ever found.

These were my people now. My family. I was good with that.

"Yes, it's true. I was a club whore and a drug addict. I've left that life and been clean for almost three years, and I plan to stay that way."

He flinched, his mouth thinning even more, and it wasn't hard to see that his entire demeanor toward me had changed. It seemed the only words he paid attention to were "whore" and "addict." If he heard "clean" and "stay that way," he didn't catch them very well.

He took off his glasses and cleaned them much like he had when he saw Kimmie at the Halloween festival. "I'm not sure I can be with you anymore. It bothers me to think you've had… sex… with other men."

His words sent a shock through me, and it was on the tip of my tongue to remind him that's how babies were made. "I'm not proud of my past, but I won't let it dictate my future."

He put the frames back on his nose and pushed them up. "That's very admirable of you, but that doesn't change what you've done. How many?"

"What?"

"How many men have you… slept with?"

"I don't know."

He glanced at a point above my head. "You don't know. Must be a lot."

At one time, his interrogation would humiliate me. Right now, it made me angry.

And I liked it.

My spine clicked into place as I stood tall and raised my chin. "What do you want me to say, Robert? I can't change what I've done, but I can change what I do now. If it's something that bugs you that much, honestly, I don't think I want to be with you either. I don't want to be around someone who constantly judges me for circumstances I had no control over. I was a kid who had no one but myself to rely on, and I did the best I could. Yes, I made some bad choices, but I've also learned from them."

He fiddled with his glasses again. Did this habit of his irritate me because of his attitude toward me now? "I'm happy you've given up that life and moved on to something more."

His tone didn't match his words. It was easy to see that he would forever look down on me in spite of how far I'd come or what I did from now on. It didn't matter how hard I worked or how successful I might be, he would always regard me as a woman who was beneath him.

"You preach about love, forgiveness, acceptance, understanding, compassion, and other stuff like that. I guess it's easier to talk about it than to live it. I am sorry that you're bothered by me now, but if what you say is true and God loves everyone, that includes us sinners as well."

He sniffed and awkwardly changed his stance. "You're right. God does love everyone, and I preach about a lot. I don't want to fall into that judgmental trap 'cause it's the opposite of what I'm supposed to think and feel, but there's a part of me that can't help it. I like you, Opal. I like you a lot, but now, when I want to kiss you, I can't help but think about how many other men have done that and more. I'm angry at myself for feeling this way, and that's something I have to face and figure out."

My anger dissipated some at his confession. "I think you're just being human."

His green eyes were wet when they rose to meet mine. "I'm sorry, and I hope you'll forgive me."

"Don't beat yourself up, Robert. I can forgive you and move on, but I think you should find someone else to cut your hair."

I turned and walked back into the salon, growing lighter and lighter with each step.

Tambre met me at the door. "You okay?"

I smiled. "Yes. Yes, I am."

CHAPTER 29

"Quit fuckin' with that thing, shithead!"

The mountain lion hissed and swiped at the stick Walt poked between the metal bars. The animal was old and skinny with a mangy coat. Not the specimen Clem was expecting for this private hunt, but it was the best he could find. They'd lugged the animal in a cage barely big enough to hold it on the back of their largest four-wheeler to the isolated cabin. The client had delayed four times over the holidays and now had delayed again. At this rate, they'd be lucky to have this fucking hunt at all. That left Clem stuck with a mountain lion that he had to feed. He'd already paid for the damn thing, and getting another one would be impossible this time of year. He hoped it ate leftover dog food.

"If that asshole don't get here soon, I'll shoot the cat myself." Clem's fierce thoughts were accompanied by a thwack of his ax as he swung to split another log. Six. Six hides had been ruined. Not because of them or their process, but because some fucking scavengers had discovered the cabin and torn into the stretching frames and upset the curing barrels. Had to be a bunch of coyotes, as those were the only ones left that might still be roaming. Normally, coyotes hunted individually but lived in packs. He didn't think they would be brave enough to approach the cabin, but there was a lot of free food laid out for them for the taking.

He'd arrived that afternoon with a spitting, hissing big cat to a huge, smelly mess. With the loss of those hides, he didn't have enough to fill the order from the taxidermy place. With the rangers combing the forests and the Dragon Runners MC activated, getting more hides was a tall order. Most of the bears were denned about now or at least should be. Two of the dens he'd marked had tagged bears wearing radio collars, so killing them would be risky. Another one had been empty, so either the bear that planned on hibernating there changed its mind or was still thinking about it.

"Fucking shit!" Another thwack cracked through the air as Clem brought the ax head down. Nothing was going right, from the dry, unseasonable weather, to the lost hides, to the client who thought nothing of making them wait with an unreasonable mountain lion.

The animal hissed and roared again as Walt ignored his cousin and continued to harass it.

"Goddamnit, I done told you to leave it alone!" Clem picked up one of the split logs and hurled it at Walt. It knocked the man back and left a streak of blood across his forehead.

"Whad'ja do that for?"

"You've got to be the dumbest motherfucker ever born. We got shit to do, so get off your ass and get it done."

Clem ignored the confused look his cousin gave him and went back to splitting firewood.

Thwack!

Thwack!

Thwack!

Firewood. One more fuckup and he'd light it all up and watch it burn.

CHAPTER 30

This was the part I liked best—the smooth glide of him as he moved inside me a few more times just after we both came.

Between his schedule and mine, taking care of Pearl and his mother, plus all the other business of simply living, we always scratched out time for each other. Some days, it was a brief conversation on the phone, and on others, we had a few hours to spend together, just him and me. That connection we'd made only got stronger, and I started to relax into it. I heard complaints on a daily basis from the salon ladies about their husbands and the annoying habits they had. One liked to pick at his feet in front of the TV. Another left beard whiskers all over the bathroom counter. Others stacked dishes in the sink instead of the dishwasher, and if they deigned to empty it, they set everything on the counter instead of putting it away in the cabinets.

Perhaps we would eventually reach the day when

we'd been together so long that we'd find those little habits irritating. But I'd take them all to keep and safeguard everything I had with this man.

"You good, babe?" he purred in my ear, still gently stroking in and out of my sated body.

"Better than good," I answered as I matched his movements.

He'd come to me this dark morning and made love to me while the world still slept. Kimmie was long gone, and I'd moved Pearl into the second bedroom in her new toddler bed. She loved her "big girl bed" but still insisted on me being in her room while she fell asleep. The full rent had come out of my pocket alone for several months now, so I didn't feel any financial hit from being without a roommate. Even better was the small savings account I'd started.

Me! With a savings account!

Bryce kissed me before slipping out of me and getting off the bed, keeping his back to me while he disposed of the condom. I frowned at the sight, as I still hadn't made an appointment to get a different birth control so we could dispense with the damn things.

"I can't stay too long, sweetheart. The chief wants us out early for a day patrol up on the western ridges before the cold snap comes." He grinned down at me as he turned around. "Finally getting some cold weather from your old stomping grounds."

Winter Storm Margie was on her way down from Canada and the northern Midwest. She looked to be a big one, but none of the others made it far enough south to do anything much. I'd yet to see three flakes of snow to rub together in these mountains. "I'll be sure to dig out my parka."

He laughed. "Want to shower with me before Pearl wakes up?"

"Think we have time?"

"Probably not." He grinned at me again. "I'm gonna hit the bathroom first and make breakfast while you get cleaned up, okay? We're expanding the patrols on the far western ridge starting today, so it'll be late before I get back home."

"Which one?" I asked as I arched my back and stretched.

He grinned and leered at my movement. "No fair doing that when I have to go to work, babe." He flopped back on the bed and gave me a quick kiss. "That's a subject I want to talk to you about. My mom is doing better and better. She's not completely healed, and I don't know if she ever will be, but she's got a lot of her strength back and is able to take care of herself for the most part. This is a nice enough place, but it's more of a temporary stop than a home. I've had my eye on a three-bedroom condo in that new development being built overlooking the town. It's between Mom's place and the Lair and not far from the salon. Got a pool, tennis courts, community building, all sorts of extras. No yard work either, so to me, that's a plus."

"Sounds nice."

"It is. Good school district."

"Does that matter?"

He rolled on top of me and pinned me to the bed. "Absolutely, it does. You get that you're moving there, too, right? I want you to see it before I make an offer."

I was stunned. We were moving in together. Asking or telling? It didn't matter to me how it was said, I wanted it. "You're buying a condo."

"Yes."

"For us."

"All three of us. If we decide we want other kids, that's cool; otherwise, I'm just as happy with Pearl. Ah, baby, don't cry."

"They're happy tears." I sniffed as I wrapped my arms around his back. He lowered his head and kissed me again, this time deeper and longer, and my belly stirred with warmth. I hoped this never got old.

He pulled at the covers until he bared my body and settled between my legs. He kissed my inner thigh before spreading me open with his fingers. "Grab my phone and text the chief that I'm gonna be a little late. When you come, try to keep quiet so Pearl doesn't wake up, yeah?"

WEATHERMAN PULLED INTO THE PARKING LOT OF THE station ten minutes after his call time. He had a big happy smile on his face and Opal's taste lingering on his lips. He loved how she writhed under his mouth while she crammed a pillow over her face to keep from screaming her pleasure, and he couldn't wait to do it again. They had only grown closer in the past weeks. Some people called this the honeymoon stage and said it would change once the shine wore off a new relationship. Weatherman wasn't so sure that was the case here, but only time would tell.

Brick and Betsey had weathered years together. He blustered sometimes about her habits, and she nagged him about his diet, but underneath the squabbling lay a clear and solid core foundation on which they'd built a life together. There wouldn't be a Brick without Betsey, nor a Betsey without Brick.

Weatherman wanted the same with Opal. The condo would be the first step. It was a big one, but if he got his way, there would be a ring on her finger before the July Fourth holiday and a band to match by the time the next Halloween festival happened. He wondered what couple they would dress up as. Batman and Catwoman? Football player and cheerleader? Doctor and nurse?

He'd barely made it into the building before all hell broke loose. Chief Wilson puffed hard and cursed harder as he ran around the office with a phone in his hand.

"Sorry I'm late, Chief. I had something to finish—"

The man waved a hand in sharp dismissal. "I don't give a shit that you were late. We got reports of a wildfire spreading between Peachtree Creek and Massie Gap."

Weatherman frowned. Winter forest fires were more common than people knew, and if the conditions were right, they could smolder for weeks before bursting into flame. The mild unseasonable weather, the dry summer and fall—hell, he was surprised they hadn't had a burn already. "How far out?"

Chief Wilson scratched his head. "Far enough that we don't gotta worry about people yet, but there's always some dumbass up there trying to do the primitive survivor thing. The fire warden has already got his people on it and 'copters on the way. From the satellite images, it's movin' fast, and he's gonna need as many bodies as he can get to contain the beast. The 'copters can only do so much 'cause a' that storm comin' in. Maybe if Margie makes it in time, she'll cool this shit down before it gets any more out of hand."

He pointed at Weatherman. "You and Fine did some training with firefighting. The fire warden ain't gonna put you on the front line, but he needs the backup. Get your asses up Lands Creek Road. Once you leave the pavement and hit the dirt, it's five miles to where they're setting up. You'll have to take four-wheelers to get there. The fire hasn't spread there yet, but it might be comin' soon. I'm headin' to the Fontana Ridge Fire Station to help the spotter send information. Get goin', boys. Time is crucial."

CHAPTER 31

I hung up and sat in my chair. The salon was buzzing with the same news I'd just heard. A wild forest fire was somewhere out there, burning and devouring everything in its path.

And Bryce was on his way to meet it.

"It's a part of my job, babe, even though I'm not a full firefighter," he'd explained. "It's probably going to be a couple of days before I get back to town, but don't worry. I won't be in the thick of it."

"Not worry? Honey, you're fighting a fire!"

"Not directly. I'm more backup personnel for this. I'll probably go help with building the fire breaks and that sort of thing. I won't get near the actual fires."

"I'm scared for you anyway."

"It's okay, baby. I promise I'll come back to you as soon as I can. I have to call Mom real quick. Would you go check on her later?" he'd asked.

"Of course. I'll get Pearl from Lori's and spend the night there."

"That would be great."

"I love you."

I didn't mean to say it out loud, but the words had to be spoken. The ones that he'd responded with were even more shocking.

"I love you too."

Such a short, simple word with a complex meaning. I'd experienced searing pain, joy, fear, courage, despair, and euphoria all wrapped up in those four letters. Now that word was expressing nervous apprehension and helplessness. My man was heading into the jaws of a beast, and I was helpless to stop it.

Courtney came in and walked straight to my chair. "I know I don't have an appointment, but my husband just called me to say he's heading up to help with the fire situation. I need a distraction. Looks like you do too. Think you can fit me in?"

"You bet."

Tambre came out of the office. "Betsey just called. The boys are gathering at the Lair and driving up to the launch site to volunteer for manual labor. That's rough country up there, but it's already been cleared. Brick is going too."

I moved away from my chair, and Courtney plopped onto it. "I guess Betsey isn't too happy?"

"Neither am I, nor Molly. Cutter and Taz went with him. Cutter's had some experience with this before." Her chin quivered. "Taz has as well, and they aren't supposed to be in the main path, but there's always a risk. A fire can turn unpredictably, and once it gets started, it's almost unstoppable."

A thought occurred to me. "Is there a threat to the town or the River's Edge or the Lair?"

Tambre shook her head. "Not at this time, as far as I know. Taz said he'd keep me updated as long as his phone holds out. The signal is real spotty up there, and there's nowhere to charge. The fire is way northeast of the Tail, so the campground should be safe too."

I picked up my spritzer bottle and put it back down, only to pick it up again. My senses were dull and out-of-body, like I was watching myself go through the motions. Maybe I should be panicking, or crying, or something like it, but I was numb. Shut down and on autopilot. "You want a shampoo too?"

Courtney's worried face nearly broke my robot persona. "I want the works."

The clatter of heels punctuated the air as Betsey arrived, and for a moment, her age showed on her drawn face. "I just came by to check on y'all before goin' over to the Costco to get relief supplies. We got us a big firebreak we keep maintained up at the Lair just in case anything ever happens that way." Her nails clicked as she waved her hand around. "Lord have mercy, I been teasing Brick for years on his paranoia, but I'll have to admit that he was right when he gets back home. I hate doing that. He always spends the next week gloating."

I saw her lips quiver before she pressed them into a

thin line that accentuated the wrinkles around them. If Betsey was worried, we should be terrified.

Then she shook it off and straightened her stance, planting both feet firmly and raising her chin high. The queen had her moment of weakness, but now she'd morphed into the leader we needed. "The Lair has to get ready for other stuff. We got firefighters comin' in from all over, and they're gonna need a place to stay that's safe. There ain't too many this time of year, but there's still people who do winter hikin' and campin' up in them woods. I'm gettin' supplies like extra toilet paper, soap, towels, bottled waters, and a lot of ready-made food we can cook fast. When y'all are free, them campin' cabins need cleanin' and stockin'. I don't know how many to expect, but I want all the workin' hands I can find."

Tambre put down the notebook she'd been holding. "I'll go with you. Opal, you're in charge here. When everyone is finished up, feel free to close early. I'll see you at the Lair, and bring Natalie and Pearl with you, yeah?"

I saw the woman's lips moving and heard the words, but it took a minute for them to register.

Now's not the time to fall apart, Opal. You're a Dragon Runner's woman, and that comes with some responsibilities. Get your head out of your ass and step up.

My internal pep talk snapped me back to the real world, and I gave Tambre a sharp nod. "You bet."

CHAPTER 32

It was Fine who spotted the tracks. Two parallel lines cutting through the woods. They were hard to spot on dry ground, but the crushed leaves showed a clear enough path to follow. It wasn't easy, but Fine had a lot of experience with tracking.

"Shows they went that way but haven't come back. Think it's more campers?"

Weatherman sighed in irritation. They had already rousted a group of hikers from their campsites and started them moving toward the base to get them to safety. The air was winter cold as usual this time of year, but the bite had a singed, smoky flavor to it. The fire still burned and was moving fast at the last radio update.

Both he and Fine had helped construct one of the firebreaks yesterday. It was backbreaking work but necessary. Table and Mute helped drive the graders that cleared the vegetation while others felled some of the trees to keep the tops from igniting and passing the flames along in the branches. The wind had already picked up for the impending storm coming down from the north and wasn't helping the fight. The fire warden had a huge map of the area and planned out where to make controlled burns to keep the wild one contained, but it had already jumped in some places.

"This area here near the creek is where I understand some people might set up a winter camp. I 'spect the smoke drove 'em out, but it's easy to get turned around and head the wrong direction. I want all y'all to make a quick run of the creek and only the creek to see if anyone is still around. Just one run, mind you, and then get out of there. Stick by the water, got it?"

Weatherman didn't know if this search and rescue type of mission was protocol, but he didn't argue. He was bone-tired and grumpy from lack of sleep. He didn't remember the last time he ate something besides the protein bars he and Fine had stuffed into their gear, and they were down to their last two bottles of water. The air was smokier and smokier, and he longed for the next time he could take a clean breath.

Still, those tracks might mean people either stuck or lost.

The radio crackled, and Fine clicked it to answer. "Repeat, over."

It was hard to hear through the static, but the faint words sent alarm through both men.

"The fire jumped the last break, and the wind changed directions. It's headed your way. Get your asses out of there now!"

Weatherman cursed long and hard as he gazed at the four-wheeler tracks. They were fresh enough to tell him that yes, someone was at the end of them, and that someone was probably still there. Maybe an old guy trying to protect a family moonshine still or a group of kids that had more daring that sense. Either way, he couldn't leave until he checked it out. "Let's go in a ways and listen for anything."

Fine reluctantly agreed, but Weatherman thought it was more because he didn't want to be left alone in the woods. They followed the tracks for about a quarter mile before stopping. This was close to the area where they'd found the bear baits some weeks ago. They shut off the two four-wheelers and waited a moment.

Weatherman closed his eyes and tuned his ears to the ambient noise of the forest. There was a low-pitched ring that resembled tinnitus; otherwise, it was deadly silent.

Then he heard it.

A scream.

It might have been a woman, a man, or an animal. It was faint, but something sounded in pain.

"Did you hear that?" he asked a white-faced Fine.

It came again.

"I heard it that time."

Weatherman sniffed the cold air. He had only one

choice. "If you want to bug out, I won't judge you, but I'm gonna go check it out."

Fine swallowed hard but found his balls and started his squat vehicle. "Let's go."

They went about another mile and a half into the thick brush. It was slow and rough, but the tracks kept going. The weird ringing in Weatherman's ears intensified, and he realized this was the beginnings of brown noise. Fire itself was silent, but the kinetic energy it gave off produced random low frequency sound waves. The beast was on its way.

Another scream reached them, and it sounded a lot like an angry animal, but it could still be a human. It was definitely closer.

"Over there!" Fine pointed to something in the distance.

It was hard to make out, but there was an old cabin among the trees. Whatever was screaming came from that structure.

"Something or someone is trapped inside." Weatherman glanced at the ground. "It's probably faster to go on foot than try to finagle this path. If it's an animal, we'll free it to take its chances. If it's a person, we can carry them back here easily enough."

The two men approached the back of the cabin with caution. Suddenly, angry voices could be heard, and Weatherman held up a fist in a muted stop command. Two men were arguing hotly, but with the brown noise interfering with his hearing, it was hard to tell what the problem was.

Fine tapped Weatherman's shoulder to get his attention and pointed at the cabin in a soundless *"Do you see what I see?"*

He could make out a large wood table with a cage on top. An angry, hissing mountain lion was spitting and swiping at the bars. Just beyond it sat a row of drying racks with curing hides stretched out. Barrels that matched the ones they'd previously found were stacked next to two beat-up four-wheelers and one brand-new, top-of-the-line Polaris Scrambler.

As luck would have it, they'd found their poachers.

Isolated in the woods.

In the middle of a forest fire.

"Fuck," Weatherman said under his breath.

"You got that right. What do we do?" Fine asked.

Weatherman unclipped his gun from its holster and eased it into his hand, pointing the barrel down. There were two rifles on their four-wheelers, but they were useless at the moment. "It's more important that we get them and us to safety. We can worry about arrests once we get out of here."

They crept closer, squatting low and taking as much care as possible not to startle the two men arguing. Through the brush, Weatherman spotted Clem Gustler and some snooty man in pretend cowboy clothes. He held a gleaming hunting rifle in his hands. Their voices barely made it above the underlying growl that seemed to radiate throughout the air.

"Would you just shoot the damn thing, motherfucker, so we can get the hell off this mountain?" Clem shouted.

"You promised me a real mountain lion hunt. It's not the same if I kill it in a cage." His patrician lip curled. "I've paid a lot of money for these putrid accommodations. It was a nasty, uncomfortable ride on that filthy machine. There are no bathroom facilities—"

"Cain't you smell it? There's a goddamn forest fire burning out there. We let that cat loose, it's gonna take off, and you won't get nothin'."

"Medicate it and it won't run fast."

Clem spat a brown stream on the ground. "That ain't no different than just killin' it in the cage. Just point your fancy rifle at the head and pull the fuckin' trigger."

Snooty shifted the long gun in his hand. "I don't want to destroy the head. I want the whole hide with the skull and head intact; otherwise, my colleagues can't tell it's a mountain lion and not some other animal."

Weatherman had heard enough. The area was primed for radiant combustion. Wildfires heated up the areas around them like convection ovens with looping heat columns, and anything that reached the right temperature could catch fire and spread farther. The colder air helped keep that possibility down, but the increased wind negated that affect. Firebrands blown into fresh fuel also kept the beast fed and growing. "Fine, follow my lead."

"Um, Bryce? I think we should…."

Fine's voice sounded panicked. Weatherman glanced over at his fellow officer, and the cold that hit his chest had nothing to do with the winter wind.

Walt Gustler stood behind Fine with a rifle pointed at the back of the ranger's head.

"Don't make no moves, Mr. Rangers. Let's git on over to Clem and the fancy man. C'mon now."

Weatherman eased his pistol back into the holster but didn't put the clip on. "Walt, you feel that heat? Are your eyes watering from the smoke? That fire is on its way, and it's moving fast. We're not here about the bears or that cougar. We're here to get you fellas to safety."

Walt licked his lips in confusion. He shifted from foot to foot and kept looking around at the trees. He'd never been known for his cognitive abilities, but the man wasn't stupid. "I don't wanna be here no more, but Clem said we gotta do what the fancy man wants so we get paid."

Weatherman stood slowly and spoke softly. "Money doesn't mean much to dead men, right?"

Walt lifted a hand to wipe his dirty, sweating brow. "You gotta talk sense to Clem. Let's go."

Weatherman lifted his hands in the air, and Fine did the same. Clem grabbed his own rifle from the table and pointed it at the two men when they suddenly walked from the underbrush into the cabin's yard.

"What the fuck? Where the hell did you come from?"

If this whole situation weren't already bad enough,

it was about to get worse. The wind picked up with several gusts. Not winter cold but one with a hot breath. Weatherman looked up to see bright orange firebrands dancing in the treetops. The constant rumbling drone flared as two large pines ignited with a whoosh.

Snooty jumped back and dropped his firearm in the dirt. "Oh my gawd! I'm so out of here."

He turned and ran to the expensive, shiny four-wheeler, plunking his butt on the seat.

"Hey, motherfucker!" Clem shouted. "You can't leave 'til you pay us!"

"Sue me!"

Clem lifted his rifle and pulled the trigger. The man screamed as the bullet pierced his spine and burst from his chest in a red spray. He tumbled from the vehicle, and his pants leg caught on one of the pedals, leaving his body hanging there half on and half off.

Walt dropped his gun and yelled, "You kilt him!"

"No shit, Sherlock!"

Weatherman snatched his pistol and desperately tried to gain some control. "Clem, this has gone far enough. Let's get on our vehicles and get out of here while we still have a chance. The fire might already have us surrounded, but if we all make a run for it, we might make it."

Clem laughed with an evil sneer. "You're one dumb motherfucker, ain't cha? You think after seeing me shoot that asshole, I'm gonna go skipping down the mountain arm in arm with your ass?"

The noise was lower and wider. More trees ignited,

and Weatherman knew the underbrush was next. Soon this whole area would be engulfed. The choices open to him and Fine were die by fire while running for their lives or die by bullet in an instant.

I'm so sorry, Opal.

He snapped up his pistol and braced for the hit he knew was coming.

Clem staggered back as a splash of red hit his chest. His mouth opened as if he couldn't believe what just happened. "You shot me!"

Walt slung the rifle over his shoulder. "Yep." He ran to the Polaris, jerked Snooty's dead body from the four-wheeler, and started it up.

Fine got his voice back. "D-Do we stop him?"

"No." Weatherman ran to the cage and shot the cheap lock off. He opened the door and jumped back as the big cat exploded from the steel bars. The animal didn't waste any time before it took off into the woods.

"Good luck, buddy." He didn't waste any more words, just waved at Fine to start running.

It was a long way back to their vehicles, and the terrain was hard to manipulate with any kind of speed. Their best bet was to get to the individual fire shelters they carried. At this point, it was the only chance they had—and a crapshoot at best. The shelters were a last-ditch effort that might or might not save their lives.

The air grew hazy with smoke. Weatherman could hear Fine's labored breathing as they ran. Another danger of forest fires was the toxic gases the flames gave off. Carbon monoxide was one, along with a concoction of hydrocarbons, nitrogen oxides, carbon dioxide, and several volatile organic compounds. This recipe brought lung damage at best and death at worst. He coughed and pulled his shirt over his nose and mouth, making it awkward to run and breathe, but he had to keep going. His eyes burned, and his mouth had a woody taste to it. His legs pumped as fast as he could make them, and he prayed he wouldn't fall. If he or Fine went down, it was over.

Another rumble split the sky.

They almost missed the four-wheelers. Fine was crying when he spotted them in the distance. "Over there!"

A bush flared up next to one of the vehicles.

"Grab the shelter! Deploy!" Weatherman yelled. His voice came out garbled, and he coughed hard to clear what he could. He snatched up the pack and tore it open as he kept running. "Get closer to the creek!"

Both men wrapped the shrouds around them to shield themselves as they ran. Their only chance was to get to a clear area and finish deploying the silvery sheathes.

They stumbled along, coughing and gasping. Weatherman's eyes watered as he searched for any open spot. He finally spotted something through the poisonous vapor. "There!"

He threw himself on the ground and rolled to get the shelter anchored. Fine bumped his side as he landed next to him, but neither man had time or breath to speak. A roasting heat rolled over them in a hot, dry wind, scorching their lungs as they gasped for whatever air they could get.

Another huge rumble crashed above. Weatherman whipped the shelter over his head and tucked himself into a ball with his hands over his ears and mouth just as the flames reached him in a deafening roar.

God, take care of my family.

CHAPTER 33

All the Dragon Runners men had returned, tired, dirty, hungry, and thirsty.

All of them except one.

I fell to my knees at the news. My legs wouldn't support me anymore.

No. No. No, no, no, no! *Not again!*

My head filled with shouting denials, and I had no idea if the words actually came from my mouth or just exploded in my brain. The heart that had begun to trust again and believe in a bright future twisted around the knife that cut it in two. Everyone I'd ever dared to love had left me. My mom abandoned me the moment I turned eighteen, and I still had no idea where she lived now. I didn't even know if she was alive or dead. I lost Rebel to the call of the white powder. Any feelings he had toward me or our child were overshadowed by his drug addiction.

Then there was Camo. My savior and support at a

time in my life when I had nothing. The man who truly loved me, forgave my sins, and promised me a life I could only dream of having had died by a random bullet in someone else's war. He'd bled out in the snow with my name on his lips.

Now Weatherman. My Bryce. In the beginning, I had tried to hate him. I tried so hard to keep him out of my life. I'd tried countless hours not to think about him or care about him or dream of any kind of future with him, but he got under my skin anyway. Lodged deeper than anyone ever had.

Rebel broke me.

Camo shattered me.

Weatherman killed me.

Somewhere distant, I heard a voice say, "Breathe, Opal."

Tambre. Calm, serene Tambre, always an anchor in the storms.

She got down on the floor and pulled me into her strong arms. I listened to her and inhaled. Betsey's floral perfume entered my lungs. She was on my other side, humming and holding me.

Gradually, I became aware of the many women, including some from the salon, in the Lair surrounding me, giving me shoulders of support in a sisterhood I'd never realized was possible. How many times over the centuries had this happened? Wives, mothers, sisters, all waiting for their loved ones' return? Praying for their safety. Rejoicing when they came home or mourning when they didn't. Firefighters, policemen, soldiers, all of them husbands, sons, brothers, standing between their families and danger at the risk of their own lives.

I don't know how long I sat there, Tambre on one side, Betsey on the other, Psalm and Lori circling. Katrina brought me a full-sugar Coke from the fridge and softly encouraged me to drink it.

"She's in shock," she whispered. "Let her process for a little while."

I heard Brick's gruff voice. "Fuck. Let me through."

The sea of women parted, and Brick grunted as he squatted down next to me. "Opal, sweetheart, look at me."

I shook my head but stayed silent. If I acknowledged him or opened my mouth, I'd scream.

He let me keep my eyes to myself, but he kept talking to me. "We don't know nothin' for sure yet. They're still out checkin'. The reception up there is real bad, and the mess with the storm and the fire fucked up GPS, but that's all. Just because we lost contact don't mean they ain't still alive. We jus' gotta wait for someone to go find 'em."

"Weatherman's mama is upstairs sleepin' with Pearl in the guest room. Let's leave her be for a little while longer." Betsey's rough tone had a hitch to it.

I think Tambre asked me a question, but my ears were filled with noise. My belly cramped, and I wanted to heave and pass out at the same time. Brick was right that we didn't know anything about what the real situation was on the mountain, but I couldn't help the direction my thoughts took. Visions of Bryce's twisted, scorched body flashed in my mind.

I remembered as a child, a house burned down in my neighborhood. I wasn't supposed to be home, but my mother wasn't tough on making me go to school. I caught a glimpse of the fat woman who lived there as they zipped her up in a big black bag. Black and red, oozing dark blood in places, her hair gone and her limbs distorted into a shape that no human body could ever obtain on its own. The harsh odor of her charred flesh mingled with the ash and wood. Sick, sweet, chemical, like no other smell. One I never wanted to experience again.

No, no, no! Not Bryce! Please, God, if you're there, not him!

"Don't faint, Opal. Keep breathing with me," Tambre coached. All I could do was cling to her and let waves of pain carry me forward.

"Finish what you got to do here, boys, and get everyone settled. Ain't no one gonna be sleepin' tonight, but best we stay in one place while we wait for news. Someone go over to her place and get what she and the baby need for a while. They're gonna stay here where we can take care of 'em."

I was lifted and cradled against a strong barrel chest that smelled of oil and leather. Brick strained a little as he carried me to the couch and gave a big sigh once he sat me down. I twisted my fingers in his cut and didn't let go.

"It's gonna be okay, darlin'," his gravelly voice

murmured in my ear. "I'm gonna take care of this shit and you at the same time. You feel like cryin', go on and do it. You need to yell, might be we'll go outside to do that so's the people sleepin' can stay that way. Only thing I'm askin' you not to do is be by yourself, 'cause I need you where I can keep an eye on you. The Runners have been leanin' on each other ever since we started. Whatever burdens us down, we share it. Long way of sayin' you can lean on me and Betsey. That's what we do."

I'd never had a father. I had one now.

When did I become a member of this tribe? Never had I experienced being a part of this family. I thought I might have had that once with Camo and the Dutchmen MC, but this was so much different from my former life. Flaws, sins of the past, addictions—all of it was washed away by the cold Nantahala River water, and what I had now was a forgiveness and love that had no limits or conditions.

The epiphany of the moment liberated something in me.

I was not alone, and I wouldn't be that way ever again.

A large crash of thunder punctuated my thoughts, followed by a torrent of hail and rain. Winter Storm Margie had arrived.

As the night wore on, I sat in the main room, half-drunk from no sleep. Betsey stayed with me, bringing me water and soft drinks. Table and Lori stayed, their kids sleeping in their room and them camping out on the sofa next to me. Mute and Kat went home. Stud and Eva came by with their girls for a little while. Psalm waited for Blue to get off work before she took her stepchildren back to their house.

The hours plodded on with lead feet. I saw the night sky fade into morning. It glowed a dull orange and would stay that way until the smoke cleared. The acrid taste of ash coated everything.

Brick was a rock. He was hurting, too, but he stepped up as the leader of this group and held it together. His strides echoed through the cavernous room as he paced and waited for the radio in his hand to speak. When it crackled, he answered and listened to whoever was on the other side before relaying the latest news to the group. Natalie was still sleeping upstairs, blissfully unaware that her son was missing somewhere in the smoldering mountains.

"They think most of the flare-ups are done, but there's still some hot spots. Margie came just in time, but she ain't done yet. The burned-up vegetation might make some of the creeks overflow, so there might be some flash flooding in a few places. Parts of the town lost power."

He walked over and squatted in front of me, and I met his eyes with my puffy, swollen ones. "They got a search and rescue team that's goin' in as soon as they say it's safe. We got a bunch of boys missing, but we're gonna find 'em—all of 'em—and we're gonna bring them home."

Fresh tears gathered behind my eyes. Would they

find Bryce, or would they find his body? I'd grieved so many times already; did I have to do it again?

The morning blended into afternoon. People came by and hung out as we waited for news. Some of the firefighters came in from the ridges, covered in soot and smoke. Betsey got them into showers and had her giant Crock-Pots of soups and stews bubbling away to feed them before they crashed in the camping cabins. Donna was there, too, having brought a case of rolls and baguettes from the Ingles bakery where she now worked. For once, she wasn't flirty or pushy with the men, just helped serve with a gentle smile.

Pearl woke up and brought her smiles and giggles to brighten the gloom. She played with several of the other kids in a big group scattered on the floor. Every once in a while, she toddled over to me to sit on my lap and cuddle. Natalie sat beside me, holding vigil. The expression on her face when she found out Bryce was missing was something I hoped I never saw again.

We spent another night the same way. I ate and drank what was put in front of me, but only because I couldn't shut down completely. I didn't cry any more, too numb to even think. My anxiety attacks hadn't made an appearance, as I was beyond them. The place I'd found was a big empty void of all emotions, and the people around me were scared that I wouldn't return.

"She ain't cried enough yet. Got it all bottled up."

"Might burst anytime. Make sure someone stays with her to catch it."

"Think she'll find her way back?"

Truthfully, I didn't want to. At least not yet. Pearl needed her mother, and I would pick up my life to be one for her, but there was a piece of me that was just gone, and I had no energy to look for it.

Mute stomped his way around the place like an agitated bull. The search and rescue people weren't allowing the civilian volunteers to help just yet because of potential flare-ups. Parts of the forest could reignite, but the hope was that Margie had dumped enough rain to keep that from happening. She was still coming down and washing the smoke from the sky, cleaning the air and the earth.

The morning of the third day, Natalie was asleep upstairs only because Betsey forced her to rest. I expected she would be making me do that soon. Maybe I'd let her.

Pearl crawled onto my lap and slapped at my face. "Mama tick?"

I roused for the first time. "No, baby, I'm not sick. Just tired."

"Go 'teep?"

Tears came, and my nose started to run. "That's a good idea. I think I'll go take a nap."

"Bish book."

I bit my lip as a fresh wave of pain hit my heart, and I couldn't breathe. My girl's favorite book was Dr. Seuss's *One Fish, Two Fish, Red Fish, Blue Fish* that Bryce often read to her. Would she miss him as much as I did?

I lifted myself off the couch that I'd barely left in three days. My back and legs cramped, but I stood up and shook some life back into my limbs. Camo would never expect me to sit on my ass this long, and Bryce wouldn't either.

The radio in Brick's hand crackled. He'd slept some, but he'd never left me alone, keeping watch over me as I'd held my vigil for Bryce.

"We found him," the garbled voice announced. The tone was hard to distinguish. Was it a happy note or a grim one?

My heart dropped out of my body, and the room spun. I heard Pearl's "Mama?" inquiry, but the white noise filling my ears covered everything else.

Don't say it, don't say it, don't say it.

Someone's hands caught me. Mute or Table or Dodge, I couldn't tell. The organs in my chest fought hard against everything.

My heart beat uncontrollably.

My lungs stopped working.

My eyes lost their vision.

My ears refused to hear.

I was shutting down to get away from the news I was sure was about to come.

Brick moved in front of me. "Opal. Listen to me."

No, no, no, no, no!

"He's hurt bad, but he's alive. They airlifted him and his partner to the big hospital in Asheville. He told the rescuers to make sure you were told so you won't worry yourself. I'm gonna get Betsey an' we'll wake up Natalie an' tell her."

Air rushed into my starved body as I took a full

breath. Then another one. And another one. My vision cleared. It was Dodge who supported me.

"You still need to sleep, darlin'. You go take you that nap for a couple hours, okay? Fauna said she wanted to cook for you, and I think now is a good time. She'll get you fueled, and we'll all go to Asheville after you've rested and showered, yeah? We got DRMC people there, too, and we'll get them updated and on-site ASAP. He'll have family around him until we get there."

I sniffed, this time crying tears of relief. "I don't think I can ever repay this."

Dodge smiled down at me. "The bill's been paid a long time, sweetheart."

EPILOGUE

"YOU'D THINK AS MUCH AS WE PAY IN TAXES IN THIS county, they'd put in nicer bleachers for graduation. My back will never be the same."

I smiled at Burna Jones's complaints as they floated around me while I worked on her hair. I'd lived in this town just over four years now, and Pearl was starting kindergarten in a few more months. She ruled the roost at preschool with her sassiness, and I expected her to do the same in "big" school.

"The caps and gowns they had weren't worth a plugged nickel." Burna sniffed. "My Hilda can do so much better than those cheap flimsy things."

I spread more of the black color onto the woman's roots as I attempted to distract her. "I understand Hilda got into the Savannah College of Art and Design."

The older woman preened, and for a moment, I saw a smile flash across her face. A brief one. "Don't know why she has to move so far away from home. We got perfectly good colleges 'round here."

"That's true, but that school is one of the best for fashion design. Plus, the grant she won will pay for nearly all the tuition there. Win-win, right?"

Other random bits of conversations floated around me as life continued to move forward.

"Tourists done flooded the town for the July Fourth holiday."

"I tried to get a table at the Smoky Mountain Bistro, and the wait time was almost two hours."

"My son got a job there washing dishes. Loves it."

I exchanged glances with Tambre, who had Fauna in her chair. I enjoyed working with the restaurant owner's corkscrew curls, but my boss was the master at the tight braids Fauna loved so much.

It amazed me how many changes I'd come through over the past few years.

Kimmie returned to her life in Minnesota. I heard from Mama J that she made a brief appearance at the Dutchmen MC compound and left again on the back of a nomad's bike toward California. That was the last anyone saw her. I hoped she found her path in life and healed herself somewhere.

People still talked about the fire that burned up so much of the forests, but to look at them now, it was hard see any damage. Scorched trees had grown back, and the black scars were covered in bright green again as the mountains healed themselves. Deer, bear, and other wildlife returned to reclaim their territories. The weather cycled through seasons. People came and went. Kids grew up, and we moved forward.

Pastor Robert still preached to his flock at his church on Sundays. He'd met and married a woman who matched him perfectly. She directed the choir for him and personified the helpmate he needed. They made a great-looking couple, and I was genuinely happy for him.

The bell rang as another client came into the salon. "Hey, Opal. I know I'm early, but I'll just sit a spell until you're ready for me," Natalie said. The cancer was in remission, but she'd decided she wanted to live her life in the fullest way possible. In other words, she didn't give a rat's ass what people thought of her. When she worked at the bank, there'd been a dress code she'd had to follow. Now she didn't care and had me color her hair to whatever suited her mood. Pink, blue, teal, and now bright purple.

"I'll be right with you, Nat." I glanced at the clock and smirked. There was another reason Natalie was early to her appointment.

At exactly four thirty, the door opened, and a little blonde tornado rushed in. "Mommy, I drew a picture for you!"

Pearl drew pictures for me every single day, but her excitement in giving them to me never waned.

"Oh, how cute! Is that a horse?"

My little girl grinned at me and cocked her head to the side. "Mommy, you're so silly. It's a dog."

I looked again at the four-legged figure. "Oh, I see it now."

"Daddy says we can get one."

I straightened up and shot my eyes to the figure coming in the door right behind my daughter. "He did, did he?"

Bryce smiled as he walked up to me. "I actually said we'd talk about it as a family. Glenda's retriever has a new litter coming soon."

I folded myself in his arms, not caring in the slightest about any onlookers. On his left cheek, neck, and underneath his uniform shirt, there were the marks left by the fire. The side of the shelter blew up from the hot wind of the blaze, and flames got to him. Somehow, he rolled himself and the shelter into the creek. Whatever guardian angel he had worked overtime that day, as he could easily have been dead from burning, drowning, smothering, or a combination of the three.

I didn't remember the frantic trip to Asheville, only that Natalie and I clung to each other as a grim-faced Brick drove us. When we laid our eyes on Bryce, he was in a sterile single room, covered in white bandages and draped with tubes dripping fluids into his starved body. Even his hands were wrapped in gauze. The burns were serious but didn't require skin grafts, at least. He was awake when I staggered to his bed and touched him to make sure he was real.

"Told'ja I'd be back." He sounded like he'd swallowed a bucket of granite gravel, but he was alive and breathing. "Love you, babe."

I'd burst into tears on the spot. "Bryce Turner, don't you ever do that to me again!"

"I'll do my best, sweetheart."

Natalie had her hugs and tears, too, and all three of us cried our way through the weeks of healing and physical therapy.

Bryce had gone back to work as soon as he was given the all clear, and when Chief Wilson retired last year, Bryce became the new chief. Officer Fine also survived but left the forestry service because of lung damage—and to be honest, he really wasn't into the job anyway.

The poaching investigation ended with the fire. Walt's body was found a few miles from the burned-out shell of the cabin. Instead of running from the flames, he'd driven right into them, either by mistake or because of Clem's death. We would never find out for sure.

The first time Pearl called Bryce "Daddy," I thought he was going to fall over. His knees gave out, and he started tearing up. My eyes were also wet when he turned his to me and smiled. "If I'm going to be Pearl's daddy, I should also be Opal's husband."

A year later, we were married, and he officially adopted my little girl. Natalie kept her bungalow, but the rest of us moved into a nice three-bedroom house just outside town. It was a fixer-upper, but between Bryce and me, plus the men of the DRMC, we renovated and turned it into the home we both wanted.

The word "happy" wasn't big enough to cover all the joy in my heart.

"What do you want to eat tonight? Ingles has a sale on bratwurst. We can fire up the grill and have us a good 'ol Fourth of July cookout," Natalie said as she joined us.

"Gramma!" Pearl exclaimed as she wrapped her little arms around the woman's knees.

Betsey had to share the title.

Tambre finished up Fauna and handed her a mirror to check the back of her head. "The fourth isn't until Thursday."

"Don't matter. I'm good with celebratin' all week."

Fauna tilted her head as she examined herself. "Who's going to the fireworks?"

"Me!" Pearl yelled and let go of Natalie's legs.

I laughed just as the timer buzzed. I shifted in Bryce's arms. "Let me get Burna sorted. Then it's your mom's turn. You need a cut today?"

He moved his hands to my hips and shook his head. "Nope. I need to go file a report about a cougar sighting on the west ridges. I'm sure it's Old Sam again. Only one of his kind here in North Carolina."

"Seems a shame that he's by himself."

Bryce shrugged. "It's better than being killed by a fire or on someone's floor as a rug. I'll take the munchkin, you bring the burgers and Mom, yeah?"

"Sure."

"See you at home, babe." He leaned down to kiss me, light and quick. "Love you."

I planned on spending a lifetime with this man and never getting tired of hearing that. "Love you too."

Behind me, I heard a familiar bellow. "I'm done!"

WE HOPE YOU GOT SWEPT AWAY IN WEATHERMAN'S journey. There's more to come, but while you wait, have you checked out ML Nystrom's bestselling DUTCHMEN MC SERIES—a darker breed of bikers?

⭐⭐⭐⭐⭐ "PHENOMENAL STORYLINES, MC DRAMA AND MYSTERY, SUPER SMEXY NSFW SCENES AND AMAZING CHARACTERS."

Iceman, Rail, Angel, and Boots, members of The Dutchmen MC, are about to meet their match as they fight hard to keep their club strong while putting everything at risk to find their happily ever after with the women destined to bring them to their knees.

WHAT READERS ARE SAYING ABOUT THE DUTCHMEN MC ROMANCE SERIES:

★★★★★ *"With every book I read from this author I fall more and more in love with her."*

★★★★★ *"They are all absolutely fantastic."*

★★★★★ *"Raw, gritty, dark, and keeps you on the edge of your seat. "*

★★★★★ *"Holy moly… dark & emotional but in such a good way."*

★★★★★ *"Wow what a wild and tumultuous ride."*

ACKNOWLEDGMENTS

Weatherman is an experiment in crossover stories. I left one of my characters high and dry in the Dutchmen MC and put her through the ringer—bad. After so much tragedy and struggle, I needed to give her a happy ending. She needed family and support, and there's no better one than the Dragon Runners MC. Bryce Turner waited for this moment, as he was set up to be the hero in Table's book. I didn't originally plan this when I made him a DRMC prospect, but he and Opal clicked, and their story was born.

Writing is a long, tough journey that I'd never get through without my team of people. Shout out to my betas, Brittany Alexander, Mandy Pederick, Franci Neill, and Kim Deister. Y'all rock!

Of course, the big one is my editor, Kristin Scearce. She keeps me on my toes and in line. I'm sure she's corrected the same grammar mistakes in every manuscript she's done for me, but she still has patience to do it again with every submission. Big thanks for her red pen and our mutual coffee addiction.

I also gotta thank Becky Johnson and the rest of the crew at Hot Tree Publishing for taking a chance on me.

Their encouragement is one of the reasons I'm still here, putting words on paper.

ABOUT THE AUTHOR

ML Nystrom has had stories in her head since she was a child. All sorts of stories of fantasy, romance, mystery, and anything else that captured her interest. A voracious reader, she's spent many hours devouring books; therefore, she found it only fitting she should write a few herself!

ML has spent most of her life as a performing musician and band instrument repair technician, but that doesn't mean she's pigeonholed into one mold. She's been a university professor, belly dancer, craftsperson, soap maker, singer, rock band artist, jewelry maker, lifeguard, swim coach, and whatever else she felt like exploring. As one of her students said to her once, "Life's too short to ignore the opportunities." She has no intention of ever stopping… so welcome to her story world. She hopes you enjoy it!

JOIN MY NEWSLETTER: HTTPS://WWW.MLNYSTROM.COM/
CONTACT
VISIT MY WEBSITE FOR MY CURRENT BOOKLIST: HTTPS://
WWW.MLNYSTROM.COM/

I'D LOVE TO HEAR FROM YOU DIRECTLY, TOO. PLEASE FEEL FREE TO EMAIL ME AT MELODY@MLNYSTROM.COM OR CHECK OUT MY WEBSITE HTTPS://WWW.MLNYSTROM.COM/ FOR UPDATES.

facebook.com/authorMLNystrom

x.com/ml_nystrom

instagram.com/mlnystrom

bookbub.com/authors/ml-nystrom

ABOUT THE PUBLISHER

Hot Tree Publishing loves love. Publishing adult romantic fiction, HTPubs are all about diverse reads featuring heroes and heroines to swoon over. Since opening in 2015, HTPubs have published more than 300 titles across the wide and diverse range of romantic genres. If you're chasing a happily ever after in your favourite subgenre, HTPubs have you covered.

Interested in discovering more amazing reads brought to you by Hot Tree Publishing? Head over to the website for information:

WWW.HOTTREEPUBLISHING.COM

facebook.com/hottreepublishing
x.com/hottreepubs
instagram.com/hottreepublishing
tiktok.com/@hottreepublishing

www.ingramcontent.com/pod-product-compliance
Lightning Source LLC
Chambersburg PA
CBHW051237210726
48287CB00002B/286